**Other Mysteries
by
Martha Kemm Landes**

# Pity the Reluctant Fan

by


Martha Kemm Landes


Elemar Publishing

# DEDICATION

I dedicate this book to all the sports fanatics out there.
And also to people like myself, who do not necessarily like
sports, but are sometimes surprised to find joy in them.

Special thanks to the Yankees fans in my life; my father,
Jim Kemm, my brother-in-law, Randy Doss,
and my husband, Daniel Landes.
All of you tried, but failed, to make me a baseball fan.

# Pity the Reluctant Fan

Martha Kemm Landes

# Sports Joke #1

I wondered why the baseball kept getting bigger…
*then it hit me.*

I flipped the channel yet again, disgusted and huffed. "Why are sports the only thing showing on Saturday afternoon TV?"

"Well Mom, if you had remembered to pay the internet bill, we could be streaming something fun right now. But no. We're stuck with only three local channels."

I turned to see Lauren, my 17-year-old daughter, hands behind her head and braiding her own hair. She was getting so good at that.

I said, "When I was a kid, we only had three channels, and I sure don't remember so many sports on TV."

As soon as I said that I twisted my mouth. Back then, besides watching cartoons, I probably spent all my free time playing outside, so had no idea what was showing the rest of the day.

I added, "In my defense, I thought the bill was on autopay. But don't worry, I took care of it this morning so hopefully we'll be back to hundreds of choices soon."

"Mom," Marie, piped up, "I hate to tell you, but some people actually like sports. And Saturdays are a good time to watch since they're probably off work." I turned to see my 14-year-old, on the couch with her nose buried in a magazine.

I rolled my head around on my shoulders and told her, "Well, I just don't get it. I would only be interested in a sport if I had some skin in the game."

I was momentarily distracted when Ree looked up from her magazine. Her face was just above the folded-down cover, making her look as if she was wearing Taylor Swift's sparkly dress. With the same length of blonde hair, Ree looked just like a younger version of the iconic singer.

I shook the vision from my head. "I'm sorry. What did you say?"

She rolled her eyes. "I said, 'When did you ever bet on sports?'"

"Oh, I haven't. I meant I'm only interested in watching a sport when your sister competes in a swim meet, or you play basketball."

Ren, her hair now in a perfect French braid, stood and stretched. "And don't forget the Olympics. You are glued to the TV then."

I nodded. "True, but the Olympics are so much more than sports. It's educational to learn about different cultures and fun to root for the USA or some underdog country. So, that's very different from a regular sports fan who just picks a random team and goes gaga over it."

Ren, now holding a comb, leaned down and ran it through the hair of our shaggy sheepdog. She told the pup, "Well, Harriet, I think Mom should find something else to do besides complain about sports. It's June! She doesn't have to teach or worry about her horrible principal for two whole months! She should go shopping with Lin, write next year's school musical, or go visit Grandma and Grandpa."

Harriet didn't react to Lauren's suggestions, but I did. Ren was right. I had a month before summer workshops started. I couldn't work at my second job at Tulsa Opinions for a few weeks since they were remodeling their client room. It was time to do something I wanted to do. Why waste my time watching television? With a click of the remote, the screen became dark.

I announced, "You're right. I am free as a bird and plan to make the best of it. What are you girls doing today?"

Pulling a handful of white cotton-like hair from the dog comb, Ren said, "I'm meeting Jennifer at the pool to see if the water has warmed up enough to swim, yet."

Ree tucked her hair behind her ear and smirked at her sister. "You mean you're going to the pool to check out the boys."

"So, what if I am? And what are you going to do? Stay inside and read all summer?"

"Maybe." Ree stuck her tongue out at her sister. "For your information, Caitlyn is coming over after a while and we're going to make plans for her birthday party in July. The theme will be either Luau or glow in the dark party!"

I said, "That sounds like fun."

Ren rolled her eyes. "Oh yeah, really exciting."

Ree waggled her head. "Well, Lauren, what are you going to do for your 18th birthday? Watch paint dry?"

I watched the two girls poke fun at each other and chuckled. I needed to plan something fun for the three of us to do this summer, or this was all they would do.

Not long after Lauren left with her swimming bag, Caitlyn arrived. The two 14-year-olds rushed off to conspire in Ree's bedroom. When I took them some snacks, the best friends were busy cutting out pictures to decorate Ree's bulletin board. Ah, to be young and carefree again.

Back in the living room, I took Edgar out of his cage and let him walk across the coffee table. I asked the giant parrot, "What do you think I should do today?'

He cocked his gray head and stared at me with a yellow eye, and spoke in the old-man voice that he picked up from his first owner, "Wanna go for a walk, Edgar?"

I snickered and answered. "You are already on your walk, buddy."

As I put Edgar back into his giant cage, he fanned his beautiful red tail and perched on his swing. I smiled and said, "You're a good boy, Edgar."

Harriet had perked up when she heard my tone of voice or possibly the word, "walk," so I told her, "Let's go out back and see if anything is blooming."

4

As soon as I opened the back door, Harriet bolted out to chase off that annoying squirrel who taunted her daily from its perch in the smallest pine tree. "Atta girl, Harriet. You're my favorite guard dog."

The first flowers I spotted were the Gaillardias. I snapped photos of the gorgeous red-orange flowers with yellow tips on each petal. It was easy to see why their common name was Indian Blanket. They were very special to me since my mom was instrumental in naming the plant our Oklahoma State Wildflower.

In another sunny spot, a group of my other favorites waited for me—Buttercups. How could there be a cuter name for a flower? Their shiny buttery petals made me smile every time I saw them.

I headed toward the rosebush, but a bright orange toy caught my eye. While walking across the lawn to retrieve it, I realized the grass had to be four inches tall and was in dire need of mowing. That was a morning or evening job since it was way too hot now.

When I leaned over to pick up the orange toy, I jumped back in alarm. It wasn't a dog toy. It was Dave!

What in the world was a fish doing way over here? I kneeled to see if he was alive, but the poor beautiful Koi was stiff and motionless. I felt sick to my stomach and started to reprimand Harriet for going fishing, but remembered she hated water and would never go near the pond. My sweet dog joined me, sniffed Dave, and backed away in disgust. The distance from where the fish lay, to the water had to be at least 10 feet. That fish could not have jumped that far. How had he gotten there? My heart sank when I realized I had to tell Marie Dave was dead. He was her baby.

Back in the hallway, giggles came from Ree's room. I hated to break up the joyful mood but knocked on the door anyway.

"Come in."

Hearing my daughter's happy voice broke my heart. I opened the door to find two girls putting makeup on each other. I cringed at how much eye shadow and mascara they had applied but focused and said, "Ree, I have some bad news."

Her smile slackened. "What is it?"

"Something happened to Dave." I winced. "He's dead."

"What? How?"

"I don't know. Come with me."

The now solemn 14-year-olds followed me outside.

Ree rushed straight to the pond, probably expecting to see Dave floating there, but I pointed farther away.

She squatted down beside the large orange fish with black speckles. With tears in her eyes, she said, "Poor Dave. Why did you put him over here?"

"I didn't. This is where I found him. I'm so sorry."

Caitlynn pushed back her hair which was almost as red as the fish. "Could he jump that far out of the pond?"

Ree checked the distance and frowned. "Something carried him here."

Caitlyn asked, "Did Harriet do it?"

Ree dried her eyes, picked Dave up gently, and inspected his body without being squeamish at all. It was uncanny how much Ree was like her scientific grandmother. Shaking her head, she said, "No, Harriet doesn't like water. Maybe it was a hawk. Look at the marks on his scales. It must have tried to take Dave but dropped him here as it flew off."

I looked at the punctures in the fish and was amazed at my daughter's hypothesis. "I think you are right, Ree. Maybe you should become a detective someday."

Caitlyn's freckled face looked up at me adoringly. "Just like you, Mrs. Kole. You are the best detective ever. You are my hero."

I smiled at my biggest fan. "Caitlyn, I'm no hero, I was just in the wrong place at the wrong time."

"No. You were in the right place to save the day."

I chuckled and thought back to the times I had stumbled into suspicious circumstances and managed to solve them. One incident occurred on a movie set. Another started when I discovered clues in an old desk, and just a few months back I found myself involved in yet another mystery in Italy.

I said, "Caitlyn, my sleuthing days are over. I'm just going to try to be a good mom and music teacher from now on."

Turning back to the sad discovery, I asked Ree softly, "What do you want to do with Dave?"

She said, "We should have a funeral." She laid him back on the grass, then the little girl in her broke down and she hugged me while she cried. I understood. We had gotten two Koi when she was only ten years old, but Ren's fish died last year, so aside from Harriet, Dave was with us longer than any other pet.

Ren arrived and was very sweet to her sister when she was told about the loss of her fish. We found a large shoebox that could fit Dave if we curved his tail around. The three girls lined it with some leftover gold curtain fabric I had salvaged from a high school stage.

We gathered in the back yard and as always with our pets' funerals, the mood was serious.

I said, "Dave looks very peaceful."

Ree agreed with a nod. "He does, doesn't he?"

Her older sister said, "Now he can swim in fish heaven with his brother, Buster."

We all nodded slowly. Was there actually heaven for fish? I hoped there was.

As the dirt was scooped on top of Dave's "casket", I couldn't help but think of the strangest pet funeral I had attended:

Becca, my P.E. teacher friend, took custody of her mother's old, apricot poodle, Peaches, when her mom passed away. We knew the tiny, blind and deaf dog didn't have long to live. Becca made the rest of our teaching team promise to help bury the dog beside her mother's grave when Peaches died.

A few months later, Becca sent us the cryptic text, "The Eagle has landed." Peaches had died. After school, we donned our black outfits and met at the nicest cemetery in Tulsa, where her mother was buried.

Becca carried a shoebox and a small shovel. Jules, the art teacher, brought a miniature headstone she had painted. Once the scene was set and the body was buried, we started the ceremony. The gifted teacher, Jana, read a poem, and I, being the music teacher, played <u>Taps</u> on a recorder.

We knew it was frowned upon, and possibly illegal to bury a dog at a people's cemetery so the whole time we kept a lookout for anyone who might kick us out or have us arrested. But all went well, and we performed our duties in honor and memory of Becca's mother and her beloved Peaches.

Dave's funeral wasn't nearly as formal as that one. It was held near the back fence of our yard with no big to-do. I was glad to see Ree and Caitlyn had washed off their heavy makeup beforehand out of respect.

Once the funeral was completed, we moved back into the air-conditioning where I started to prepare dinner. Considering the situation, I opted for grilled cheese sandwiches and soup rather than the fish sticks I had planned.

The doorbell rang just as I opened the can of soup. One of the girls must have answered it because, within seconds, the distinct shrill voice of Caitlyn's mom assaulted my ears. Only a year ago, Trish had been one of my least favorite people, but things changed and despite her haughty demeanor, she was now almost a friend. Almost.

Trish stood in the living room with her nose in the air. "I hear you had a death in the family?" The woman could stand straighter than anyone I'd ever known. I self-consciously pushed my shoulders back and improved my posture every time I was around her.

I nodded. "Yes. He was the last Koi from our pond. Now Dave and Buster are both gone."

She raised an eyebrow and gave a slight nod. "That's too bad. Personally, I've never found a reason to have any sort of pet in or outside of our house. They are messy and loud, require food and care, and then they die. Whatever is the point?"

She must have seen my reaction because she quickly amended her statement with, "But I'm sure it was hard to lose a special fish." Her face did not show much compassion, but at least she tried.


After the mother and daughter left, I made the sandwiches without burning them for a change and poured the soup into the first bowl. Unfortunately, when I turned around to place the pot on the stovetop, I tripped over Harriet and crashed to the ground.

I'm not sure if I blacked out in the fall or what, but when I opened my eyes, both girls stood in the doorway, with mouths open.

There was a muffled but urgent, "What happened? Is that blood?"

Blood? I quickly assessed the situation. I was lying on the kitchen floor with a sharp pain in my side. When I turned my head, all I could see was red. I gasped. Was that my blood? I rubbed my hands along my body for an injury. Even though I didn't feel a wound, there was still a pain at my waist, I focused on my daughters. "Did I get stabbed?"

A worried Ren leaned in and studied the scene closely. Her face relaxed. "Wait, that's not blood. It's tomato soup."

Her little sister put a finger on the floor and started to lick it.

Ren shouted, "Eew stop, Ree! It may very well be tomato soup, but it has also been on the floor." She turned to me and asked, "Mom, are you okay? Did you hit your head?"

I moved my head around. "No, but my side hurts."

She checked me over and said, "I don't think you are bleeding."

Ree wiped her finger onto her jeans. "Gee Mom, I thought you were lying in a pool of blood, but there you are just lounging in a pool of tomato soup." She smirked.

"Well, I'm not exactly lounging. And I'm sorry you're disappointed that I wasn't stabbed and bleeding. Help me up, please."

They helped me to sit up. I winced. "You didn't happen to record my graceful landing, did you? I'm curious if I hit something when I fell."

They shook their heads. I looked at the mess. Besides the whole saucepan of soup, my bowl lay shattered on the floor. I frowned at the mess. "How is Harriet? I tripped over that silly girl. She's always in the kitchen hoping for handouts."

Ren looked around the corner into the living room. "She must have run away when you tripped. She looks fine. Not a drop of soup on her."

As the girls helped wipe me off, Ree said, "You should change clothes."

Ren nodded. "Yeah. You look awful. Here, just put your clothes in the washer so you don't drip on the new carpet." She was always the practical one.

Ree said, "While you clean up, we'll finish fixing dinner, Mom. And for your information, I am glad you didn't get stabbed." She started to hug me but backed away when soup dripped into my bra from my hair. Who could blame her?

The shower pepped me up and upon close inspection, I only had a small cut on my finger from the shattered bowl. There was no discernable abrasion on my side. Must have just pulled a muscle.

We ate cold grilled cheese sandwiches with beef and barley soup since tomato soup didn't sound so good to any of us anymore.

To cheer the girls up after such a weird day, I said, "You know, we haven't discussed anything special to do this summer. Any ideas?"

Ever since my divorce from Todd nine years earlier, I had worked an extra job to make enough money to take a trip or do something fun while we were all off from school.

Ren said, "Well, I probably can't take off work for long. You know not just anyone can do what I do, and this is their busiest time of year."

That's the problem with kids getting older - they become independent and get jobs. Lauren did have the strangest summer job though, taking underwater photos at a swim school. She spent most of her shift in a pool underwater.

Ree shrugged. "I don't care what we do." She sighed, "I just keep thinking of how sad the backyard will be from now on."

I brightened. "We could get more fish. You always wanted to get a white Koi. This is a good time of year to get them, so they can acclimate before winter."

She said sadly, "Nah. That's OK. I just wanted one to keep Dave company. There's no point now."

Ren said, "Yeah, let's stick to indoor pets that can't be picked up by hawks and tossed onto the lawn to suffocate."

I grimaced. It had been a gruesome way to die. "Well, start thinking about what you want to do this summer."

After dinner, my body ached. I took ibuprofen and asked the girls, "Could one of you mow the back yard tonight? My side really hurts, and I want to run to Grandma and Grandpa's. I'll give you extra allowance for it."

When Ren agreed to do it, I said, "Thank you! And don't forget to put on insect repellant or you'll get eaten alive. Ree, can you do dishes?"

She nodded. Gee, they were so agreeable. Maybe I should appeal to their sympathy or get rid of WIFI more often.

On the drive to my parents' house 20 minutes away in Tulsa, I texted my sister, Kim, and asked her to meet me at Mom's.

I arrived at the house I'd lived in from my birth until I got married. I entered through the unlocked front door and heard my folks watching *America's Got Talent* in the family room. "Hi, kids!" I hollered in order to be heard above the super loud singing group.

Dad paused the recording and smiled. "Well, look who came to see the old folks." He stood and gave me a hug. I loved that he was such a softie.

On point, Mom popped up and said, "Pity! Are you hungry? I made a Crumb Cake."

My mouth watered and I grinned. "Like I'd ever turn that down."

Kim and R.A. arrived and there were more hugs. My brother-in-law's big Santa Claus beard always tickled my neck when I embraced him, and I loved it.

Kim said, "Pity, can you cut my hair real quick?"

"Sure. Let's do it outside." I yelled into the kitchen, "Mom, I'm cutting Kim's hair out back, then we'll come in for cake, OK?"

"That's fine. Just don't use my sewing scissors."

"Wouldn't dare." We all knew not to use the scissors with the ribbon tied through the orange handle. Those were for fabric only.

I grabbed a generic pair from the junk drawer and a comb then followed Kim to the steamy back patio. Summer evenings in Oklahoma just didn't seem to cool down at all. I slapped at a mosquito as Kim sat on a stool. The only good thing about this time of day was the fireflies that lit up periodically just above the grass. So cool.

Although we are both brunettes with similar features, my hair couldn't be more different than Kim's. Mine had body and could be dried straight or left wavy. Kim's was curly and nearly impossible to tame. She had trouble finding someone who cut her hair just the right way. I figured out the trick years ago, so I was her go-to and very cheap hairdresser. Our oldest sister, Kay, had stick-straight blonde hair. Go figure.

As I snipped away, Kim said, "Do you have something fun planned to do with your girls this year?"

I frowned. "No. Usually, I've got June and July planned out by now, but this year I was a slacker."

She cocked her head. "Well, you were pretty busy with end-of-school stuff and dealing with Dr. Love and his newest crazy schedule."

"True." I smiled, remembering I wouldn't have to hear the horrible principal's whiny voice for at least two months. "Now hold still so I don't cut your ear off."

Minutes later, while savoring the yummy cinnamon cake, I recounted the death at our house today. I frowned. "It was pretty sad, especially how he was murdered."

Mom pointed her fork at me. "Now Pity, please don't get involved in solving another mystery."

"Right. I don't want to hear that you hunted down the hawk to get revenge," Dad said with a smirk.

I scoffed. "It hasn't even crossed my mind. Besides, how would I even go about interrogating a bird of prey?" I considered this. I had enjoyed deep conversations with Edgar, so maybe it wouldn't be so different.

R.A. frowned at me. "Was that Ree's fish that died? Wasn't he like five years old?"

"Almost."

Kim said, "He was really fun to watch swim around the lily pads. He practically glowed underwater."

I sighed. "Can anyone think of something I can do with my girls this summer? Maybe an inexpensive trip or something memorable for our last one before Ren graduates?"

Mom said, "Isn't their dad getting married in July? You'll have to plan around that."

I groaned, "Ugh. Yes, their wedding is set for July 4th. And that's all the girls hear about from Shelly. They are not very excited."

Kim swallowed her bite of cake. "Why would anyone get married on Independence Day?"

I put down my napkin and launched into an impersonation of Shelly, my girls' annoying soon-to-be stepmother. Blinking my eyelashes, I crooned, "Oh, Hot Toddy, just think…every year when the fireworks go off, they'll be celebrating our anniversary!"

That got a laugh from everyone at the table.

Dad turned to me with a suggestion. "You and the girls can always spend a week at the creek. That's an affordable option."

Just the thought of going to my favorite place on earth made my heart swell. I said, "A week at the cabin would be heavenly, but we are already meeting you there the day after the wedding. I mean, we wouldn't dare miss the 14th Annual Jim Kole, International, Invitational, Big Sugar Creek, 4th of July, Ping Pong Tournament, even if it is on the fifth of July this year."

Dad gave a mischievous smile. "Good, because I'm upping first prize to $14 this year."

I chuckled at his dollar-per-year increase. R.A. gave a smug smile at me, so I pointed my fork at him.

"You and your boys better not come in first, second, and third again! This is my year to win."

I turned to the whole group and said, "But I'm thinking of something extra to do with the girls that we don't normally get to do."

"Why not buy something fun," R.A. snapped his fingers, "like a swimming pool?"

My eyes widened. "What? That would be perfect, but aren't they super expensive?"

He answered, "An inground pool is, but you could get an above-ground pool." He pulled up his phone and googled prices. "Look, you can get this for under $500. It's pretty big." He handed me his phone.

Wow! The pool in the picture was much nicer than I expected at that price. Maybe I could do that. I said, "Great, but what about assembly?"

R.A.'s eyes twinkled. "If I get to use it, I'll help build it."

I cocked my head. "Well, that's a given."

He grinned. "I've even got a buddy who can probably help. And what about Mike?"

I twisted my mouth. "Mike?"

Kim stared at me. "Your boyfriend?"

I made a face. "I know who he is…but he's going out of town, and I don't know when he'll be gone. I'm sure he'll help if he's here."

Dad said, "Where is Mike going?"

"Oh, he's going with a policeman friend on a baseball tour of the East Coast. He'll go to games in a lot of different stadiums." I rolled my eyes. "He's excited, but I can't imagine anything worse than being on a bus with a bunch of baseball fanatics and going to all those baseball games."

## Sports Joke #2
Did you hear about the slow swimmer?
*He could only do the crawl.*

I was giddy when I got home and ran inside to tell my girls the new plan. Ren and Ree were watching a movie on Netflix so apparently, our internet had been turned back on.

I put my hands on my hips. "So, are you sitting down?" They stared at me as if I was crazy since both were in prone positions on the couch and floor.

"What would you think about me buying an above-ground pool for our backyard?" Before they could respond, I jumped in, "I know it's not as fancy as a real in-ground pool, but it would be deep enough to swim a little and would cool us off this summer. And I can afford it. What do you think?"

Ree's face was bright. "I'm in! Can I have a swimming party?"

"Of course. Just so long as you know that nobody can jump off the house, dive off the ladder, or anything else stupid since it won't be more than five feet deep."

She nodded and I looked at Ren, who was a little more discerning. She lifted her shoulder a bit. "I guess it would be fun, but I may not invite all my friends over."

I was a little sad that she might be a little old to enjoy it. Why hadn't I done this when they were younger? I nodded. "Whatever you want sweetie. But would you use it?"

She must have given it more thought because her eyebrows lifted and she said, "Of course, I would. I'd like to get in it today."

"Ok then. I'll research how to build a deck around the pool, so we don't get grass in it. I hate grass in pools, don't you? I'll talk to R.A. about it tomorrow and plan to buy one soon."

That night Mike called. "Hi, Pity. What's up?"

Just hearing his smooth and confident voice made me relax. We had met last October when the tall, handsome policeman kept me out of trouble during a frantic and dangerous week. Somehow, despite my crazy antics, he stuck around.

I filled him in on all of the day's excitement.

He said, "I'm sorry about Marie's fish. And what a bad way to die - kind of the opposite of drowning."

"Just horrifying. What did you do today?"

"I spent the day with Sally and Jesse since Scott is still overseas. Kind of a bad time for him to be deployed with her baby due in just a month."

"You are a very sweet brother and uncle. Did I tell you how much I enjoyed her shower? I'm surprised she doesn't want to know its gender with all the reveal parties going on now. How is she doing?"

"She's great. Jesse's getting very excited about being a big brother."

"Awe. Cute. So, when is your big baseball trip?"

"We leave on Wednesday, but if you and R.A. need help setting up the pool before I leave, I'll be free in the mornings. Or I can help after I get back."

"I'm not sure if we'll be ready this week, but we may need your assistance when you return. Thanks."

"I'm sorry I had to work tonight since we missed date night."

"It's ok, Mike. Someone's gotta patrol the streets. Hey, as long as you're on duty, could ya keep an eye out for a suspicious-looking hawk flying around? Maybe take him in for questioning. I mean that's a perk of dating a police officer, right - asking him to help solve a mystery?"

"You are a complete nut, Pity. Listen, I'm off tomorrow evening if you want to do a movie and dinner."

"I gladly accept that offer."

"OK. I'll pick you up at five."

The next day, R.A. came over to check out the location for a 16-foot, round pool.

As my brother-in-law measured, I bit my lip and pointed to my pond. "Will we need to fill it in to have room for the pool? I mean it is in the middle of the yard."

He rubbed his beard. "Either that or take down your shower doors."

Shocked, I said, "We can't do that. They are our privacy fence. We'll need them more than ever with a swimming pool."

I know it was weird to have shower doors in a backyard, but I loved them. Years ago, I planted eight glass doors on end like dominoes. The artsy wall they created was very useful as the doors let light through for my flowers but being patterned, nobody could see through them.

R.A. rewound his measuring tape with a snap. "Well, then are you willing to give up the pond?"

I held up a finger. "Hold on."

While he walked off the perimeter, I ran inside and asked the girls about it. I returned right away and said, "Okay, they agreed we can lose the koi pond since we have no koi. Can we make a 16-foot circle with my garden hose so I can visualize where the new pool will be?"

He helped me pull the green hose out and make an outline. As soon as we set it out, and part the hose dipped into the pond water, we knew it had to go.

I stared at the lone lily pad and said, "Oh well, it had a good run. I might miss the frogs croaking at night, but without Dave and Buster, it doesn't seem right to keep it. Hey R.A., do you think I can make a deck out of pallets? I heard you can get them for free from the hardware store."

R.A. chuckled. "It should work, but you'll have to screw in wooden planks across them or someone might fall through the slats."

I nodded, getting even more excited about the upcoming pool installation.

That evening, once Mike and I had ordered our meals at Zio's Italian Kitchen, I sat back marveling at the beautiful Italian décor. I took a sip of my Cab Sav and said, "Whoever designed this restaurant must have been to the same Roman villa I stayed in last February. It looked just like this."

Mike smiled, showing his dimples. His gorgeous eyes twinkled as he said, "Maybe we should go to Italy together, sometime."

I started to sweat; maybe due to the wine, but probably from the thought of being with him on a romantic Roman holiday.

With a weak voice, I said, "That sounds amazing." For fear I might melt right there in public, I cleared my throat and changed the subject. "So, when we get the pool up, Jesse will have to come and swim. My girls just love your nephew. It might be nice to let Sally have a break before the baby comes." I leaned my elbows on the table, feeling a twinge in my side, but sucked it up and said, "Now…tell me about this baseball tour. Where all will you go?"

His face brightened, making him even more irresistible. He leaned across the table. "Well, we fly into Baltimore, and the next day we take a bus to DC to sightsee and then go to a Nationals' game."

"There is a baseball team called the Nationals?" I considered this and made a slow nod. "They are in our nation's capital? Well, then I guess that name makes sense."

"Yup." His eyes lit up as he spoke faster, "Then we go to Philadelphia and tour Independence Hall and the Liberty Bell, then go to a Phillies' game that night."

"So, you fly to Philadelphia?"

"No. Bus. The next day we ride the bus to New York City to a Yankees game."

I put down my fork. "Wait. That's an awful lot of games—three games in three days? Won't you get sick of baseball? And what about riding so long on a bus?"

He laughed at my horrified expression. "Well, if you think seeing three games is too many, we're actually doing six games in six days. The cities out East are close together, so there won't be that much time on a bus."

I cringed. "Better you, than me. I'm sure you've figured out I'm not much of a sportsperson."

He nodded. "I've noticed."

I didn't say it aloud but could think of a lot of activities better than sitting through six ball games—like lying in the middle of a floor covered in tomato soup. I smiled. "Well, visiting all those cities sounds amazing anyway."

The server brought my pesto pasta, and I took a bite. The flavor was delicious, almost as good as the pasta I had in Rome. I swallowed and said, "So, where do you go after New York?"

"I think Boston. I'll text you my itinerary, so you'll know where I am at all times."

After dinner, we went to the newest *Mission Impossible* movie. After sitting for so long, I could hardly stand straight with my side pain. I felt like I'd fallen from a cliff like Tom Cruise did in the film.

Mike squinted at me. "Are you OK? You're walking funny."

Not wanting to admit to my soup stunt, I said, "I'm fine. I must have sat in a weird position."

🩹

The next morning, I drove to Urgent Care to see if one of my ribs was cracked. On my way, Mike called me in a panic. "Pity, I'm not sure what to do. Mac can't go on the trip. His dad had a heart attack and isn't doing well."

"Oh no! I'm so sorry. I hope he recovers."

"I know. He's a really nice man."

I pulled into a parking spot and said, "So, what are you going to do about your trip? It's day after tomorrow, right?"

"I called the trip organizers and found out it was too late for Mac to get his money back, but someone could take his place since the tickets were already purchased." He hesitated then said in a rather meek voice, "I don't suppose you would want to go along with me?"

I was glad I wasn't driving, or I may have run into something. I was also glad Mike couldn't see my face, for it was not pretty. All I could think was how awful going to six baseball games would be. Sure, hanging out with Mike would be great, but riding on a bus with 50 baseball fanatics sounded horrible.

Frantically, I brainstormed other ideas and suggested quickly, "How about R.A.? He loves baseball."

"Oh…so, that's a no from you?"

He sounded so disappointed that I said, "Well, let's see if there might be someone who would appreciate the games first, and then if not, I'll consider going." Oh crap, did I just say that?

Mike said, "OK, I'll give him a call. Whoever goes would have to share a room with me. Hope he wouldn't mind that."

Wait a minute. Staying six nights in a hotel with Mike was an enticing argument, but I stayed strong and replied, "Oh, my brother-in-law is very easygoing. He has shared rooms with me on Tulsa

Opinions work trips and he never complained." I crossed my fingers that R.A. could go.

Since I arrived early for my appointment, I stayed in the parking spot by the clinic and called Kim and told her everything. She said, "I think R.A. has a big job next week so he probably can't go."

"Oh, dang."

"Come on, Pity. You could handle that trip. It would be fun for you to go with Mike. Kinda romantic too. And you love all the places they're going."

I twisted my mouth. "Yeah. And I've never been to Baltimore."

"There ya go! I think you should jump on it."

"Well, maybe he'll find someone else who can go. I don't have the extra money for a trip like that, anyway. If I did, I'd take the girls somewhere fun instead of getting a dinky pool with a rickety homemade deck."

"Oh. They're gonna love the pool. Just wait and see what happens. But keep an open mind, sis."

"Okay, I will." but I wasn't sure about that.

I stewed over the trip in the waiting room, and while the doctor examined me. I even fretted about it while getting an X-ray.

When I left radiology, I went back to the doctor's office for the results. She said, "We don't see any fractures. It's probably a soft tissue injury."

"What does that mean?" I bit my lip, waiting for the gruesome diagnosis.

The pretty young doctor cocked her head. "A bruise."

"Oh." Why did I feel disappointed that it wasn't something more complicated? I whined, "But it hurts when I breathe or push on it."

The petite blonde doctor said, "Then don't push on it." She smirked then turned serious. "Bad bruises can be very painful. It will take a while to heal. You'll have to be patient."

Great. Patience was not my virtue. Ever. But I got a great idea and sat up straight. "So, it wouldn't be safe for me to travel on an airplane or ride on a bus for extended periods, right? And sitting through six baseball games is a bad idea."

She smiled. "No. That would be fine. And that sounds like an amazing trip."

I almost asked if she wanted to go instead of me. But I wasn't keen on this cute young doctor staying with Mike in his hotel room.

She added, "Just have someone else lift your suitcase so you don't strain your side. Otherwise, you can do anything you want."

I gave up on the excuses, thanked her, and drove home. I still hadn't heard from Mike. Maybe he found someone else and was making plans.

I logged into my bank account and was happy to see I had plenty in savings, but knew it had to last all summer. Some people believed teachers had it easy with summers off, but most of us had only one month before preparations for the next school year began. Our salaries were very low and there was nothing cushy about teaching. But I love my job and wouldn't change it for anything.

I would, however, change my principal, Dr. Love, in a heartbeat. But that's another story.

Could I handle money for the pool and the trip if I had to? The phone rang interrupting my quandary. "Hello?"

It was Mike and he sounded frustrated. "Well, R.A. has to work. Joe is taking a vacation with his family. Jack is working security at a concert this weekend, and Simon is having knee surgery."

I wasn't sure what to say, so I cleared my throat and mumbled, "Um. Wouldn't we need to pay Mac back? How much would it cost?"

I heard him take an excited breath. "Oh, don't worry about it. I'll pay Mac back if you'll go with me."

What? That had been the only true excuse I had left. I mean, the doctor permitted me to go, I didn't have to work this month, and the girls and the pets could be taken care of.

I said, "I hate for you to do that. It's probably a lot of money."

"It's fine. I've wanted to take this trip for so long that I'd pay pretty much anything to go. And besides, I want you there. It would be a lot more fun with you than Mac anyway."

I took a deep breath and winced at the pain in my ribs. This sweet guy was winning me over. I said, "Let me talk to my girls before I commit, but you strike a very hard bargain, Officer Potter."

When the girls returned from seeing a *Barbie Movie* sequel, I made them pose by the fireplace in their pink outfits for a photo. Then I explained the situation. I sort of hoped they would give me a good reason to stay home.

Ren said, "You should do it, Mom. You loved those cities when we took our East Coast trip. It would be fun for you to go back."

I cocked my head. "Yeah, but you're forgetting one thing. I don't like baseball and there is a game every frickidy-frack day."

"What's not to like about it? You love being outdoors. And you like people, hotdogs, and beer."

Ree said, "And you like Mike."

"True, but…um, I would have to share a room with him." I waited to see what they thought about that.

Ree said, "So? You're an adult. You can handle it. Just don't do anything you don't want to do."

I stared. How had my 14-year-old matured so much? I scrunched my nose. "Do you mind being sent to your dad's house so soon after my extended trip to Italy?"

Ren groaned. "Shelly is going to be a nightmare just weeks before her wedding. Do we have to stay there the *whole* time."

Ree bobbed her head in agreement.

"Well, you need to stay with your father on his regular nights, but I'll see if your grandparents can host you a few nights. And maybe you can spend a night or two with Jennifer and Caitlyn."

I looked at my calendar and gasped. "Lauren! If I go, I'll miss your 18th birthday! That settles it. I'm staying home."

Ren said, "Don't worry, Mom. I've already decided about my birthday this year. I want to wait and celebrate it at the cabin over the Fourth of July weekend–after the wedding. Is that, OK?"

My heart pounded as I realized I had forgotten my own daughter's birthday, but her calm reaction helped to slow my poor thumper. "Really? You're not just saying that so I will go on the trip?"

Ree joined in. "She's not. Ren told me about her plan yesterday. She was jealous that Eli got to spend every birthday at the cabin."

That was right. Their cousin always celebrated his July 3rd birthday there. I smiled and said, "Alrighty then."

It was settled. I called Mike and gave him the news.

He said, "That's awesome. You won't regret it. We will…"

I butted in, "But I'm paying for all of my meals and souvenirs."

He bubbled with joy. "Okay. We'll have so much fun, and I'll make sure it's not only about baseball. We can dine at local places, eat crab cakes and Philly cheesesteaks, and see the sights. You just need to give me your information for the airline ticket and your shirt size."

"What? Why do you need my size?"

"Because you're going to get a Ballparks and More T-shirt!"

"Ooh! That's cool." I did love me some swag.

That night, sitting at Mom's dining table, I whined, "What if I don't like the people on the bus? And what if they don't like me?"

Mom put her hand on mine. "They'll love you, Pity. You'll probably make lots of new friends. You always do."

With my elbows on the table, I took a bite of her homemade strawberry shortcake. "But I don't know anything about baseball. What will I even talk about?"

"You'll be fine."

Dad came in holding something behind his back. "I'm going to loan you my lucky charm."

He handed me the faded blue hat he wore often over the years. I studied the design and a guess. "Is it Yankees?" I figured it might be since that was his favorite team and there was a Y on it.

He grinned. "Yes. Every time I wore it to one of their games, they won. You can borrow it but please don't lose it."

I popped it on my head. "Thanks, Dad. I'll wear it when the Yankees play and treat it like gold."

He shook his head. "I still can't believe *you*, of all people, get to see the new Yankee Stadium and I've never been there."

I brightened. "Dad, I have a great idea. Why don't you go on the trip with Mike? You love baseball and would have a blast."

He chuckled. "It does sound like fun, but I would just slow everyone down. Now tell me, who are playing the Yankees?"

I pulled up the new MLB app on my phone and said, "Looks like we'll see them play twice. Once against the New York Mets and then the Orioles, but I'm not sure where that team is from."

In unison, Mom and Dad said, "Baltimore."

"Oh, ha! I get it. Baltimore Orioles. Maybe their mascot is a bird." I laughed at the idea.

My parents looked at each other and rolled their eyes. Oh boy, I would be the worst one on the trip if this was their reaction.

"What other ballparks do you go to?" Dad bit into a strawberry.

I scanned the itinerary. "The Nationals in DC. The Mets. Phillies and then Red Sox, so I'm guessing Chicago?"

Dad said, "No, Chicago has the White Sox. Boston has Red Sox."

"What's with all the socks?"

He sat up straight to explain. "The Chicago and Boston teams are the oldest in baseball. Years ago, players wore long socks, so they created nicknames for the colors they wore, and the names stuck. It sounds like a fascinating trip even if you aren't a baseball fan."

I pondered what he just told me while scraping my plate and asked, "Dad, can you give me a quick lesson on how baseball is played and explain some of the rules? I don't want to be a complete idiot."

"Of course. Come with me."

He pushed himself up from the cherry dining table and led me to my old bedroom-turned-office. I smiled when he pulled up a picture of a baseball stadium on his computer screen. Thankfully, my parents had joined the 21st century quicker in getting the internet than they had in buying a microwave. I never thought they would get one.

Sitting in his office chair, Dad swiveled around to me. "You do know I tried to get you three girls to watch sports with me on television, but none of you were interested. I had hoped you learned something along the way. I even took you to see the St. Louis Cardinals when you were a kid."

I winced at being such a terrible daughter.

From over my shoulder, Mom said, "Jim, Pity was only four when we went to St. Louis." At least Mom provided one excuse for my ignorance.

Dad pointed to the pennant on the wall that read "Tulsa Drillers." "Well, we also took you to Drillers' games. But if I recall you were more interested in the songs the organist played and eating ice cream than watching the games."

I studied Dad's shelves, lined with Cardinals and Yankees paraphernalia. There was even a box of baseball cards featuring favorite players he had collected over the years. Poor guy. Until now, I'd never thought about how much he might have enjoyed having a son—or at least a daughter who was interested in sports. No wonder he enjoyed going to Lauren's swim meets so much.

He said, "So, Pity. Let's start with what you *do* know about baseball."

I took a breath. "Well, there is a pitcher and a catcher, and three strikes you're out. I know that from the song, *Take Me Out to the*

*Ballgame*, which I can sing and play on the piano with my eyes shut." I had to brag about the one baseball thing that made me an expert.

Dad's eyes widened, realizing how much work he had ahead of him in my crash course.

I continued, "And there are players who stand out on the little white squares to keep the batter from going around the big square."

Mom said, "Bases and it's a diamond, not a square."

And that's about how my lesson went. There was so much to learn about outs, balls fouls, and strikes. Why hadn't I paid attention when Dad tried to teach me years ago? Maybe some of the terms would stick in my brain, so I wouldn't humiliate myself around Mike.

Back home, I told the girls that Mom and Dad would be happy to have them stay there anytime. With two nights scheduled with friends and several with their dad, they would be fine.

I stood to go start packing and groaned.

"What was that for?" Ren raised an eyebrow.

"Oh, I'm still a little stiff from my tomato soup incident. The doctor said I'll be fine eventually."

"You need to stay out of trouble on this trip. You don't want to embarrass Mike."

"I'll be on my best behavior."

In my room, I gathered the things I would need for the trip. Since I liked to take little gifts for people I met while traveling, I dug through my stash of small garage sale finds for something small.

In my box of tiny flashlights, I found the 25 Oklahoma keychains I had bought recently. This was exciting. They were small, and easy to pack, and I only paid $5 for the whole lot. I put most of them in my suitcase and a few in my purse. You never knew who you might want to thank with a treat.

It was time for the most important question—what to wear to the games? My weather app indicated a chance of rain for most game days and the temps would be hot. I found a small umbrella, a cheap poncho, and my light rain jacket. I popped them in a stack to pack along with shorts, skorts, and two pairs of jeans. I figured it would be casual dress but threw in a sundress just in case.

But I needed to have some baseball clothes so I would fit in with the other people on the bus. The fans would probably be wearing team-of-the-day shirts and I didn't want to stand out by wearing regular clothes.

All I had so far was Dad's Yankee's hat. I searched Amazon for generic baseball-themed shirts with one-day shipping since I was leaving so soon. Wow! Such cute shirts. I ordered two but saw another design that was so simple I could make one with my new vinyl-cutting machine. I hopped to it and found a plain white T-shirt, then uploaded the design, and ironed the vinyl onto it. Easy peasy.

The day arrived. It was time to board the plane for Baltimore. When Mike picked me up at 4 a.m., he was more handsome than usual. I, on the other hand, was pretty sure I looked like a gargoyle at that time of day. The 6'4" guy leaned down, kissed me, and carried my heavy suitcase as if it were a marshmallow. I didn't even have to tell him about my sore ribs.

Mike was so excited that I was so glad I hadn't passed up the trip with him.

I wondered if spending a whole week together would change our relationship. I just hoped it changed for the better and not the worse after he saw my bedhead.

## Sports Joke #3
How do football players deal with their problems?
*They tackle them head-on*

After a long layover in Atlanta, we landed at the BWI airport in Baltimore. The cutest, tiniest shuttle driver, Shamika, drove us to our hotel. I don't know how she did it, but she lifted and tossed our giant suitcases into the van without a problem. With her cool accent, she explained how she immigrated from Nigeria a few years earlier. Shamika couldn't have been over five feet tall and looked to be about 14 years old. As she drove to the hotel, I asked her for a place that had good local food - maybe crab cakes.

She said, "Oh, you have to go to Timbuktu for that."

Surprised the Saharan city had crabcakes, I said, "Jeeze, Timbuktu? That sounds too far for us to go for dinner."

She shrugged and said with her cute accent, "Nope. It's just over there. I will drive you when you are ready. It's the best place around."

I said to Mike, "Who woulda thunk Timbuktu was in Maryland?"

When we arrived at the Holiday Inn, I was a little relieved to see our room had two queen beds—not that I mind sleeping with Mike. We had dated for eight months, but having choices and space was always good. I chose the bed closest to the bathroom and unloaded all my hair and beauty stuff on the counter by the sink while Mike lay on his bed watching a golf game. Whatever. I lay next to him and texted my family that we had arrived safely.

At five o'clock we made our way downstairs to the breakfast area for the meet and greet. I bounced into the room, ready to meet the people on our tour. To my disappointment, everyone sat in little cliques, and nobody looked up. A family of five, including a darling little boy, sat at a table together. They all wore Yankees hats similar to Dad's. Another group, of three loud couples sat at a table, laughing. Four men, who looked alike, played cards together as if they had been there for hours. Maybe they weren't even on our tour.

Several couples wore assorted team ball caps. One couple stood out because they were unbelievably tan. Maybe they lived on a beach, had a farm, or worked outside a lot. Or perhaps they owned a tanning bed. I would ask them about that once I got to know them.

When nobody invited us to sit with them, we found a table in the back. At the table next to ours, two blonde gals sat decked out in Dodgers shirts. On the other side of us, a teenage boy sat with an older woman. Perhaps it was his grandma. Two young men with matching red hair poking out from under their Yankees hats sat across from each other at another table.

I scrunched my nose at one guy who sat alone and looked creepy—well he had dirty hair and a scowl, anyway.

Another forty-something, balding dude sat by himself and wore a big cross on a chain around his neck. He didn't look much like a rapper, so I figured he might be religious.

I was surprised at how many Yankees fans there were, and even more shocked at the number of women on the trip without male partners. Their fathers must have been thrilled to have daughters who liked sports. Sorry, Dad.

A couple sitting in front of us caught my eye because they were drinking from cans of beer. She had long dark hair and sat a foot taller than the short stocky man she was with. Something about the couple was familiar. Did I know them? In a friendly voice, I leaned over. "Wow, where did you get the beer?" If they sold them at the hotel, I might want one.

Without turning to me, she spoke in a flat voice, "Liquor store."

Gee, she wasn't too keen on being my friend.

The teacher in me wanted someone to get the meet or greet part of this "meet and greet" going.

I whispered to Mike. "What a great beginning. Nobody is talking to anyone but the people they came with."

He patted my hand. "It's okay. We'll get to know them later."

Finally, a handsome man with salt and pepper hair, entered the room. He wore a green, 'Ballparks and More' t-shirt. Ooh. Was that the shirt I was going to get?

He announced, "My name is Rob. I'll be your Ballparks and More guide for the next seven days. Keep your schedule handy and I'll let you know if there are any changes. Now, I'll come by and get your names and phone numbers."

He proceeded to stop at each table, which seemed odd because we gave that information at registration. It took 15 minutes for him to make the rounds, while we all just sat and watched.

Then he said, "I want to make sure you all know that we have a priest on our tour. If you need to speak to him, he is available. Father John, can you raise your hand?"

The guy with the cross raised his hand and people clapped. He stood and said, "Just call me John."

Hmm. That explained the cross on his necklace. Even though I wasn't Catholic, it was good to know a man of the cloth was nearby.

Rob said, "OK. See you here tomorrow at 9 a.m." He turned, got on the elevator, and was gone.

What? That was it? No ice-breaker games? No 'tell us your name and where you are from?' How weird. I mean, it would have only taken ten minutes to introduce ourselves. Oh well, as much as I wanted to rule the world, I was not in charge.

As we stood to leave, I turned positive and said to Mike, "Maybe we'll get nametags tomorrow?"

"Maybe." He seemed as confused as I was. "You hungry?"

"Always."

Mike asked the desk clerk if Shamika could take us to Timbuktu. That sounded so funny, but the woman said, "I'll let her know you want to go. You'll love that place."

We did love that place. I got wine and a ridiculously large seafood platter that was amazing, but Mike's crab bisque was unforgettable.

I gave him some cash to help with dinner and while he paid the server, I walked to the lobby. As I left, I overheard him ask, "So, do most people get crabs here?" It was a good thing we were in a seafood restaurant or that question would have sounded pretty rude.

I asked the host if they had Timbuktu shirts or mugs. "I want to remember this amazing place when I get back to Oklahoma."

"We only have caps for twelve dollars." He handed me one.

"Ooh. It's so cute. I love it. I'll take it!"

I grabbed my wallet, but he said, "You're so excited, I want you to have it. Besides, I own the place and can do whatever I want."

I thanked him and gave him an Oklahoma keychain, vowing to wear my new hat the rest of the trip, except when the Yankees played.

After Shamika took us back to the hotel, we collapsed into our separate beds with full bellies and fell right to sleep.

The next morning, as I put on my sleeveless 'Play Ball' shirt I ordered from Amazon, I made a face at Mike and said, "Why are you wearing a drugstore hat instead of a baseball hat?"

"What?" He narrowed his eyes.

I pointed to the emblem. "It's a Walgreens hat. Why wear that to a ballgame?"

He looked in the mirror. "This isn't Walgreens. It's for the Washington Nationals. And it's called a cap."

"You are kidding, right? It is the same red W."

"It is not."

I didn't want to argue, but knew I was right and even googled Walgreens so I could see their W logo. Yep. Same.

We packed our bags for our next hotel. I checked my keychain supply in my purse. Then we took our luggage down to the lobby to meet everyone, but nobody was there. Even the breakfast room was empty. I checked my watch. 9:02 and said, "Where is everyone?"

Mike said, "Maybe they're already on the bus?"

We rushed outside and I climbed the steps to the bus while Mike and the driver loaded our bags in the luggage compartment. The bus was packed, and the only seats left were in the very back row by the bathroom. Oh, brother.

We rode for an hour and a half, feeling every bump in the road on the way to our nation's capital. It would have been okay, but it was so hot on the bus that I started to feel sick. Everyone fiddled with their vents, but the bus never got cooler.

By the time we made it to the National Mall, I was about to throw up. Mike wet a napkin with cold water from my water bottle and placed it on the back of my neck. I looked up as we approached the Washington Monument. It was so impressive I wanted to ignore my nausea but couldn't. When we finally stopped, we traded the bus heat for a 95-degree outdoor temperature. At least it wasn't stuffy.

As we stood outside the bus, I asked our guide, "Is the A/C broken? I'm feeling sick riding in the back of the bus in this heat."

Rob shrugged. "Last one on the bus gets the worst seats."

I wrinkled my lip and almost said, 'Well you should have told us to be on the bus at 9, not downstairs at 9.' But he was right. We were the last and deserved to be the rotten eggs. Unfortunately, the thought of rotten eggs made me gag.

Then Rob said, "And Mac turned the temperature down. It should cool off soon."

"Oh, that's good." But I wondered who the heck Mac was.

I hoped Mike wasn't embarrassed that I had already complained, but figured he didn't want me to barf on him, either.

I had to cool off, so made a beeline for the Lincoln Memorial Reflecting Pool. All I wanted to do was jump in, but nobody was swimming in the 18 inches of water, so I couldn't. A few people sat on the side with their feet dangling in, so I followed suit and took off my shoes. Ahh. How did that cool me off so quickly? I scooped water into my hands and wet my arms down which felt even better.

I heard nervous tapping and looked back and saw Mike's foot. We only had an hour here, so I put my shoes on and followed him.

The Lincoln Memorial was just as magnificent as when I'd seen it before. The marble statue of his detailed face and body just screamed dignity. If I wasn't already in love with the Tulsa Golden Driller statue, I might choose Abe as my favorite stone man.

We took selfies with Lincoln and some with the Washington Monument in the background, just beyond the reflecting pool. I sent the pics to my girls right away.

It was my first time visiting the Vietnam War Memorial and I was in awe as we walked along the wall etched with 58,000 names. So sad.

As we headed back to the bus, I overheard Rob tell someone on the phone, "Jeeze, I've already got a complainer. It's gonna be a helluva trip with some of these people."

My face turned red since I knew who he was talking about. I vowed not to complain anymore, even if I ended up sick as a dog.

## Game 1

### San Francisco Giants vs Washington Nationals

We made it across town to the ballpark without incident despite the sweltering hot bus. Apparently Mac, whoever he was, had not turned the air down very much.

I heaved my purse onto my shoulder, ready to exit the bus, but Mike said, "Um Pity, I forgot to tell you some stadiums only allow little purses or none at all."

I froze. "Well, that would have been nice to know. I didn't even bring a small purse."

He scrunched his nose. "Sorry. But your shorts have pockets. Can you put your wallet in there?"

Figuring he knew the rule, I stuffed my license, credit cards and cash into a front pocket and phone in the back. With my new Timbuktu hat on my head, I held my arms out to the side. "Guess this will have to do."

Mike wasn't kidding. When we got to the entrance, a woman in front of us was stopped from entering. The security guard said, "Your purse is too big."

I strained my neck to see her large bag, but it wasn't large at all. In fact, it was so small I figured he was joking, but he frowned and pointed to a sign. 'No purse over 5"x7".

The frantic gal said, "But we rode an Uber here and I have no place to put it."

I held my breath as the drama unfolded. The guy shrugged and her shoulders slumped. She took out her important items and I watched in horror as she threw her purse in the trash! Unbelievable.

Being in the sisterhood, I considered consoling the lady but figured she might be creeped out by a stranger's hug, and just let it be.

Once we entered the huge Washington Nationals stadium, I stood at the top of our section and looked over the ballpark. After taking it all in, I turned to Mike. "What a pretty pattern on the field! It looks like a green quilt. How do they do that?"

"It's lawn striping. They use a lawnmower, followed by a roller that pushes the grass down. When they mow in different directions, the sun hits the bent grass to make that effect."

I gaped at Mike. "You sure are smart about baseball fields. Here, I want to take a photo of you at every ballpark." I positioned him down a few steps so I could see the name, "Nationals" over his big body. He gave me an irresistible smile, and I gulped then clicked.

"OK, let me get one of you."

I wasn't sure why he wanted one of me. I dripped with sweat, but I posed in my new "Play Ball" shirt and gave him a cheesy smile.

By the time we found our seats, I was so hot that I left right away to buy a cold drink. I choked at the $10 price for a Coke, but at least I got a souvenir Washington Nationals collector's cup with it. It had beautiful cherry blossoms printed all around it. I stood in the shade and savored my cold, expensive drink and watched as other members of our group found their seats.

How weird. The only people wearing baseball shirts were those two blonde gals who wore different Dodgers shirts today. The four men who looked sort of alike, wore matching shirts that read, 'Outer Banks.' Maybe they were from North Carolina? Was this how I would have to find out where people came from? I pulled out my phone and I started making a list, so I could identify who was who on our tour.

I made a trip to the bathroom where a total stranger said she loved my shirt. Maybe I did fit in with baseball people.

When I finally rejoined Mike, he asked, "Are you feeling okay now? It should start cooling off soon."

"Yes, the cold drink did the trick. But why isn't everyone on our tour wearing baseball shirts? I mean there are a few in Yankees outfits, and those Dodgers gals, but the others are in everyday clothes."

"Maybe they don't care that much. Or maybe they only like one team."

"Well, at least you're supporting Walgreens with your hat." I punched his arm.

He corrected me. "Walgreens *cap*."

I laughed at my funny guy. Mike owned a "cap" from each MLB team and brought one for each ballpark we were going to visit. As I looked around, I noticed other people wearing the same W. Hmph.

The gal next to me wore a Yankees hat. I asked, "Are you a Yankees fan?"

"Oh yes, we live in Long Island and always support them."

Her accent was adorable. It was so New Yorkish. Internally, I copied her accent then said, "I'm Pity. This is my boyfriend, Mike. We live just outside of Tulsa, Oklahoma."

"I'm Ava and this is my husband, Vince."

I nodded at Vince. Yippee. I finally met somebody on our tour.

Ava leaned over. "Did you say your name was Betty?"

I smiled. "No. But that is my mom's name. I'm Pity with a P." I gave her my usual explanation. "My real name is Kitty but when I was born my sister couldn't say her Ks and called me Pity. The nickname just stuck."

"Interesting, but hello, Pity. Have you been on a Ballparks and More tour before? This is our first one."

"No. I wouldn't be here, but Mike's best friend had to back out due to a family emergency and I took his place." I scoffed, "I don't even like baseball."

She squinted as if she was really confused.

After that reaction, I realized I probably shouldn't have announced that. It might diminish their excitement. I backpedaled by repeating Ren's comment, "But I love the outdoors, hotdogs, beer, and all the cities we'll see on the trip. I expect it will be loads of fun." I added, "And who knows? Maybe I'll become a baseball fan?" I had to chuckle to myself at that improbability.

When we stood for the National Anthem, I followed Mike's lead and took off my Timbuktu hat. I placed it over my heart and then cringed as a singer butchered the song with unnecessary vocal acrobats. As a music teacher, I'm more of a purist with the song. It didn't need such embellishments. When the woman's last, eternal note finally ended, someone yelled, "Play Ball." Ha, maybe they read my shirt!

I tried to focus on the game and the rules Dad had taught me, but I had so many questions. I leaned into Mike. "What is that timer for?"

He smiled, apparently happy to explain. "Oh, that's the new rule. The pitcher only has a certain amount of time to pitch the ball. If the time runs out on the pitcher, it's a ball. If the time runs out and the batter isn't ready, it's a strike."

"Hmm."

He looked at my confused face and said, "You should be glad of this new rule because the games go much faster now."

"Well then, I like that rule."

Across the field, an enormous screen showed replays which were fun to watch. When teams switched places, cameras caught live footage of fans eating, cheering, and enjoying the game.

Mike looked at me and did a double take. He raised his eyebrows. "I'm glad to see you are enjoying the game so much."

I turned to him with a fixed smile. "The game? No. I'm trying to look pleasant; in case I'm caught on that big screen."

He smirked and turned back to the game.

Suddenly, big hearts and lips with the words 'Kiss Cam' covered the huge electronic screen. When an unsuspecting couple appeared on camera, they lit up when they recognized themselves. They kissed each other. How sweet. I watched as a few more couples kissed on demand. The best one was when a man holding his baby kissed it on the cheek. Adorable.

I practiced the surprised look I would make if the Kiss Cam focused on Mike and me.

Mike caught me. "Okay, now what's with that goofy expression? You look like you just won the lottery."

"It's a secret." I wasn't about to tell him the truth.


As much as I tried to focus on the game itself, I spent more time watching the vendors walking up and down the aisles selling drinks. They each had their own style of pitching their food or drinks. I tried to keep track of the different ways they got people's attention. As I was typing the sing-songy "Beer, Beer, Beer, Beer, Beer!" into my phone, the 14-year-old boy from our group came down the steps.

He told the older lady in front of me, "Memaw, a guy gave me a button for visiting Nationals Park for the first time."

Before she could react, I leaned over and asked him, "That's so cool. Where did you get it?"

He said, "Go to Fan Services - just up the steps to the right."

"And it's free?"

"Yep."

I jumped up from my seat as if it was on fire and crawled over Mike. At the top of the steps, there was a man at a little table wearing a 'Fan Services' shirt. He gave me a button with 'First Game' printed on it and the word, Nationals beneath. I said, "Thank you! Could I possibly have one for my boyfriend too?"

He handed me another one. As I pinned my button on my shirt, the man said in a hushed voice, "Would you like to see the presidents up close?"

I froze, then unable to contain my excitement, I shouted, "Sure! Who wouldn't? How can I do that?"

"Well, come up here right after the 4th inning. You can have your photo taken too."

"Wow. Thanks!" I could hardly believe my luck. My photo with the president of the United States? I hadn't heard the commander-in-chief would be at the game tonight. But we *were* in the nation's capital. Maybe it's commonplace for the POTUS to attend ball games. Man, if the president ever came to Broken Arrow or Tulsa, there would be a huge to-do for weeks in advance.

Wearing my button proudly, I sat between Mike and Ava, bubbling over with the excitement of meeting our nation's leader. I tried to get Mike's attention to tell him about it, but he was so engrossed in the game that I didn't want to interrupt him.

I tried to find the score among all the billboards lining the field so that I could catch up, but there were so many numbers it was confusing. Oh yeah, Dad had said to look for an R - since runs were the baseball points. Found it. The Nationals were ahead of the Giants.

During a break, I gave Mike his button and started to tell him how I was going to meet the president, but I was interrupted by a loud announcement over the speakers.

"It is now time for the president's race."

A race? Like a running race? I stared wide-eyed at the field. Why would our president race someone at a ballgame? Then out of the dugout came four giant-headed guys dressed like presidents! There was Abe Lincoln, George Washington, Teddy Roosevelt, and another one whom I guessed to be Thomas Jefferson. It was as if Mt. Rushmore was coming to life on the ballfield.

Good grief. Of course, the real president wasn't racing, or even attending the game. I couldn't believe my naivety. So, that was who I could have my picture taken with—four mascots. I was such a goof.

I focused on the race since it was too cute to miss. At first, George Washington was in the lead, then Lincoln came up, but Jefferson ended up taking first. Poor Teddy Roosevelt was left in the dust. Now, that was real entertainment!

I turned to Ava. "Aren't they adorable?"

She giggled. "So funny."

I told her, "The guy who gave me this button said to go up to up to Section 13 if I want to meet them. Do you want to go with me?"

"Sure!"

I explained what we were doing to Mike, and we ran up the stairs. We lined up behind a man with his grandson. After just a few minutes, a big crowd had gathered behind us. I told Ava, "I'm such a dope. I was just sure I was going to meet the real president."

She laughed. "You've never heard of the racing presidents?"

I shook my head. As we waited, I said, "So, what do you do on Long Island?"

"I'm a retired nurse, which comes in handy when watching grandkids."

"Very handy. I'll try not to bug you with blisters or papercuts."

"I'll be happy to help with any ailments. What about you?"

"I'm an elementary music teacher, raising two teenage daughters on my own. Well, they do have a dad, but he's pretty useless this month. He's getting married to a bridezilla in a few weeks."

Two buff men wearing black t-shirts reading, 'Secret Service,' set up barriers to keep everyone in line. How cute—it made sense. The four famous presidents need to be protected.

In a flurry of noise and excitement, the 10-foot-tall presidents ran up a ramp toward us. Their giant heads bobbled as they bounded over and stood against a wall to pose for pictures with the father and grandson who were in line in front of us.

When it was my turn, one of the "secret service agents" took my phone. I positioned myself in front of the presidents and glanced back and looked up, and up, and up to see their faces. Now I knew what it felt like to be an ant. I made several poses, laughing the whole time.

After our photos were taken, we giggled on our way back toward our seats. As I followed Ava, one of the red-headed guys from our tour rushed past me holding his stomach. I watched as he ran to the men's restroom, and hoped he made it in time. I considered mentioning it to Ava since she was a nurse but figured it was a personal problem so I didn't want to embarrass the poor guy.

Back in my seat, Mike handed me a hotdog.

"Ooh. Thanks!" Between bites, I told him all about how I thought I would meet the actual president, then showed him the silly photos.

He laughed and said, "You look so tiny. Even if they aren't real presidents, those photos are good souvenirs."

When a beer vendor came by, I bought us each a $14 can of beer. Wow! Ballpark food and drinks were sure expensive! With five more games and meal prices like this, I wouldn't be able to even afford the screws for the swimming pool deck.

I looked down and saw a splotch of mustard on my shirt. After wiping it, I searched the ballpark app for stadium bag and food policies. Hmm. At most ballparks, you were allowed to carry individual-sized snacks and an unopened water bottle if carried in a clear bag. Good to know! I now had a mission to find one.

As I scanned to see if anyone was carrying one of these bags, I saw an older couple from our group talking to Father John. I guess it was good to have a priest on the tour. Maybe he even took confessions.

When Mike's phone rang, he motioned that he'd be right back and took off up the stairs. I tried to focus on the game while he was gone but instead, I surveyed other people and their food. Aha! A woman with a big clear bag walked up the steps. Through it, I could see her wallet, a bag of Cheetos, a brush, and some M&M's. Her clear bag had Phillies printed on the side.

Nice. We would be in Philadelphia tomorrow, so maybe I could buy a bag so I could take my own snacks to future games.

When everyone cheered and stood, I jumped up to see what was going on. I studied the scoreboard and figured out it was the Nationals who had just gotten a point, or technically, "scored a run." I was getting the hang of this baseball thing. I copied the teenage boy from our tour and yelled, "Yay, Nats!" But by being so loud and responding late, people stared at me.

Mike returned but he was out of breath and sweaty. He said with a frown, "Pity, I have to leave."

I squinted. "Oh. Okay. Is the game over? I'll get my stuff." I grabbed my collectible cup and trash.

"No, Pity. I have to go home…back to Tulsa."

"What? Why?" That didn't make any sense. I stared at him.

He was frantic as he spoke. "Sally's in labor a month early. Scott is still overseas. My parents can't travel from Utah now because they have bad colds. I have to be with her and help take care of Jesse."

I put my hand on his. "I'll go too." I stood and almost knocked my pretty beer cup from its holder. "Better yet, why don't I go help Sally, and you stay for the baseball games? This is your trip."

He held out his hands. "No. She asked for me specifically, and she's really scared after her problems with Jesse's delivery. You should go ahead with the tour, and I'll be back in a few days, once she's settled and I know she's Okay. Besides, I already called and got a flight out of DC. It leaves in an hour, and I'll be at the hospital in Tulsa by midnight. I'm so sorry Pity, but I promise I'll be back."

As much as I wanted to scream, 'Take me with you,' I tried to stay calm for his sake. "Well, don't worry about me, Mike. Just be there for Sally, keep me in the loop and please try to come back."

"I will." He leaned over and gave me a big, juicy kiss that would have been perfect on the Kiss Cam. Furthermore, the kiss was the most affectionate we had been in weeks considering the business of school ending and traveling. I was really going to miss him, now.

He leaned across to Ava and Vince, who had heard the whole thing, and said, "Please take care of my Pity."

They nodded and he rushed off.

I took a deep breath and began to worry about him and Sally. But then it hit me; Mike had said, "My Pity." I couldn't help but smile.

Wait! How in the world did I end up on a baseball tour by myself?

## Sports Joke #4

Why was Cinderella kicked off the basketball team?
*She ran away from the ball.*

A bit later, on my way to the bathroom, I ran into our guide, Rob, standing above our seats with his arms folded in front of his chest. I frowned and said, "I guess Mike told you he had to leave?"

Rob said, "That's too bad. He was looking forward to the games."

"I know." I frowned. "I hope he gets back soon. Oh, do you know when we will get our Ballparks and More T-shirts?"

There was a loud cheer, and Rob craned his neck around me to see who had made a hit. "Oh, they'll send them to one of our hotels."

"Cool. Do you know what color they will be?"

He rolled his eyes. "No. I'm not in charge of the T-shirts."

Okay then. This guy was not a very friendly tour guide, or maybe I was just really being obnoxious. Before I turned to leave, I asked, "Say, is that guy from our group all right?"

He furrowed his brow at me, so I clarified. "He's tall, with red hair, and came with another guy that looked kinda like him? He ran to the bathroom maybe 40 minutes ago and he didn't look so good."

Rob scoured our group and said, "I'll find out." He headed down the stairs and spoke with the other red-headed guy, who bolted up the steps past me. Rob followed him with a worried look on his face.

As I stood at the top of the stairs, pondering the situation, I noticed a woman and a kid sitting in high-top chairs overlooking our section. When they turned their heads, I realized it wasn't a mother and child, but the tall woman and short man I had spoken with at the meet and greet. It was a good thing that wasn't a kid because the short man was downing a 16 oz beer.

I finally figured out who the two reminded me of. With their extreme height difference, her long black hair, and his mustache, they looked like live versions of the dastardly Boris and Natasha from the "Rocky and Bullwinkle" cartoon videos Dad used to show me. I suppressed a giggle as I stared at them. How had they managed those fancy seats up top anyway? Whatever.

Back in my seat, I leaned over to Ava. "So, what quarter is this?"

Ava leaned back and stared at me. "Wow. You really don't know anything about baseball, do you? They are called innings and we're in the 7th." When she saw my dazed look, she added, "Of nine."

There was a commotion behind us. When I heard the word, ambulance, I worried about the guy I saw running to the restroom.

It wasn't two minutes before rumors about the red-headed guy started to fly: 1. He had fallen down the steps. 2. He choked on something. 3. He had been hit by a foul ball.

None of these made sense to me and I added my two cents worth to Ava and Vince. "Well, after we took photos with the presidents, I spotted him running toward the bathroom holding his stomach. I sure hope he's ok."

The last inning took forever as I worried about Mike, Sally, and the guy with the tummy ache. The Nationals finally won, and Rob led us back to the bus. Comments from other passengers ranged from the score of the game to concern for our fellow traveler.

My seat in the back of the bus was lonely. Poor Mike. I still couldn't believe he had to leave.

Rob took the microphone and said, "I am sad to announce that a young man, Jason, from our group, has taken ill. He is in the hospital with some sort of stomach problem. It does look like he will recover. His cousin, Michael, is with him now and will keep us updated."

My shoulders relaxed, happy that he would be OK. I settled back in for the two-and-a-half-hour ride to Philadelphia. Since it was evening, it wasn't as hot as earlier, but they sure needed to fix the A/C. I spent the drive time texting photos to my girls, Kim and Mom.

I made a Facebook post with selfies of us in DC, at the game, and a picture of me with the presidents. I didn't share the situation of Mike and his sister with the world.

It was impossible to sleep on the ride with the heat and loud laughter coming from the front of the bus. So, I started making my list of people on the bus to help keep them straight. It came naturally to me, after having so many students to keep track of year after year.

I started with the people I knew and wrote down Ava and Vince–Long Island. Jason–the guy who got sick and his cousin, Michael. And of course, Rob–the guide. That was it. Since I didn't know any of the other 45 names, I would use distinguishing features to identify them.

After hearing an exceptionally loud squeal, I sat up on my knees to see who was making the racket. It was those two blonde Dodger gals who were sitting across from Rob in the front row. They seemed to be flirting. Hmph. At least someone was having fun.

I could see quite a few other people from my vantage point in the way back, and jotted notes as I scanned the bus.

The priest, Father John, sat alone five rows up debating baseball stats with the man sitting in front of him.

A lone guy was taking up both seats right in front of me. Oh, it was that big guy with gross hair. Today his dirty-looking hair even stuck to his head. I caught a glimpse of his profile and noticed he had a creepy mustache that made me shudder.

I looked ahead at the four guys who were dressed alike. They were in some grand discussion about one of the plays that should have gone to the Giants. They acted like they might be brothers.

A light glared in my eye, and I looked between the seats in front of me and saw Gross Hair Guy's phone screen. Eew. He was looking at photos of a naked woman. I put my phone down and leaned against the window so I couldn't possibly see any more of that. Ick. Could this day get any worse?

Arriving at the new hotel, I got my key and wheeled my suitcase to my room, hoping Gross Hair Guy wasn't in the room next to me.

Upon opening my door, I frowned when I saw two big queen beds staring at me. Poor Mike. Poor Sally. I hoped she would have a safe and easy delivery.

My side hurt when I lifted my suitcase onto the rack—yet another reason to miss Mike. He had done all the schlepping. Buck up, Pity.

After getting ready for bed, I called my girls. "So where are you gals staying tonight?"

Ren, on speaker phone, said, "We're at Grandma and Grandpa's."

Ree piped up. "Grandpa showed us slides of you when you were a girl, then pictures of us when we were little. It was pretty funny."

I smiled, picturing Dad's complicated setup with the standing slide screen and the projector on a metal TV tray. His round slide tray clicked whenever he advanced to the next photograph. I could just feel the heat from the light and fan blowing on me. How many times had I watched our family trip photos from their couch? Hundreds for sure. Dad was old school, and I loved it.

I told the girls about Mike having to leave the tour.

Ren sucked in a breath. "Will you be OK until he gets back?"

"Oh, I'll be fine. Hopefully, it will just be a day or two."

"Tell Mike we'll be glad to watch his nephew if he needs us to."

Ree added, "Yeah. Jesse's so cute. We'll watch him for free."

"That's sweet and Mike may need you. I'll give him your number. Have you been to your dad's house?"

"Yes. And Shelly is horrible."

I exhaled. "Now keep in mind, she's just excited about her wedding, so cut her some slack."

Ren huffed. "No, you don't understand. She told me since I'm her maid of honor, I have to read a poem at the wedding."

"That's not so bad. You can do that."

"But, Mom, she wrote it herself and it's about her! I already read it and it's awful! I can't do it." Had I heard Lauren, right?

Ree said, "But that's not the worst thing. Remember the peach-colored dresses she picked out for us?"

I pictured the hideous peach dresses with giant, puffy sleeves. The long skirts had layers of lace resembling an ugly pink doll cake I'd once seen on a Pinterest fail. "Yes. How could I forget those?"

Ree whined, "Well, forget them. Now she has bought us red, white, and blue dresses that still drip with rows of lace. They look like the American flag! I will die if I have to wear one."

I made a face and cleared my throat. "What does your dad say?".

They both squawked, "Nothing."

I tried to be diplomatic. "Well, maybe nobody you know will come to the wedding."

Ree said, "Ha! Shelly already invited Caitlyn's family because she knows how rich and influential her dad is, him being a judge."

"And get this," Ren added, "Last week, Chris's parents bought a Cadillac convertible at Big Jack's Cadillacs. Apparently in June, if you buy a car, you get an invitation to the wedding! So, now Chris is going to be there too. Mom, you have to help us!"

I pictured all those Cadillacs showing up at Big Jack's ranch for the wedding. Then I cringed at the thought that my girls' friends would see them in hideous flag dresses. I said, "Okay. I'll call your dad but I can't promise anything."

"Lauren, are you excited about your birthday tomorrow? I still can't believe I'm missing it. Want me to call you at 5:04 a.m. to commemorate your birth at the exact time you were born?"

"Um. No. Call a little later, please."

🏏

At breakfast, I didn't see Ava and Vince, so I looked around for an empty seat by someone else who looked friendly.

One woman spoke quietly with the priest at a table. How nice.

Everyone else was deep in conversation with one another, except for the grandma and the teenage boy. I asked, "May I join you?"

"Of course." The woman smiled, acting as happy as I felt.

I learned they were from Oregon and the grandson, Isaiah, was 14, just as I had guessed. As he talked, I wondered if Ree would think he was cute.

How sweet of the grandmother to take him on a baseball trip. I decided when I had grandkids, I would take them on trips, even if it was to baseball games, operas, or car racing. I never wanted to spoil my kids and didn't really have the money to anyway but if I ever had grandkids, I just might.

When the bus arrived, I made my excuses, threw away my paper plate, and rushed out to get a better seat this time. Some people had marked their territory with bags or jackets, but I found an empty spot four rows from the front and plopped myself down. Whew. I could even see out the front window behind the tiered seats. Much better!

Across from me, a man sat talking with the priest, who took notes and comforted the man. After a few minutes, the guy left and moved to another seat. Father John seemed pretty popular.

When the four guys, who looked sort of alike, boarded, I got an answer to one of my questions. They were indeed brothers. I knew that because their matching green shirts read, 'Mom's favorite.'

When they sat in the row behind me, I turned and asked, "So, who is the oldest?"

The guy with a gray goatee sitting across the aisle said, "I'm the oldest and the smartest."

The one sitting next to him boasted, "But I'm the best looking."

Behind me, the man pointed next to him. "I'm older than him by four minutes and have much more experience."

I had to laugh at these characters.

"But Mom saved the best for last." That comment came from the last brother, of course.

As I studied the twins, I could see they were identical, but since one had a beard and the other didn't, it hadn't been obvious at first.

I said, "It must be fun to see how you would look with a beard, or a different haircut just by looking at your brother."

The two nodded and I continued, "I always wanted to be a twin. Nice to meet you. I'm Pity Kole."

The twin with the beard said his name was Harry and the one without introduced himself as Barry.

I said, "Thank heavens the one of you with the beard is Harry or I'd never remember which was which."

Harry asked, "Are you here alone?"

"My boyfriend was with me but had to leave for a family emergency. He should be back in a few days."

Barry said, "Wow. I hope he doesn't miss too many games."

I agreed and turned back to the front and checked for a text from Mike. Finally, there was a brief message. 'Sally's OK, but no baby yet. Send good thoughts.'

I closed my eyes and sent good thoughts and a prayer that all would go well. I replied, 'Done,' and added, 'Oh and Ren said she and Ree can watch Jesse anytime you need them.'

I gave him Ren's number, and closed with, 'By the way, it's Ren's birthday, so it would be cool if Sally had the baby today. Keep me informed, please. I miss you.'

That was my cue to call Ren. Of course, since it was still only 8:30 in Oklahoma, I woke her up. I tried to keep my voice down since the priest was sleeping. "Happy birthday sweet pea! Do you have fun plans for today on your REAL birthday?"

"Hi, Mom." She sounded groggy. "Yeah, Ree and I are going to see that new Ryan Gosling movie with friends. Then Chris is taking me out to dinner. But we have to spend the night with Dad and Shelly…they can have her parents over to celebrate."

I was distracted when I saw someone sit beside the sleeping Father John and open the priest's notebook. What a snoop.

I returned to my phone call. "Oh, so you'll get to hang out with the famous, Big Jack! That's cool. Sounds like a nice day! I wish I was there to give you your 18 swats on your butt."

"Thanks. You know how much I love those." Her voice was sarcastic, but I figured she missed me and my silly traditions.

"Oh, I left an envelope for you under my pillow. Make sure to go get it before you head out today."

"Ooh. Thanks, Mom. I will."

"I'm heading to Philadelphia now. Have a wonderful birthday!"

I looked toward the priest, but the snooping guy was gone.

When the bus dropped us off in front of Independence Hall, I was pumped. This was history! It was even more historical than four racing presidents. I mean the actual Constitution was signed here!

I took the tour and tried to soak in as many facts as possible. Afterward, the Dodger girls invited me to join them at a Philly cheesesteak place. The gals were fun and wow, that sandwich was good. There was enough meat on one bun to serve a whole ball team! Oh my, I was starting to use baseball references.

As we ate, I asked, "So, where are you from?"

One of them said, "Los Angeles, of course."

The other joined in. "That's why we call ourselves Deb and Diana, the Dodger's Divas."

I guessed that meant the Dodgers were also from California. I said, "How cute!" then added, "I have a sister in L.A. It's the only place I ever get to go to the beach since I'm landlocked in Oklahoma."

Diana brightened. "Next time you go see her, you have to go with us to see a Dodgers game!"

I forced a smile. I had no intention of going to another baseball game after finishing this trip. But getting together with 'The Divas' might be fun. I gave them a real smile. "Yeah. I'll call if I go out there. So, are you two married?"

They wrinkled their noses and spoke as one. "To each other?"

I laughed. "No, I meant to other people. I'm just curious why two gals would go on a baseball tour."

Deb nodded. "Well, I have a boyfriend, and Diana is widowed. We just really love baseball and figured it would be a fun trip."

"Oh. Good for you." What else could I say?

Diana added, "And I can't get enough of those uniforms. There is nothing sexier than a guy in baseball pants." She pretended to swoon, with her hand on her forehead.

I hadn't even noticed the uniforms. I'd have to check them out. I said, "So, I heard you two chatting with Rob. Is he single?"

Looking a little disappointed, Diana said, "No. He said he's been married for 20 years. He's such a doll."

Deb said, "Lucky wife."

Again, I was confused. He was good-looking but didn't seem like that much of a catch to me. Whatever.

After eating as much as we could of our Philly Cheesesteak sandwiches, we got in the long line to tour the Liberty Bell.

A guy walked past us as he left, and said to his friend, "Well that was a waste of time. It was just a big bell. How boring."

Deb, Diana, and I snickered at his comment. I said, "He's probably the same guy who wrote that ridiculous review of the Grand Canyon. I mimicked the reviewer with a sassy voice, "It's just a giant hole in the ground. No roller coasters or even Dippin' Dots."

The girls laughed as we inched our way inside. I was excited to see the copper bell made in 1752. The last time it rang was in 1846 for George Washington's birthday. When I got closer, I marveled at America's symbol of freedom. The three-foot-tall bell was suspended on its original yoke of elm wood. I studied the details and inscriptions and could see where they had tried to repair the crack. Ain't history grand?

Diana was busy putting on lipstick so I said, "Deb, can you get a picture of me standing in front of the bell?"

Deb took my phone but just as I posed with my signature smile, a toddler ran under the railing that protected the famous bell. The teacher in me took over and I hopped over the barrier to grab her. Unfortunately, I missed her hand and tripped over my own feet. I ran a few steps with my arms outstretched trying to keep from falling, but as if in slow motion, I flew towards the National treasure. And to my horror….my head banged smack into the Liberty Bell.

BONGGG! A loud metallic sound reverberated in my skull. There I lay, sprawled beneath the giant bell. Just before I blanked out, a thought rushed through my gonged head–If I lived to see another day, I could write a mystery and call it *Death by Liberty Bell.*

I heard faint voices and opened my eyes and saw Deb, Diana, and a security guard standing over me with their mouths moving. I couldn't decipher what they said with the clang of the bell still echoing in my head. They helped me stand up and walked me over to a bench.

After a few seconds, I finally understood the security guard's repeated question, "Are you okay, Miss?"

I croaked, "I think so. Did someone grab the little girl?"

Just then a young mom walked by holding the toddler who was in mid-tantrum. Lucky for me, the little girl's shrieks were muted by my stupor. Sometimes it's good not to hear everything.

I asked the guard, "Am I in trouble for ringing the bell?"

"Well…no. We could tell it was an accident. But keep in mind, the security of the Liberty Bell is our job, not yours."

I twisted my mouth. "I'm really sorry. It was just instinct."

He said, "Are you sure you're okay?"

I gave a weak smile and stood up, feeling less woozy than before. But my left side hurt, as well as the right. Why was I so clumsy? I looked around and realized everyone in the entire place was staring at me. I just wanted to get out of there, and urged, "Let's go, girls."

Deb and Diana escorted me out of the building.

I shook my pounding head. "How embarrassing!"

Diana said, "What were you thinking to go after the little girl?"

I closed my eyes, partly in pain, but mostly in embarrassment. "It's second nature. I'm an elementary school teacher, so kids are my business." I scoffed. "You should see me in the grocery store. When I see children running around, I usually interfere so nobody gets hurt. Sometimes the parents are thankful that I grabbed them, and sometimes, not so much."

Deb rolled her eyes. "I hope I caught your stunt on your camera."

I hoped not. Even though I wanted to know how I had fallen in the kitchen just days before, I wanted to forget all about this.

Deb held my phone up so my face could wake it up. She looked over my shoulder as I opened the camera app. Oh yeah, there was a shot of me smiling. That, I could handle.

She leaned over and said, "Keep flipping. I took a lot."

Diana joined us as I scrolled. In the series of photos, I leaned, then hopped, then ran off balance, then fell and hit the bell.

I closed my eyes and said, "Why me?" The gals laughed and I couldn't help but crack up, too. Oh, great. Now I was making Liberty Bell jokes about myself–crack up–ha.

I said, "Oh my gosh, I'm glad this is only on my camera and not a video anyone could send to America's Funniest Home Videos."

Diana put her hand on my shoulder. "Are you sure you're, okay? We can probably find an Urgent Care."

I put my hand to my head, thinking I must have the hardest skull in the world. "It's just a little bump and it doesn't seem to be growing. I'll be fine." I pointed to the visitor's center. "Before I go, I want to buy a little Liberty Bell to commemorate the event."

Deb raised an eyebrow skeptically and dug in her purse. "Here, at least take some Ibuprofen."

I thanked her, took two pills, and assured them I would be fine.


Back on the warm bus with my Liberty Bell souvenirs, we made a quick stop at the Philadelphia Museum of Art, so we could take pictures of the Rocky Balboa statue. Most of us wanted to run up the

72 steps and pose like the iconic movie boxer. I couldn't exactly run with my head and both sides of my body aching but managed to climb to the top while humming the Rocky theme song, 'Gonna Fly Now'. Without my girls or Mike alongside to share the experience of the iconic movie location, it seemed anticlimactic.

While standing at the top of the stairs overlooking Philadelphia, people from our tour motioned for me to join them for a group photo. A woman standing about 15 steps below us, took a picture while we all posed like Rocky finishing his training montage.

I was halfway down the steps when people started screaming. I turned to find an older man lying sprawled out on the steps.

A little boy from our tour group ran to him. "Abuelo! Abuelo!"

The woman who took our photo yelled, "Papi!" and rushed over.

The man tried to sit up, but he winced in pain. Two young men helped him to a sitting position. He looked to be all right until he tried to stand up. He cried out in pain and pointed to his foot. The guys slung his arms over their shoulders and carried him down the steps. I recognized the family of five I had seen the first day.

I made it back to the base of the stairs and asked the guys, "Is there anything I can do?" They shook their heads no, so I backed up to give them room. One guy was on the phone, seeking medical help.

The old man kept saying, "Empujado. Empujado."

I didn't speak Spanish, but thought he was asking for those Spanish meat pastries. He must really be hungry. It was an odd thing to say while in pain, but who was I to judge? I was always hungry!

When I settled back in my bus seat, I started worrying about the older man. At least we both had stories to tell—mine at the Liberty Bell and his at the Rocky steps.

I wished the man hadn't mentioned meat pies, because it made me hungry. Maybe I should have saved the rest of my sandwich.

Harry leaned over the seat and asked, "Are you excited to tour Citizens Bank today?"

I made a face. "Why are we going to a bank? I thought we were going to the Phillies stadium."

You would have thought I was a stand-up comedian the way all four brothers laughed. His twin, Barry, said between snorts, "That is the name of the Phillies ballpark."

I crinkled my nose. "Why?"

The priest cleared his throat and spouted, "It's named that because the bank agreed to a 25-year, $95 million deal for naming rights to the stadium. The bank can advertise on billboards, merchandise, and more." He said this as if he was spewing facts from a book. He must be an expert at baseball as well as religion.

"Hmm." I nodded flatly when he continued to ramble on with more facts about the ballpark, which were of no interest to me. I just stared at the red B on his hat, wondering what baseball team that stood for. Braves, Broncos, Bears, or Bulls, maybe?

I turned my attention to the front of the bus when Rob announced, "Señor Herrera is being transported to Pennsylvania Hospital to get checked out. We hope he didn't break a bone. Please keep him and his family in your thoughts."

Ava asked, "And how is Jason doing in the DC hospital?"

Rob answered, "He is much better, but they are running tests. We hope he'll be able to join us soon." He turned off the microphone.

Oh my. How sad. I looked back at the two empty rows where the family sat with the grandpa earlier. They must have all stayed back with him. I jotted down the name, Herrera, on my phone note as people began to discuss the two unfortunate incidents.

## GAME 2
### Baltimore Orioles vs Philadelphia Phillies

When we got to Citizen Bank Park, I was less than thrilled to discover we were to take a tour of the stadium before the game. With my head still pounding, I considered staying on the bus, but I had promised Mike I would take photos, so I begrudgingly joined the tour.

We were split into groups of 18, and I followed a friendly old guide named Joe. He knew everything about the Phillies and had been a guide ever since he retired from teaching 20 years ago. I smiled. Of course, a former schoolteacher would be a good guide.

People asked lots of questions and Joe shared facts about the players, the retired numbers, and how the ballpark was built. I took lots of photos and even recorded the guide, so I could share the details with Mike since I would never remember, much less care about them on my own.

I frowned when I realized I still hadn't heard much from Mike. I moved off to the side so I could text him. 'Hey, is Sally OK? I need a baby update please.'

When there was no immediate answer, I joined the group again and stared at a photo on the wall of a strange fuzzy creature. I raised my hand, thinking I finally had a good question for the guide. He called on me. Full of confidence, I asked, "So, what is this odd green creature with a horn for a snout?"

The whole group looked at me with incredulity as if I said I'd never heard of Big Bird or Popeye the Sailor Man. Then, as if it had been rehearsed, they called out in unison, "That's Phillie Phanatic!"

My eyes darted from the brothers to Vince and Ava, to our driver, to Father John to Gross Hair Guy, to the super-tanned couple, and other baseball fans I hadn't met or identified yet. When they all stood with mouths open, I shrank back, humiliated.

In the total silence, I finally said, "Uh. I'm not much of a baseball fan. I guess I just never heard of him."

Thankfully, Joe answered my question in a kind tone. "Phillie Phanatic, spelled with a PH by the way, is one of the best-known and most beloved mascots in sports. He's even in the Mascot Hall of Fame."

He moved on to another group of photos, but I was still embarrassed. I stayed in the back and didn't even pay attention to find out who was the best Phillies hitter of the 1970s.

Harry hung back and patted me on the shoulder. "It's okay, Pity. My girlfriend didn't know who Mr. and Mrs. Met were." He chuckled at the insanity and rejoined the group.

I guessed that was supposed to make me feel better. But who the heck were Mr. and Mrs. Met?

As I moved forward, Gross Hair Guy stopped in front of me, standing way too close. He gave off a sour odor as he spoke. "So, what happened to the guy who was with you yesterday?"

I looked at the big man and wondered if it was his breath that smelled so rank or if it was his hair. It was practically matted to his head. I said, "Well, he got called home for a family emergency, but he should be back tomorrow." I had no way of knowing when, but figured I had to say something.

He leaned his hand against the wall, blocking my way. When I looked around his big body, the group was nowhere in sight, and I panicked. "Oh look! The group is getting pretty far ahead of us." I took a step forward, but he didn't let me pass.

He breathed, "We can catch up later, but since we're both alone on the trip, why don't we make the best of it?"

## Sports Joke #5
Why did the police officer go to the baseball game?
*Someone stole second base.*

Ick! The greasy-haired jerk had me trapped. For some reason, I pictured the scene from the movie *Oklahoma!* when sweet Laurey was stuck in a buggy with the creepy hired hand, Judd Fry. The rest of the party was ahead of them going to the box social. Here I was, just like the innocent Laurey, desperate to get away from the disgusting man.

Wait. I wasn't sweet, nor innocent, and the scene wasn't from a Hollywood movie where everything worked out. I had to think of a way to get away from the guy. My mind whirred and I stood tall and replied, "I will not make the best of it with you."

He lifted an eyebrow and started to say something, but a voice with a familiar New York accent said, "Pity, are you alright?"

Relieved, I yelled, "Yeah Vince, I'm coming." I ducked underneath the Gross Hair Guy's arm and pretty much ran to my new friend.

Ava met us and said, "What was that about?"

I exhaled, trying to get the icky smell out of my nostrils then hooked arms with her. "I don't know, but I don't want to be alone with that guy ever again."

Ava, Vince, and I walked as a trio for the rest of the tour. At one point, after riding an elevator up several floors, we stood outside of the media room where announcers would do their job. I took photos overlooking the ballpark.

Joe warned our group, "Don't get too close to the edge. Renovations are ongoing and the new railings haven't been installed yet." He held his hand to his mouth and said conspiratorially, "I'm not supposed to bring you up here yet, but hopefully I can trust you to be safe."

Already scared of heights, I cautiously looked over the side. Wow, that was indeed a big drop-off. My stomach somersaulted at just the hint of falling that far.

The other half of our tour group joined us, making it very crowded on the small platform. I noticed Memaw telling Isaiah to stand back so he didn't fall. Good idea.

We were free to take photos before going back downstairs so I stood far away from the edge, taking a selfie with the empty ballfield in the background.

When I heard a scream, I yanked my phone down from my face and saw people staring over the edge. As I ventured closer, my stomach lurched when I spotted a woman lying crumpled on the seats below. It was the blonde gal who was extremely tan. Her arms and legs were bent in unnatural positions after the 15-foot fall. Feeling faint at the sight, I stepped back.

The tanned man, whom I assumed to be her husband, rushed down the steps, calling, "Marcia!"

Joe's face turned pale as he used his walkie-talkie to call for medical assistance. Then he commanded, "I need everyone to follow Simon down the steps to the team shop and wait there."

I swallowed the bile forming in my throat and along with Ava, Vince, and another 30-plus people, we followed the other stadium guide downstairs to the Phillies team shop.

After witnessing the horrible sight, I walked around the store in a daze. The shop was full of jerseys, caps, jackets, socks, and more, all in red, blue, and white. For once I wasn't in the mood to shop. I sure hoped the lady would be ok.

Ava came over and said, "Come here, Pity." She walked me to a wall of Phillies' backpacks and lanyards and pointed to a clear bag just like the woman had carried up the steps yesterday.

Even though we were still dumbfounded by the accident, Ava and I took the bags to the register and bought them. I purchased a Phillies keychain for Mike while I was at it.

About 20 minutes later, Rob arrived, looking worn out. He called us all together and said, "The medic checked Marcia out. She is in a coma, but her brain waves look good. She has fractures in both arms and a leg, as well as substantial bruising. Hopefully, she'll regain consciousness soon." He closed his eyes and added, "Promise me you will all stay safe from now on?" After everyone nodded 'yes', he said, "Now, let's go watch the Phillies/Orioles game."

I trudged to my seat, hoping the horrible image of the gal sprawled across the seats so unnaturally would leave my mind soon. I was glad to sit beside Ava and Vince again and said a silent thanks that I didn't have to sit anywhere near Gross Hair Guy.

Ava and I discussed the series of unfortunate events. I mean, one or two problems were possible, but three were far-fetched in any scenario. I had a sinking feeling they were not all accidents. On top of those, there was my Liberty Bell stunt, but I kept that to myself since it was fully on me.

The game was fine, but I spent a lot of time studying the players' uniforms—especially their pants. The Dodger divas were not wrong. Something about those stretchy tight pants and the fit men inside them was alluring—much more so than with football or basketball uniforms. At least I had a new appreciation for baseball.

I wiped the sweat from my forehead. Even at 7:30 at night, it was so hot and humid I wished I had worn my sleeveless shirt again instead of this thick t-shirt with the ridiculously giant words, "Summer Nights and Ballpark Lights."

I perked up when the weird-looking Phillie Phanatic appeared and pranced around on the field. "Ava, did you know who that was? And what is he supposed to be anyway?"

"He's a flightless bird."

"He doesn't look anything like a bird to me." Just then, a big orange and black mascot ran on the field. I pointed. "Now *that* looks like a bird. Oh wait, the Orioles are playing. Is that a Baltimore Oriole?" I remembered joking with my parents about Baltimore having a bird as a mascot and shook my head.

"Pity, you got that one right off the bat."

"Yeah." I chuckled, "One mascot figured out. Hey, you don't happen to have any Ibuprofen, do you?"

"Sure." She dug into her tiny purse and gave me a few pills. "You ok?"

I smiled, debating whether to tell her about my embarrassing moment or not. I opted against it and said, "I just feel like the liberty bell is clanging inside my head."

She nodded as if she understood.


Later during the game, there was a loud roar, and I watched as a ball flew into the stands. A whole group of people reached for it, some even wearing baseball mitts. When the tallest guy caught it, people cheered. Wow. Did he get to keep the ball? Maybe I would get lucky and catch one. I should start paying attention to the games, or one could clock me on the head. That would be all I needed after my two recent falls.

My stomach growled so I climbed the steps to find something affordable to eat. I walked around the food court, or whatever they called it, and I chose a soft pretzel with cheese and a Coke. That would do the trick. I juggled my cardboard container while taking photos for Mike. Then, looking out over the ballfield, I called the girls' dad.

As I waited for Todd to answer, I saw the short man and tall woman, a.k.a. Boris and Natasha, in a deep discussion. They were again sitting in seats above the stairs. How strange that they never sat with nor talked to anyone from our tour.

There was an empty seat beside them, so I took it and put my pretzel box in my lap. He finally answered. "Hey, Todd. Are you alone?" I had to ask this because Shelly was known for listening in on calls and spewing her two cents worth.

"Yeah. Shelly's with her mom trying out wedding cakes."

"So, you don't get to taste the cakes too? Never mind. Look, Ren and Ree are pretty upset about a few things: Number one–having to read Shelly's poem. And two–the dresses. Especially the dresses. Have you seen them? Can you do anything about it?"

"Oh, you know Shelly. She jest wants the wedding to be her special day. The girls can handle it and Pity, it's none of your business anyways."

His new fake hick accent drove me crazy, but I ignored it and spat, "My girls *are* my business!" I gave an exasperated sigh. "OK, so maybe Lauren can handle the poem, but have you seen the dresses? They sound awful."

"Yeah…" I could picture him rubbing his beard. "I saw 'em alright. But what am I supposed to do?"

"You get a backbone and help your daughters for once, Todd."

"Well, Pity. If you come up with somethin', you jest let me know."

Unbelievable. I had no response to that and hung up. How in the world had my ex lost all control of his own life? He used to be more of an overly confident bully. Now he was a pushover. My pulse thumped wildly, and I worried I might join the throng of people with health problems on our tour by having a heart attack.

I smiled at Boris and Natasha, feeling kinda bad that I named them after cartoon characters. After eating most of my big pretzel, I asked, "So, how did you swing those cool seats?"

They stared ahead like zombies, and without looking at me, the woman finally answered, "Nobody was sitting here."

I finished my pretzel and stood. In as friendly a tone as I could muster, I said, "Well, I hope you are both enjoying the tour."

After no response, I threw my trash away and headed off to my seat to visit with people who acted less like robots. I might even try to watch the game.

I spotted a man walking away from the priest, leaving Father John sitting alone in an aisle seat. Maybe he could help with something that had been nagging at me for months. I spoke politely as I approached. "Hi Father John, do you have a minute?"

He scooted over so I could sit next to the aisle, but he didn't take his eyes off the game.

"I'm sorry to bother you while you are watching the game, but I have a few Catholic questions."

He raised his eyebrows at me. "Are you thinking of converting to Catholicism, my dear?"

"Oh no. I'm Methodist, but I was in Rome recently and there was an incident." I looked around to make sure nobody else was listening. "So, I accidentally stepped on a priest's robe and tore it. Is there some special prayer I should pray so I'm not condemned for my actions? Do you take confessions and does this even warrant a confession?" I babbled on, "I mean, the Italian priest wasn't angry with me when it happened. I just want to clear my conscience."

He scoffed, "You're not going to Hell just because you stepped on his robe." He then adjusted his tone as if he just remembered he was a priest and took a kindlier approach. "And yes, I do take confessions. You are absolved, my dear." He made the sign of the cross and put his hand on my hand.

Wow. That was fast. "Good. I have been very concerned." I grinned and stood, then finally asked, "So what is the B for?"

He squinted.

"On your hat?" I pointed to it.

"Oh. Red Sox. I'm from Boston."

I wondered why there weren't red socks on the hat, but asked, "Is that where you work? Or practice? I mean, preach? You know…do the sermons?" Heck, I wasn't sure what Catholics called it.

He pinched his lips and tried to look around me to see the game. When I moved aside, he said, "Yes, I serve at The Body of Christ Chapel."

"Oh, that's cool. Well, thank you for absolving me of my sin." I moved on down to my seat, wondering if I said anything that made sense during that whole exchange.

The game finally ended with the Phillies winning, and we boarded the bus for an hour-and-a-half drive to New Jersey. It was crazy how close together the states were in this part of the country. Since it was so late, I planned to sleep on the bus, but my phone lit up with a long-awaited text from Mike. It read, 'Call me when you can.'

Even though I was dying to hear the news, I hated to disturb anyone by yammering on the phone. I shouldn't have been so considerate because the Dodger Divas were still flirting with Rob and carrying on with loud laughter in the front row.

I sent Mike a reply. "I'll call from New Jersey in about an hour."

The stuffy bus was uncomfortable, but I managed a catnap anyway. It was almost one a.m. when we arrived at our hotel. As we prepared to get off the bus, the bus driver, who I finally learned was named Mac, took the microphone and announced, "You'll be happy to know the air conditioning should be fixed by morning."

Everyone cheered, but I may have been the loudest.

Once in my room, I called Mike. "Sorry it's so late. How is Sally?"

"She's great. The baby was born at five o'clock this afternoon, but there were complications, and it was touch and go for a while. I didn't want to try to call you at the game to explain."

I asked, "How is Sally?"

"Great, but she's waiting until Scott gets home to name her."

I sucked in a breath. "So, it's a girl?"

"Oh yes, I probably should have led with that." He yelled, "It's a girl! She's beautiful with dark brown eyes. She reminds me of you."

I blushed as he gave me more details. I was glad all was okay, even though it sounded like a difficult delivery.

He said, "Oh before I forget, Ren and Ree picked up Jesse from Sally's friend's house this afternoon and they played with him until our neighbor came over to watch him. They were so great. They plan to get him from daycare tomorrow and keep him all evening. He just loves those girls."

I smiled to hear Lauren took the time to do that on her birthday. "That's nice and so cool the baby was born on Ren's birthday. So, Mike, can you meet me here tomorrow so you can go to the Yankees/Mets game?"

He let out a sigh. "No. I'll have to miss it." They won't release my sister and the baby from the hospital for a few more days. Mom and Dad may fly to Tulsa on Tuesday, and then I can try to meet you. I'm so sorry, Pity. This is not what I had planned."

"I know."

He perked up. "So, how is the trip? Are you starting to like baseball? Have you met anyone fun?"

"Uh… like baseball? Not really. I have enjoyed hanging out with Ava and Vince and those four brothers are fun. But you won't believe what happened…" I didn't tell him how I rang the bell or even about the encounter with Gross Hair Guy. I did inform him of the guy who got sick, the man who fell down the Rocky steps, and the woman who broke both arms. I shuddered and added, "It was just awful."

"Damn. That sounds terrible."

I said, "One funny thing happened while the old man lay on the steps. He kept talking about empujados. I guess he was kind of out of it or else was really hungry."

"What? Pity, you are thinking of empanadas."

"That's the word. I love those things." I frowned, then admitted, "But that's not what he said."

"Well, the word empujados means pushed."

I scoffed. "Pushed? Why would he repeat that word?" I froze as it sank in. "Wait. Do you think the grandpa was saying he was pushed down the Rocky steps?" My mind started to race.

Mike said, "If that's the word he used, then yes. It sure sounds like a lot of unusual problems on the trip. No matter what, you need to be careful."

I didn't want him to worry so I said casually, "Nah. Things always happen in threes, so I'm sure it'll be smooth sailing from now on." I crossed my fingers and changed the subject. "Mike, have you ever heard of the Phillie Phanatic?"

He laughed. "Of course! He's the most popular MLB mascot."

"Well, I don't get it, I'd rate those racing presidents way higher than that oddball any day."

After we hung up, I took some more ibuprofen and then thought about the strange injuries.

I was extremely chipper the next morning. The lump on my head was almost gone and my right side didn't ache as much as my left side. I was a new woman…on the mend. What really had me excited was the tour of New York City. I had been there several times before but never grew tired of visiting The Big Apple.

Since I wouldn't have time to change before going to Mets Stadium, I dressed like a real New York baseball fan and wore Dad's hat and a Yankees shirt I'd ordered online.

I cooked a waffle in the hotel breakfast area. As I waited for the beep, I noticed a woman having a quiet conversation with the priest. The two of them shut their eyes and Father John held her hands in his. Oh, that was nice. There sure had been a lot of people meeting with him. Were they all confessing something?

After breakfast, I bounded onto the bus for the hour-long ride into the city. The moment I stepped on board, I could feel cool air. I turned to Mac and said, "You fixed it!"

"Yes. I'm sorry it took so long."

"I'm so relieved now that I don't even care."

I had just settled in my seat when a man I'd never met sat beside me. I stared at his shaggy brown hair sticking out from under a hat with a big A on the front. He wore small round glasses like John Lennon's, or maybe Harry Potter's, and gave me a quirky smile. What was he doing there? I'd never even noticed him before, which I guess wasn't that shocking with 50 people on the tour. "Can I help you?"

He held out his hand. "Hi. I'm Grant Green from Tupelo Mississippi. Aren't you the one who wore the Tulsa shirt at the meet and greet?"

He must have used a whole bar of Irish Spring because his fragrance was strong. I shook his thin hand, afraid I might crush it, and raised an eyebrow. "Yes?"

He beamed. "Is that where you are from?"

"Well, I live in a suburb called Broken Arrow, but I was raised in Tulsa."

His face brightened as if I announced I was from Paris. I waited for an explanation. He took a deep breath and each of his words built with excitement, "Do…you…know…Hanson?" He lifted his eyebrows and his shoulders in anticipation of my answer.

I twisted my mouth. "Hanson? The singing group?"

His eyes widened as he nodded. "Yes! They're from Tulsa, right?"

I stared at him. Why was a man in his late 40s or early 50s so interested in the musical brothers who hit the charts in the 1990s? With eyebrows narrowed, I said, "Yes, they live in Tulsa. But it's a city of 400,000 people so no, I don't know them personally."

"But you see them around town, right?"

Did he think everyone in Oklahoma just walked around town all day greeting each other as if it was Mayberry? I shrugged, "Well, I did see them cross a parking lot to their car once back in the nineties. But that's the closest I've ever been to them." I laughed, thinking that would shut him up.

"So, you saw them? In person? Were they nice?"

I had to refrain from laughing out loud and reiterated, "I was in my car, and they just walked by." What was up with this guy? Sure, Hanson was a cool group, but why was he so excited about them?

The guy raised his eyebrows, comically. "Do you think if I came to Tulsa, I could meet them?"

I exhaled at his bizarre question. "I have no idea."

He crinkled his nose and then perked up. "Maybe I could stay with you, and you could show me around."

With that, I looked around to see if he had escaped from his caretaker and wasn't even supposed to be on our bus. But nobody seemed to be looking for him. I cleared my throat and looked through his thick, round glasses and into his eyes. "Grant, I don't believe staying with me is a good idea. I have children."

He waved me off. "Oh, it's fine that you have kids. I have children too. They are named Isaac, Taylor, and Zac."

I was flummoxed but managed to say, "Wow. You and your wife must really be fans to give them those names."

"I am, but she just went along with it." He shook his head. "We didn't see eye to eye on things, so she's not in the picture anymore."

Somehow, it didn't surprise me that this oddball was divorced. "And your boys don't mind being named after the Hanson brothers?"

"They're fine with it, but my Taylor is a girl and she's silly. Recently she started telling people she was named after Taylor Swift. As if?" He took a deep breath and bragged, "But yeah, I've been a fan since day one in 1997. I've seen Hanson in concert 14 times—once for every tour. They are such a wholesome group." He gazed with a faraway look. "I'm crazy about two things: Hanson and Braves baseball."

*Crazy* was the key word. He pointed to his hat and said, "The Braves are my team. And I see you like the Yankees."

I said, "Well, I don't really have a favorite team." He blinked a few times as if that made no sense. I fidgeted, wishing he would leave and said, "Well, nice to meet you, Grant, but I need to get back to…"

I tried to come up with an excuse and said, "text my boyfriend." Yeah, good thinking, Pity. Maybe he would get the hint.

But he didn't. He ignored me and turned serious, "It would be really cool if you could take me around Tulsa because I don't drive."

That did it. The more this Hanson freak spoke, the more I was convinced I was being recorded for some reality comedy show. I studied the man for a hidden camera. Who was this guy and how could I get rid of him? I pulled myself up onto my knees to give wide eyes to the twins behind me. The four brothers were wearing light blue shirts today that read Tar Heels. What the heck was a tar heel?

I interrupted Harry and Barry's heated discussion. "Hey guys, can you help me out?"

Harry said, "What do you need?"

How could I tell them the guy was bothering me? "Well…" I made my eyes big and motioned toward the clueless guy next to me.

Barry caught on and said, "Hey buddy, Pity's boyfriend may be upset that you are talking to her while he's gone for a few days. You should go to your seat now."

"Oh, yeah. Sure." Grant was nonplussed and said, "We'll talk about our plans later." He stood and moved to the back of the bus.

I swiveled to the brothers. "Thanks. That was bizarre. He invited himself to stay at my house in Tulsa so he could meet Hanson."

Harry wrinkled his nose. "Hanson? The MMMBop guys?"

I nodded.

He asked, "Do they still perform?"

I nodded. "Oh yeah. They just released a new album, but I sure as heck don't know them personally."

Barry pointed back. "And he wants to stay with you? Weird. Who is that guy anyway?"

"No idea. I'm still waiting to be introduced to everyone." I waved my hand across the seats.

Harry said, "Yeah. It was a strange meet and greet with no meeting or greeting. When I asked Rob about it, he said it was better for us to meet each other organically."

I nodded, thinking that was a weird plan, but it made me feel better to know I wasn't the only one who needed a little group bonding. I just hoped I wouldn't organically meet any more odd ducks like the two who had glommed onto me.

# Sports Joke #6
Where does a hockey player get all his money?
*From the tooth fairy.*

I faced the front of the bus for the rest of the ride, which was much more comfortable with the working A/C. I smiled when Ren sent me a long text describing her jam-packed birthday. She loved the gift cards I had left for her and planned to go shopping today. "Can you believe Sally's baby was born on my birthday?"

"It's so cool."

I rode the rest of the way, smiling that Ren was having a good birthday. I was also stoked to see the sights of the Big Apple.

Our day in NYC was awesome. It would only have been better if I'd been with Mike or my family—or if we had enough time to see a Broadway show. But alas, the focus of the tour was baseball games, not going to musicals. It gave me an idea and I instantly googled Broadway Musical Bus Tours. They did have some, but only for day trips. I'd be happy to ride a bus full of musical lovers and could just imagine all the singing that would go on.

We started the day by taking a ferry into Manhattan. As we rode on the big boat filled with locals and tourists, I pictured immigrants seeing the Statue of Liberty for the first time as they approached the United States. Lady Liberty was, and always would be, an awe-inspiring welcome sight.

When the Ferry docked, Rob introduced us to a cute gal waiting at the terminal. Crystal was a cheerful Ballparks and More guide who lived in the area. She had been hired to show us around the city. She was a hoot, dressed in baseball-decorated clothes including her hat, backpack, and even down to her baseball shoes. With Crystal's quick pace, it only took us ten minutes to get from the dock to the Wall Street Charging Bull. It would have only taken another five minutes to reach the 9-11 Memorial, except 'some of us' stopped to buy $5 NYC hats from a street vendor.

I caught up with the group and was taken aback by the beauty of the Memorial. How tragic that thousands of people died due to the attack on September 11th. As I walked around the acre-sized pool, I scanned the names etched into the border wall. Halfway around, I reached the names of firefighters and EMT's. Overcome with emotion, I sat on a bench to gather myself. What a dark day in history.

When we all rallied in a spot across the park it was so hot and humid that I was a big sweat ball. Crystal noticed us fanning ourselves, and like a magician, pulled folded paper baseball fans from her backpack. I thanked her for mine and walked around fanning the faces of people who hadn't snagged one. When I found myself standing in front of Gross Hair Guy, I fanned him, too, or would have felt rude.

He lifted an eyebrow suggestively. "You know…you should ask before you blow me."

I backed away, disgusted, and vowed never to go near him again. I turned around and nearly ran into the Hanson freak. I wasn't about to fan him and rushed over to Vince and Ava who were standing in the shade of a tree. Out of breath, I said, "Hi, guys. I probably should stick with you from now on." I told them about Gross Hair Guy's comment and the odd Hanson fan.

Vince said, "You must be a magnet for weirdos."

The bus took us to Broadway and 42$^{nd}$ Street. Crystal announced, "You have two hours to tour Times Square on your own before going to the game."

Ava, Vince, and I, did so many touristy things; We ate Ray's Pizza and New York Cheesecake and then shopped for souvenirs. After taking selfies under the giant electronic billboards we saw the naked cowboy, who wasn't technically naked but wore tighty-whities with 'Naked Cowboy' printed on the rump. With his cowboy hat, boots, and guitar, he was quite a sight. Only in New York!

It practically killed me to walk past the TKTS booth without buying a discount ticket for a Broadway show. Next time…

As we walked back to the bus. I asked, "Are you two excited about this game?"

Vince smiled. "It's going to be a heck of a subway series."

I didn't ask him to explain, for fear I would show my ignorance again. Since both the Mets and Yankees were in Ney York City, where people rode the subway daily. I figured that's why it was called a subway series.

Crystal rode with us to Citi Field, popping up to the microphone now and then to tell us fun facts about the teams we would see. She was a much more fun and entertaining guide than Rob.

## Game 3
### New York Yankees vs New York Mets

When we found our section, the tall Natasha and short Boris sat up top again. Did they have beer cans surgically attached to their hands? I waved to them but as usual, there was no reaction. Why did I even try?

As I walked down the steps, Gross Hair Guy winked at me, and then two rows down, the Hanson dude waved at me. Lucky me. Ick.

Once in my seat, I relaxed to be seated by Ava and Vince. I posted photos of New York and the ballgame on Facebook with the heading, 'Game three of a baseball tour! Wish you were here!'

Sometime around the 4th inning, the people behind me cheered. I turned around and saw the two red-haired cousins walking down the stairs. How cool that they could meet up with us in New York. Jason looked pale, even more so than the fair-skinned guy had before.

After they sat right behind us, I turned and said brightly, "I'm so happy you feel better. Did they find out if it was something you ate?"

Jason started to talk, but he held his throat as if it hurt. He pointed to the other guy who said, "Sorry, my cousin can't talk now. They had to pump his stomach, so his throat is raw. Unfortunately, it looks like he was poisoned."

I gasped, but Ava asked, "Food poisoning?"

He replied, "No. They found a chemical in his bloodstream and sent a sample to the lab. We should know something soon, but whatever it was is out of his system now."

Jason whispered something else to his cousin who told us, "He thinks something was put in his soft drink because it tasted bitter."

I made a face. "What? In your cup at the first stadium?"

They both nodded. "Who would do that?" I asked, "Did you ever leave the cup alone after you bought it?"

They looked at each other and Jason whispered to his cousin again. His cousin explained, "I guess when I went up to smoke, he left the cup in the holder by his seat when he left to get a hot dog. When he came back and took a drink, it hit him like a brick."

I cringed. "That must have been when I saw you run to the bathroom. I'm so sorry I didn't check on you."

"Well, at least you told Rob, who alerted me, and we found him before it was too late. Thank you for that."

Before turning around, I said, "We should all stick to factory-sealed drinks from now on." To emphasize this, I picked up my new clear plastic purse, pulled out the water bottle I'd brought from the hotel, and took a swig.

After I turned around, my spidey senses tingled. Was there imminent danger? Poison was scary. And what about the Hererra man saying he had been pushed by someone? Then I remembered the tanned woman who fell yesterday. Had Marcia been pushed, too? As far as we knew, she was still in a coma, so nobody could ask her. I couldn't shake the foreboding prickle on the back of my neck.

From now on, I would watch our fellow travelers like a hawk for any unusual activities. Of course, thinking of a hawk made me sad for poor Dave, our fish. I shook that thought off and wondered if anyone in our group acted suspiciously, but hunger got the best of me and I changed my focus.

"Ava, I'm running up to get some of the amazing-looking nachos I saw earlier."

"OK."

Just before I reached one of the main concession stands, I spotted Rob walking along the corridor at a fast pace. He looked both ways, acting paranoid as he walked. I had to follow him.

I tailed our tour guide as he wove in and out of the crowd scanning everyone as he went. When he paused at a bratwurst line, I stopped next to a popcorn kiosk so I wouldn't be seen.

The gal behind the popper said apathetically, "Lahge or smwall?"

I stared at the girl wearing a red and white striped apron. What was she talking about? I caught on and said, "Oh, no. I'm just hiding…"

When Rob took off down some stairs, I told the lady, "I've gotta go. Maybe I'll get some popcorn on my way back." I raced down the steps after him, looking right and left. He must have gone down another flight. I took a few steps down, but dang it if he didn't turn around and climb back up toward the floor I was on. After running back up, I scanned the area for a place to hide. I opened a door behind me and jumped into a room. That was close!

I opened the door a crack and watched our fearless leader scout the deserted area for something or someone. I couldn't go out with him standing right there, so turned and checked out the room. Oh my! It was full of crazy, fun costumes. Two of them were giant Baseball heads. I was in heaven. My costume closet at home wasn't half as cool as this.

One outfit lay folded on a bench, so I picked it up. It was a darling hotdog costume–complete with squiggles of mustard and ketchup. I held it up and realized it was adult sized. Most of my costumes only fit kids, so I was extra excited. I peeked out the door and Rob was still standing there looking like he was waiting for someone.

I just had to try it on! I stepped into the hotdog and pulled it up over my shoulders. It fit perfectly over my clothes. Why wasn't there a mirror handy so I could take a picture of myself or at least see how I looked? I started to take it off when another door opened.

A gruff voice yelled, "You're late! What-a-ya waitin fer? Yer own personal dressa?"

Flustered, I said, "Um. I just…"

Before I could say more or turn around to see who had spoken, the hotdog was zipped up the back. I sputtered, "You have the wrong person. I'm…" I turned and found myself face to face with a giant talking mug of beer. It was the best costume ever, complete with a handle and bubbly foam dripping over the top of the mug.

The grumpy beer urged, "If ya don't getcha head on quick, ya won't get paid."

Wasn't this mug even listening? I was obviously not who he believed I was. I stammered, "But, I was just trying…"

Suddenly he slammed the top of the hotdog onto my head, essentially shutting me up. It was dark and smelled so much like onions I almost gagged. Mr. Beer told me something, but I couldn't hear and worst of all, I couldn't see anything. Worried I might suffocate, I lifted my hands to take the hat off, but he swiveled my headpiece around. Suddenly, I could breathe. I also could see through a mesh area behind the swirls of mustard and catsup. Whew!

He yelled "Showtime!"

What did that mean? Was I supposed to sell hotdogs? If I could trip over a real dog in my kitchen and fall into the Liberty Bell wearing regular clothes, I sure wouldn't be able to walk around in this getup and sell hotdogs. I was baffled.

He urged, "Come on, Wiener! We're late. Pizza and Popcorn are already in place."

I followed Beer out the door I had entered and was shocked to see Rob standing in the corner in a heavy embrace, kissing a woman! Wasn't he married? That must be why he was lurking around. In my stupid costume, I couldn't see who he was with, but she had blonde hair. Deb or Diana maybe? So weird. At least he would never recognize me in this getup.

Beer yanked my arm and led me to an elevator. As we descended, I demanded, "You have the wrong person. I was just looking around. I don't even know what's going on."

"Oh yeah? Well, Wiener's substitute was a no-show, so you're the Wiener now. No time to change."

"But what are we doing?"

The door opened, revealing the baseball field. He said, "Racing."

I froze. Racing? Racing like the presidents? Was I, dressed like a hot dog, supposed to compete against a beer, popcorn, and pizza? I'd never been in any race before and was a complete klutz. I could not do this.

He startled me by shouting, "Move it, Wiener!"

As I inched onto the field, a loud voice announced, "Place your bets, Mets! It's time for the race of the concessions."

Beer grabbed me again and pulled me, so I stood between him and a giant box of popcorn. He growled, "When the gun goes off, just run. Doesn't matter who wins. The crowd will go wild."

I puffed out a big breath of air. This was definitely the weirdest thing I had ever gotten myself into.

The announcer yelled, "On your mark, get set…" Then there was a bang! I ran with the others but lagged behind. I was in no shape to race anyone, especially in a bulky costume.

I scanned the stands for our group but couldn't find them. When I faced forward again, my hotdog head did not turn with my head. The mesh had twisted around to the backside.

Everything was dark again. I was discombobulated, confused, and disoriented. Which way to run? Where were the others? I lifted my hands to straighten my hotdog head, but it was stuck and wouldn't turn back to the front. Perhaps I should have stopped running, but I wasn't sure how far we were to run around the track, so I just kept going. Luckily, the ground became soft underfoot, which made it easier to get traction.  Even inside my muffled, gross-smelling head covering, I could hear the crowd yelling. Someone must be close to winning. Good! This stupid race would be over soon. I listened for the announcement of a winner, praying I wouldn't smash into a wall or a person as I ran blind.

The sounds grew even louder. Should I stop running and just stand still? What was I supposed to do? I did what any self-respecting wiener would do–kept running. After what seemed like forever, I was forcefully thrown to the ground and tackled like a football player. Ouch! I sure didn't expect that.

I lay there still for a second and could smell fresh cut grass, which was much better than the previous Wiener's onion breath.

My tacklers helped me to my feet, laughing all the while. Were all the runners stopped in this way? If so, it was a weird tradition. I was, at least, happy that I could rest.

When the hotdog top was finally lifted from my head, I was blinded by the lights of the ballpark. But once my eyes adjusted, I was shocked to see thousands of people standing and pointing at me. Had I won the race? Something told me I had not. Upon closer inspection, I discovered I was standing in the outfield, beyond second base, while Beer, Pizza, and Popcorn stood together on the gravel by home plate.

The more telltale sign that I didn't win was that everyone was laughing–at me!

After I was ushered out of the stadium and back to the costume room like a common hotdog criminal, I was met and bashed by the other concessioners.

Beer growled, "I told you to snap the head to the body or it could twist around."

I shrank back and meekly said, "I didn't hear you say that."

Popcorn shook her head. "Novice."

Pizza scoffed and said rudely, "Don't you know that no one, except players, is allowed on the field and certainly not on the diamond?"

The more they talked, the more I felt like a dummy. I said, "I'm sorry I ruined the race. I didn't ask for any of it." But I realized by putting on the costume, I had indeed asked for trouble. I asked quietly, "So, who won?"

Beer said, "Pizza."

Pizza grumbled, "But, it didn't matter. All the attention was on you–the crazy wiener running onto the field."

I gulped and undogged myself, folding the costume in silence. The others left, grumbling about my stupid stunt. I sat down on the bench, feeling like an even bigger dope than usual.

A man wearing a suit entered and I stood quickly, hoping to escape before he recognized me as the interloper hotdog.

He stopped in front of me and said, "I understand you took the place of Wiener at the last minute. What is your name?"

Oh no. This was it. I fessed up, "I'm Pity Kole from Oklahoma. Look, I'm sorry. It was all a misunderstanding. I was in the wrong place at the wrong time. And I didn't mean to run onto the field or square or emerald or whatever you call it, but my hotdog head twisted around, and I couldn't see where I was going."

I hung my head and apologized again. "I shouldn't have put on the costume, but it was so cute, and then this guy…well, anyway, if there is a fine for crossing into forbidden territory, please let me know how much and I'll pay right away. I…"

He interrupted, "Hold on." He took out a pen and paper and wrote something. I cringed, wondering how much I owed.

Then he said, "There is no need for you to pay us, Pity."

His eyes were kind as he continued. "I just wanted to thank you. The crowd loved it so much, that we hope you might come back for an encore performance next week. You are climbing the ranks as our favorite concession, as we speak."

It took a moment to comprehend what he said. He wasn't mad at me? I giggled and said, "That's really funny but I live in Oklahoma. I'm on a baseball bus tour and we leave town in the morning, so I'll have to pass. I'm just glad I didn't ruin the race."

"Far from it." He handed me the paper.

When I looked at it, I gulped. It was a check for $200. I said, "Seriously? You're paying me?"

"Of course. Since you aren't on the payroll like our other racing concessions, I hope this will do. Thanks Pity. Have a safe trip back to Oklahoma." And just like that, the man was gone. I was dumbfounded by the way the situation turned out. I only hoped that none of my tour friends recognized me as the goofy hotdog running out onto the field. I felt confident that I was too far away for them to recognize me. That was good. I put the check into my bag.

When the Star-Spangled Banner began, I walked back toward my seat. On the way, I stopped and bought popcorn from the gal whose cart I had hidden by, then walked down the steps.

That was when all hell broke loose from the tour group. I heard, "What were you doing dressed as a hotdog?" "Why did you run away from the race?" "You were so funny." Etc. etc. etc.

I didn't stop to reply but kept walking to my seat, humiliated. When Ava and Frank pelted me with the same questions, I told them what had happened and ended with "…so you see, my head wasn't on straight."

"We've been saying that since we met you," Vince laughed.

"Ha ha ha. But how did you recognize me from so far away?"

Ava cocked her head. "Remember the Jumbotrons? Your face was that size!" She pointed to the giant screen and I winced. She said, "It was hard to miss you. I took pictures and shot a video."

She texted me the ridiculous photos as I was hauled off by ballpark employees and a video of a crazy hotdog with flailing arms running wildly across the field. It was too funny.

I said, "Just something else to embarrass my children."

Ava and Vince left to get food. Why was I so paranoid? Trying to solve a mystery was how I ended up in that mess. Rob wasn't trying to hurt anyone. He was having a clandestine meeting. That was all.

I told myself to just relax, then took a deep, cleansing breath. It wasn't so bad being at a baseball game; the weather was cool, people were happy, the popcorn was salty, and the score was close.

I focused on listening to the New York accents around me instead of reliving my stupid race. One stadium vendor cracked me up by yelling, "Who's drinkin' bea hea? When he walked by me, I asked him to repeat it so I could record him. When he did, I sent that video to Mike, after buying one of the man's beers, of course.

When someone sat in the seat next to me, I turned to check out the nachos I assumed Ava had bought, but the person beside me was not Ava. It was Gross Hair Guy.

He gave me a sleazy smile and murmured, "I thought I'd watch my Yankees with my girlfriend while her guy is away."

I almost choked on my own spit. Just as I opened my mouth to say, 'What the heck?" The creep put his arm around the back of my chair. Eew. I leaned forward so that his sweaty arm didn't touch me and frantically looked for someone to save me. Wait a minute. I didn't need anyone. I could handle this. I turned to him and said, "You should get up now or I will call security."

"Settle down, Honey. I'm just enjoying the game like you are. I watched you run a bit ago and wanted to see that big hotdog smile up close."

I was horrified and was about to leave, but suddenly everyone around us squealed and pointed at the Jumbotron. I looked up.

To my horror, my face and that of Gross Hair Guy filled the enormous Kiss Cam screen as if we were a couple!

## Sports Joke #7

Did you hear about the soccer player who lived past 100?
*He's still alive and kicking.*

No, No, No! How embarrassing! Gross Hair Guy saw the screen too and gave a sleazy smile just before he leaned forward to kiss me. Thousands of people waited for me to reciprocate.

Disgusted to see the creep's fat lips come closer, I reacted by shoving him away. I yelled, "I said, leave me alone!"

Did I imagine it, or did the entire stadium turn silent? The crowd witnessed my repulsed face as I pushed him away, but I didn't care. I cringed at the jerk's audacity and moved to an empty seat.

The Kiss Cam switched to a different surprised couple who did as anticipated and gave each other loving kisses.

The cousin behind us asked, "Are you bothering this lady?"

Gross Hair Guy scoffed. "Oh, she's just being playful. I think she likes having me here." Then he winked at me.

Before I could object, a security guard from Mets Stadium approached us and asked if everything was OK. I felt safer knowing employees had witnessed his unwanted advance and were checking on me.

The creep told him, "I was just kidding around."

I said, "Thank you for coming. Yes, he was definitely bothering me, but he will leave me alone from now on, right?"

I glared at Gross Hair Guy. He stood, stepped back into the stairway, and saluted me. "Yes, Ma'am."

The security guard leaned in. "If you have any more problems, let us know."

Ava and Vince passed the guard on their way back down the steps to their seats. Ava said, "What was that all about?"

"You don't even want to know," but I explained the whole thing to them anyway.

Vince shook his head. "That's it. We are never leaving you alone, again."

I closed my eyes, still upset by the encounter, and then froze when I saw my friends' drink cups. "You two left your fountain drinks in your cup holders. What if that jerk came down here to poison us?" I took a deep breath and said softly, "At least take a sniff before you have a drink."

Ava tasted her drink and gave it a thumbs up. Then she escorted me to buy the most amazing nachos I'd ever eaten.

At one point, while scraping the remaining cheese from yet another cardboard bowl, two mascots wearing those giant baseball heads I'd seen earlier bounded playfully onto the field.

Ava pointed. "Pity, it's Mr. and Mrs. Met!"

I nodded. So that was who Harry was talking about. As I watched the giant ball-headed characters dance around the track, I wondered; If I made $200 as a substitute Wiener, how much did big-time mascots make? Maybe I could start a new career if Dr. Love kept driving me crazy at school.

Thankfully, the rest of the game was uneventful. The only real disappointment of the night was that the Mets beat the Yankees. As we walked to the bus, most of our tour group, who were Yankees fans, moped in silence, as if someone had just died.

Father John, however, was very vocal. He gloated, "It's about time someone put those damned Yankees in their place."

Now, I'm not around a lot of Catholics, or many ministers for that matter, but that didn't sound like something a member of any clergy would say. His comment demonstrated how weirdly dramatic people could become when their team won or lost. It was just a game, for heaven's sake.

Back on the bus, I walked slowly past Rob and Crystal, scouring the passengers for a blonde who may have been Rob's illicit partner. The only ones who fit the look were the Dodger Divas and they never went anywhere without the other.

As for the foreboding feeling from earlier, it had lessened. I felt safe in my seat. Harry and Barry were behind me, in case I needed them. Gross Hair Guy was sitting way in the back and the Hanson lover was nowhere to be seen. The know-it-all priest wore headphones, so he was quiet too. The only real sound was the Dodger Divas' never-ending giggles as they flirted with Rob.

I relaxed as we rode a few hours to New Haven, Connecticut, close to Boston, for tomorrow's game. With so much time to think, I wondered if the Herrera grandpa had truly been pushed. I hated to think someone tried to hurt the older man. If it was a person from our tour, the only one who came to mind was Gross Hair Guy. I didn't know what he was capable of. I searched the group to see if anyone else seemed suspicious, but they all looked innocent—of course, they were asleep.

Once I collected my suitcase from under the bus and had my new room key in hand, I entered another lonely hotel room.

I called Dad, hoping he was still awake at 11:30, Tulsa time. When he answered, I relaxed at the sound of his sweet, calm voice. I told him about my first Yankees experience.

He asked, "I'm so glad you were able to go, even if they didn't win. Are you starting to learn the game?"

"Sort of. Mike taught me about the new timing rule before he had to leave. You wouldn't believe how many Yankees fans there are on this tour. Did you see the photo of me wearing your hat?"

He laughed. "Yes. Kim showed it to me. I just don't understand why that lucky cap didn't work for you."

"Maybe it will work better in Yankee Stadium. Look, it's late, so I'll let you go. Tell Mom I miss her and will call her tomorrow."

Next, I called my girls and said, "It's hard to keep track of where you girls are."

"We're at Dad's tonight," Ren said.

"I hope he doesn't mind me calling so late."

"Oh, they're still up watching a recording of *90 Day Fiancé* so Shelly can get last-minute ideas for her wedding," Ree said.

I had seen the show and that sounded like the worst place for ideas, but I said, "Well, I called your dad today about the dresses. He can't stop her, but if we come up with a brilliant idea, maybe he'd go along with it. I'm going to make it my mission, so you don't have to be dressed like frilly American flags."

They both said, "Thank you, Mom."

I changed the subject. "I'm proud of you girls for taking care of little Jesse."

Ren said, "He's so cute and funny."

Ree added, "He says his Rs like Ws so he calls us Wen and Wee."

"Awe. Cute. Has he seen his mom and new baby sister?"

"No, but they might come home from the hospital tomorrow or the next day. How is your trip going?"

I had to answer carefully, so as not to worry them. "Well, Philadelphia and New York City were great!" I told them how sad the 9-11 Memorial was and about visiting Times Square.

"Did you see the naked cowboy?" This came from Ree who had been grossed out to see him standing around in underwear.

"Yes. I did and he made my day—not."

Ren asked, "Are you meeting some nice people, or are they all baseball freaks like you were worried they would be?"

"Well, they are definitely extreme baseball fans, but I've met some very nice people and even a few fruitcakes." I hadn't decided if I would ever tell them about Gross Hair Guy, so I said, "When I get back, I'll tell you about the weirdo who wants to stay with us so he can meet Hanson in person."

They both said, "What?"

I chuckled. "I'll save that story for later and I may even tell you how I became a fan favorite hotdog."

There was silence on the other end of the line.

"Mom, are you drunk?" This came from Lauren.

"No. I'm not. But I am exhausted. It's tiring riding on a bus for hours and staying in a different city and hotel every night."

Ree said, "You sound like a rock star complaining about being on tour."

"Yeah, but I'm not on a cushy bus getting paid millions of dollars at each stop. I get to sit through a bunch of 2 ½ hour baseball games."

Despite the late hour, I wasn't sleepy and went down to the lobby to peruse their snack shelves.

As I was getting out of the elevator, Grant, the Hanson fan approached. He was so preoccupied by messing with his headphones, that he didn't notice me pass him. But before the door closed completely, it slid open again.

He said, "I almost didn't see you."

Oh, brother. I turned to see Mr. MMMBop standing with a wide smile. "Oh, Hi. Grant, right?"

He gave me a salute. "Yes, Ma'am. So, about my visit to Tulsa…you wouldn't need to chauffer me. I could just go with you on your errands and maybe I'd see one of the Hanson brothers around town."

Oh, good Lord! He had to be kidding. Frustrated, I said, "You know, I've been running errands all my life and have only seen them once, so I don't think that's the best way to catch them in the wild." A brilliant idea popped into my head. "Why don't you see if there is a Hanson fan club in Tulsa? That might be a great place to start."

"Good idea. I'll google it, now. Thanks, Pity."

Without waiting to see if his elevator went up, which I was pretty sure metaphorically his did not, I scooted into the lobby. The tall woman and her diminutive husband, or whom I assumed him to be, sat on a couch with no expression. They were drinking beer again. What an odd couple. They didn't even act like they enjoyed their drinks. But what did I know? Maybe they were friends with the gal who fell and were worried about her. I waved, but it was like they were made of stone, or perhaps stoned, for they ignored me yet again.

Father John was leaning over the counter talking to the desk clerk, probably mansplaining something to her. He nodded at me when I walked past, on my way to the tiny convenience shelf for snacks.

When I returned to pay for my little pack of Oreos and bottled water, the priest was gone.

I heard someone else talking and turned. Rob stood off to the side, on his cell phone. Maybe he was asking when we would get our T-shirts. But instead, I heard him say, "I know, but it's more difficult than last time. What am I supposed to do?"

I sure wouldn't want to oversee this accident-prone group, so I opted not to bother asking him about the shirts. I headed up to my room and conked out.

I was groggy the next morning because I only got five and a half hours of sleep. We had to be on the bus by 8:30 so we could make it to Boston on time. How were we supposed to keep up with such a whirlwind schedule? After showering I put on the white T-shirt that I had designed with big red baseball stitching around the armholes. It was the trickiest design I'd made with my new vinyl cutting machine and I was proud of the results. I stood at the mirror and laughed. I looked like a big baseball with arms.

As I sat at breakfast, glancing over our tour group, I was relieved not to see Gross Hair Guy. Grant sat at a table alone wearing a Braves hat and headphones–I had no problem guessing who he listened to.

When the four brothers walked in, I read their shirts. "Green Monstah." I might as well give up trying to figure out the meaning of their shirts. This one really confused me.

When the Dodgers Divas appeared, I urged them to sit with me. I whispered, "I just don't want this one guy to sit here."

Deb nodded in understanding. "The creepy guy on the Kiss Cam? What was that about?"

"I'm not sure, but I seem to attract interesting characters. I'm pretty sure he's harmless, but who really knows? Say, have you been on one of these tours before?"

"No, but we might go on the one that goes to Texas."

The girls complimented me on my shirt. With a voice a little too chipper for such an early morning, Diana asked, "Can you make some shirts like that for us, but add Dodger Divas?"

I chuckled. "I'm new at it, but maybe? Hey, speaking of shirts, look at all the die-hard Yankees fans. I can't believe they are still wearing Yankees T-shirts even after they lost."

Deb stared at me and wrinkled her nose. "Well, that's what a true fan does, Pity. Don't you have a favorite team?"

"Uh…I don't actually like sports, but I do root for my daughter's swim team if that counts."

The girls spoke in unison, "Why don't you like sports?"

I was distracted when a little dark-haired boy wearing a Yankees hat walked by me with a plate piled high with eggs, bacon, and a banana. Wait. That was the little Herrera kid. Was the whole family back? He sat at a table alone, but shortly after, the other four joined him, including the older man on crutches.

I waved at Deb and Diana. "I'll explain later. I'll be right back."

I walked to the Herreras' table. "Hi! I haven't met you, yet. My name is Pity. I'm from Oklahoma. I just want to welcome you back."

I turned to the older man. "I'm so sorry about what happened in Philadelphia, but it looks like you are up and around now."

The whole family stared at me as if I had interrupted a private moment. I waited for someone to say something. Perhaps they didn't speak English?

Finally, the little boy said, "Hi, I'm Joey. I'm almost nine." The adorable boy held out his small hand for me to shake.

I shook it and said, "Hi, Joey. I guess you had to miss the Yankees game yesterday, huh?"

He looked down at the ground. Shoot, why had I brought that up? I said, "Well if you had been there, I'll bet they would have won. You are a pretty big fan, right?"

He looked up and smiled. "They are the best."

I said, "Who is your favorite all-time Yankee?"

"Joe DiMaggio! I'm named after him. He helped win nine World Series and set the record for the longest hitting streak in baseball."

How did a little kid know all that? I said, "Wow, that's cool."

Of, course I wanted to ask the grandpa if he had been pushed, but didn't know how to bring it up. Instead, I said, "Well, I hope you all enjoy the game today!"

They all smiled. Maybe they did understand English but were just quiet people.


The Dodger Divas and I rolled our suitcases out to the bus and left them with the others to be put in the luggage compartment. As I took a step up toward the bus, Mac lifted the big door. Seconds later, somebody screamed.

Oh great! I squeezed my eyes tight. Did someone else fall? This was getting ridiculous. I stepped back down to find a group of people staring at the open, empty luggage space.

As I moved around the gathering crowd, I could see that the compartment was in fact, not empty. The body of a man lay motionless in the baggage compartment. My eyes grew wider as I realized it was Gross Hair Guy.

Ava rushed to the compartment, climbed inside, and checked his pulse. She shook her head and said, "He's dead."

# Sports Joke #8
Why was the tennis match so loud?
*Because all the players raised a racket*

I stood speechless, staring at the lifeless body. How had he ended up inside the luggage compartment? Had he been in there all night? Oh my gosh. Why did nobody notice he was missing? So many questions. I was queasy but looked around to see if there was anything I could do.

More panic ensued as new people witnessed the horror. Rob pulled out his phone and dialed 9-1-1 for help. Mrs. Herrera sheltered little Joey's eyes from the gruesome scene and urged him back into the hotel lobby.

Rob made an announcement. "I've called for assistance, but please, everyone go back inside the hotel until we find out what we should do."

By this time, people still on the bus started coming down the steps to see what happened.

I intercepted Memaw Mary and Isaiah, thinking they didn't need to see the body, and walked them back to the lobby. "There has been an accident, and we are to stay inside." I whispered to Mary, "It appears a man was trapped in the luggage compartment overnight and he died."

She looked at me in horror. "Oh my! How could that happen? Thank you for keeping us from seeing that."

Once everyone was inside, I ran back out and found Rob, who was making another call. "I know you are busy, but please let me know if there is anything I can do to help."

He looked up and pointed to the driver who sat on the curb with his head in his hands. "Can you console Mac? He feels awful for shutting him in there last night."

My heart just broke for the man. How would you ever be able to forgive yourself if you thought you caused a death? Perhaps the job of comforting him was a better fit for the priest rather than a music teacher. Oh well, I gathered myself together, made my way to the bus driver, and sat beside him.

"Hi, Mac. My name is Pity. I'm sorry we've never met. Is there anything I can get you? A cup of coffee, maybe?"

He dropped his head. "I just can't believe I didn't see him in there. He helped me unload the luggage last night and honestly, I don't even remember shutting the door, but I must have. It's all my fault." He wiped his tears away with his sleeve.

"No. It was a terrible accident. Nobody is going to blame you."

"Well, they should. I'm in charge of everything that happens on my bus. I'll be fired at the very least and who knows, I may have murder charges on my hands."

How horrible to have so many awful thoughts going through his mind. Poor guy. I said, "I'm sure it was an accident. You're going to be ok. I'm going to get you some hot tea. Maybe it will calm you down. Just sit here and I'll be right back."

The hotel lobby was crowded with somber tour members standing around. Someone said, "Poor Howard."

So, Gross Hair Guy's name was Howard.

As I filled a Styrofoam cup with hot water, someone bumped into my arm, spilling the hot liquid on my shirt. I jumped back and shook the fabric so it wouldn't burn my skin. I looked up and found Grant standing mere inches from me."

He said, "Oh, I'm so sorry. Let me clean that up. He grabbed a napkin and reached towards my chest."

I jerked back, held up my hands, and said, "No. That's OK. It's only water."

He grimaced and said, "Hey, at least that guy won't bother you anymore." He shrugged and walked away.

That was a crass thing to say. Honestly, what a weird guy.

After refilling the cup, I dipped the little bag several times and took the green tea outside. A police car and an ambulance arrived and parked on opposite sides of the parking lot, lights flashing. One officer spoke with Rob while the other took photos of the scene. Medics stood by waiting to take the body away.

I handed the tea to Mac, who took a drink. "Thank you. I'm waiting to be interrogated." He took a deep shaky breath and let it out slowly.

"Do you want me to stay with you? I have nowhere else to be."

"That would be nice." He looked at me for the first time. "What was your name again?"

"Pity."

After a few moments of awkward silence, I watched another police car arrive. A plain-clothed officer joined Rob. I said to Mac, "So, you say you don't remember shutting the door? Is there a chance someone else shut it?"

Mac closed his eyes. "I don't remember. I must have shut it, but I always double-check to make sure it's empty."

When the two officers approached us, the plain-clothed man motioned for me to leave. I touched Mac's shoulder. "You've got this."

As I made my way inside, Rob caught my eye. "Thank you for doing that."

"Sure. Anything else I can do?"

He looked tired. "No. I'm still waiting to hear what I'm supposed to do. The company has ordered another bus to take you all to Boston. I'll probably have to stay here to handle things. Maybe you could let everyone know that much. Tell them law enforcement may want to interview them."

"Okay. This is just awful."

"Indeed. We had a few things happen on the last tour, but nothing horrible like this."

Seeing Rob so upset, I was confident he wasn't responsible for any of the incidents on the trip, even if he was having an affair. Another thing was certain; Gross Hair Guy was off my suspects' list.

Inside the breakfast area, everyone spoke in hushed tones. The four brothers bombarded me with questions as others stared at me, wide-eyed, awaiting information.

I announced in a serious tone, "Rob asked me to give you an update." I told them what I knew and warned them that we all might be questioned.

It wasn't long before the detective came in. I watched the man in a suit go from table to table, asking questions. The scene reminded me of our first night's meet and greet, but with grave undertones.

When he came to me, he asked my name and reacted by saying, "Ahh. Your name came up several times. You're the one who pushed Howard away at the game yesterday?"

"Yes, but he was trying to kiss me, and I didn't want him to."

"Do you know anyone else, other than yourself, who might want to harm him?"

I studied his face to see if he was joking, but he was serious. "What? Just because I didn't want to kiss him doesn't mean I wanted him hurt or dead!"

He held up his hands. "Don't worry. We're just checking all angles. You aren't a suspect yet."

Even though the word 'yet' bothered me, I was more interested in the fact that he was looking for suspects. I said, "So, you don't think it was an accident?"

He snapped his notebook shut. "The truth will come out. We dusted for fingerprints and have everyone's contact information. If his death was intentional, we'll find out, eventually."

After the detective left, our group started getting antsy. Luckily, Rob came in and announced, "We have another bus coming to take you to Boston. I'll stay behind, but you'll be well taken care of. When it arrives, come on out and transfer your things from the old bus to the new one."

Minutes later, an identical-looking bus drove up.

When we were called to move our belongings to the new bus, I glanced at the luggage compartment and was thankful the body had been moved to the ambulance. No need to see that sight again. While grabbing my backpack from my seat on the first bus, I looked back to the spot where 'Howard' had sat. My stomach lurched at the realization the guy was actually dead.

As I moved to the new bus, Crystal, the guest guide, surprised me with a bright, "Hello again!"

So, she would be our temporary guide again while Rob dealt with the police. I said, "Hi, Crystal. Thanks for coming to the rescue."

"Well, it's a good thing I'm still free today." She leaned forward and said softly, "I'll try to keep people's minds off of the accident."

"Good idea."

I climbed the steps and found Deb and Diana already sitting in the front two seats. How did they get there so fast? Well, this time, they wouldn't be giggling with Rob, since he wasn't going with us to Boston.

I found the same seat on the second bus and put my stuff down on the seat next to me. As much as I missed Mike, I did enjoy having elbow room.

I looked through my window and saw Rob standing beside the bus in a deep conversation with Crystal. He was probably giving her tips on how to handle things.

Father John interrupted me by saying, "I will try not to upset you after seeing what happened to the last guy who made you mad."

I stared at him in disbelief. How did someone so callous ever become a priest?

Once the bus was loaded, Crystal popped on board and said, "Hi everyone. I'm still Crystal. Looks like I get to take you to my favorite stadium today, Fenway Park. Our new driver is Don. Let's give him a hand for bringing the new bus to us."

We gave Don polite applause, and she continued, "Due to the circumstances, we will start mandatory roll calls each time we get on and off the bus." I could sure see why that might be a good idea.

She straightened a paper in her hand and started reading names. As she did, we answered, "Here," just like in elementary school. I had never heard most of the names, of course, and tried to keep track but it was difficult because I couldn't see everyone.

Finally, we began our two-hour ride to Boston three hours late. I settled in for the long ride. The mood on the bus was solemn. I needed something to do. Why hadn't I brought a knitting project or my computer? I hadn't even brought a book since I planned to hang out with Mike the whole time. At least I had my phone and the handy USB plug on the bus to charge it, so I played a game.

The microphone squealed and Crystal held it away from her until it stopped. "I think we could all use a pick-me-up. It's time to play baseball trivia." In a singsong voice, she added, "And I have prizes!"

I smiled. Of course, she did. I was already jealous that I wouldn't be getting a prize in this game, but I sat up to listen anyway.

She started with, "In what year did Roger Maris break Babe Ruth's all-time homerun record?"

Father John yelled, "1961! He hit 61 home runs."

Crystal said, "Right!" She scooted down the aisle and let John choose something from a bag. I strained my neck to see what the prizes were but couldn't tell.

Back at the front of the bus, she asked, "What Major League pitcher holds the record for throwing the most no-hitters?"

Father John yelled, "Nolan Ryan!"

Crystal repeated her journey down the aisle and asked the next question while standing beside me, "Who is the oldest Major League Baseball player to play in a game?"

Again, Father John blasted, "Satchel Paige. He was 59 years old."

Gee, that priest sure knew his baseball stats, but why didn't he let anyone else answer? Crystal must have thought the same thing because she said into the microphone, "Maybe people should raise their hands, so others can get a chance to answer and get a prize."

John rolled his eyes, but as she continued, I was happy to hear more people answer. It all sounded like mumbo jumbo to me.

When Crystal asked, "What's the oldest Major League Baseball Park still used today?" Isaiah raised his hand, and she pointed at him.

The teen answered, "Fenway Park. It was built in 1912 and that's where we are going today." He gave a cool teen shrug when he got his prize. I learned something. We were going to a very old stadium.

As the questions continued, even little Joey answered one right and received a prize. Smart kids. There were so many questions that everyone answered, except for me. Then Crystal let people ask their own baseball trivia questions.

Father John was the first to ask some obscure question. When nobody could answer, he answered it himself. Then Harry, behind me, asked a question that captured my attention.

He said, "Who here, knows why Pity doesn't like baseball?"

I was embarrassed by the attention. Most people were confused by the question and probably didn't know who the heck Pity was.

Barry said, "Let Pity answer that herself." He pointed to me.

My face turned red as the entire busload awaited my answer.

When Crystal handed me the microphone, I cleared my throat and sat up on my knees on the seat so people could see me. "Um, for those who don't know me, I'm Pity Kole. I live in Broken Arrow, Oklahoma. All the men in my life love sports - especially baseball. But, please let me clarify; I have nothing specifically against baseball. It's just that I don't like sports in general." I shrugged. "I just don't understand the hype. So, I'll go ahead and list some things about sports that baffle me." I compiled a quick list in my head.

"First of all, why do baseball players steal a base, but they really just leave it there?" A few people smiled.

"Why do wrestlers compete for a belt when they don't even wear pants?" There were a lot of chuckles at that, and I continued.

"Why do baseball coaches wear team uniforms, but basketball coaches wear suit jackets?" There was some discussion on this, so I waited then kept going.

"Why do football fans wear team jerseys to watch football, but swim team fans don't wear team swimsuits to swim meets?" This created some giggles as they visualized how silly that would be.

"Why do people get quiet when a golfer starts to swing, but yell loudly before a batter does?"

Harry said, "That's a pretty good question."

"It irks me when people get snacks during a football halftime when the marching band is the best thing about the game." I was ready to hold my ground about marching bands but was glad when nobody debated me.

"Why do fans yell at referees and umpires but not at the judges at gymnastics meets?"

"Why is fighting allowed in ice hockey, but not in golf?" This elicited a few laughs, but I was coming to my finale and continued.

"And how in the heck am I supposed to keep the competitions straight? There are games, meets, matches, Bowls, tournaments, cups, opens, series, and grand slams. And…why, with almost every championship, do they consider themselves failures if they don't come in first—even though they beat everyone else to get to the finals? I'm just so confused by it all. And that's why I don't like sports!"

I took a deep breath and let it out. The bus was silent. Had I made a huge mistake? After a long span of nothing, I said, "So am I kicked off the tour now?" That got a laugh from the crowd and a few folks even clapped.

Crystal brought me a little keychain that said, 'Biggest Sports Fan.' I laughed. "That is so appropriate."

When the rest of the group resumed visiting, Crystal leaned into me. "So, your boyfriend had to leave? You should get a much bigger prize for being on a baseball tour alone when you don't enjoy the games."

"It's okay. I've had more fun than I thought I would, well until this morning anyway."

She nodded and moved back to the front. I worried that even though I still didn't know many people's names, they all knew mine and figured I was a big old dope.

As if to confirm my dopiness, Father John leaned across the aisle and handed me a piece of paper. I was surprised to see he had scribbled down all my questions and weirder yet, he had answered each one. Didn't he realize my questions were rhetorical? I wasn't asking for someone to explain the odd sports traditions. Jeez.

I looked up at him and attempted to be polite. "Thanks?"

I crammed his paper into my bag and willed Mike to come back to save me.

I must have had magical powers, because just then a text popped up from Mike, reminding me to take lots of photos of Fenway Park. Ha. As if I wouldn't automatically take pictures. He added, 'Make sure to get a good shot of the Green Monster.'

Well I sure would, if I saw the thing. I started to ask the twins about the monster since they wore something about it on their shirts, but they were watching a video on their phones and laughing.

## Game 4

### Atlanta Braves vs Boston Red Sox

We arrived in Boston and the bus driver, Don, dropped us off outside Fenway Park. Crystal said, "We only have an hour and a half before we tour the stadium, so go get lunch and meet us back at this entrance." She pointed to a gate.

When I stepped down from the bus, Ava said, "Pity, do you want to have lunch with us at our favorite place?"

"You've been here before?"

"Several times. We love it."

As we entered a place called The Bleacher Bar, Vince said, "Check this out. See how that window is open? We are at ground level and can look onto the center outfield of Fenway Park!"

Even though the game hadn't started yet, it was cool to see the field as if we were practically on it. What a fun place to have lunch.

The Fenway Park tour was informative. I learned that some of the seats were the originals from 1912! The tour guide was a local Bostonian who had the best accent ever, or should I say, 'evah?' She said, "Let's go upstehs to get a wicked view of the Green Monstah."

I was excited to finally see this creature, but when we reached the top and I looked where she pointed, there was no monster at all–not even a mascot. People took pictures, but all I saw was a baseball field.

Vince leaned over to me and said, "Can you see where we ate lunch? It's right there by the Green Monster."

I looked across and found the glass window by the field. "Yeah, I see where we ate, but I still don't see a monster."

He laughed. "That's the nickname for the green wall."

Now, I was confused and honestly, disappointed. "That wall is the green monster? Why is it called that?"

"Well, it's green and it's called a monster because it's difficult to hit a ball over the 37-foot wall."

"Aha," I nodded as if it made sense. I took some photos for Mike, but still couldn't fathom why he cared about a silly wall.

The guide took us down into the dugout. Everyone was excited to go into the little cubby area where I learned that the players sat there while waiting to go on the field.

The guide said, "This pahk is one of only two who still have manually operated scoahboahds. Make sure to wahtch as someone opens the little doahs in the monstah to flip the numbahs."

I loved her accent and tried to recreate it in my mind. I also looked forward to seeing the little people pop out during the game.

After the tour, we were all supposed to go check into the new hotel and relax before the 7:30 game. I had no desire to sit on a bus any longer or go to a dumb hotel when Boston was calling! I wanted to forget all about baseball, tours, injuries, and especially the death for a while.

I found Crystal and asked if I could please take an Uber to Quincy Market and Faneuil Hall to do some sightseeing and shopping.

She said, "Sure, a few others are going out on their own. Besides, you're an adult. Do what you want, but thanks for letting me know so I don't worry when I call roll." She continued, "You do have your ticket to the game on your phone, right?"

"Yep, and I have my clear bag too." I held up the bag with a bottle of water, my wallet, and Oreos in plain view.

"Okay. We'll see you later, then."

I told Vince and Ava that I was heading out on my own and asked if they wanted to come. They looked surprised and said, "We would, but we want to rest and unpack. Are you sure you'll be okay alone?"

"I'll be fine and if I see a random hotdog costume, I promise I will not put it on."

They laughed, but I wasn't about to tell them some of the things that had happened to me as a tourist in Rome just months ago. But this was America. What was there to worry about in Boston? Then two things crossed my mind: The Boston Marathon bombing and the Boston Strangler. But I needn't worry about those  everyone responsible for the attacks was caught years ago.

I ordered an Uber with my new app, thinking my girls would be amazed. A driver named Jamal picked me up only ten minutes later.

As I sat in his backseat, I sent a text to Ava with Jamal's name and car number and wrote, 'Just in case I'm kidnapped.'

Of course, he didn't kidnap me. He was very pleasant and dropped me off just where I requested. He said, "Enjoy the mahket."

I stepped outside and music filled the air as local musicians played along the busy walkway. I stopped to listen to a violin player and then shopped at some outdoor kiosks. The atmosphere was festive, and I smiled as I watched a talented group of teenagers in matching shirts dancing on the steps of Faneuil Hall.

Ahh. This was so much better than riding the bus to a hotel.

When I heard a familiar voice, I turned to see Father John exiting a car. Well, that made sense since he was from Boston.

What didn't make sense was the woman who walked up and kissed the priest…on the lips.

# Sports Joke #9
Why do golf announcers whisper?
*Because they don't want to wake up the people watching.*

Wait. Weren't priests supposed to be celibate? I watched the gal lock arms with Father John. They walked together into a white brick building with huge columns, acting a lot like a couple.

I started to follow them, but I spotted Grant talking to a pushcart vendor. I guessed he was another tour member who had ventured out on his own. He was wearing his Atlanta Braves hat and shirt, which made sense since that was who Boston was playing today. Grant was digging through the merchandise, probably looking for a Hanson shirt.

Before I could turn away to go find Father John and his "girlfriend," Grant picked up a large knife. I watched him inspect it.

I snuck closer so I could see better, and leaned casually against a big column, trying to look inconspicuous. The cart he stood by was full of antique weapons. He touched the blade of the knife and nodded with a smirk. Yikes!

A woman interrupted my sleuthing and said, "Would you like to try a sample of this perfume?" She held out a small packet.

"No thank you." I tried to look past her, but she blocked my way. Then she said, "We also have special Greek moisturizers for your face. It will make all your wrinkles disappear."

I stared at the woman. Wrinkles? I was only 46. So now I had to wear readers and worry about wrinkles, too?

I honestly felt hurt and said, "No thank you." When she finally moved aside, I saw Grant walking away carrying a bag. Had he bought the knife? And if so, why?

I followed him until he entered a booth and bought tickets to watch the Dino Safari Exhibit that I had seen ads for during the drive. I had no desire to see twenty giant moving dinosaurs while in Boston.

My to-do list was long, so I needed to get cracking. It included four important items: Eat Boston cream pie, a lobster roll, and Boston Baked Beans. I also wanted to find Boston Red Sox socks for Mike.

I passed several street performers as I made my way to the building Father John had entered. I stopped by a plaque that read Quincy Market. Wow! It was the first food hall in the United States and had been around since 1826. Amazing.

The busy old place sure offered a lot of food options. I was still stuffed from lunch, so couldn't eat one of the delicious looking "lobstah" rolls I had dreamed of but found a donut shop and bought a Boston cream donut. It wasn't exactly a Boston cream pie, but it hit the spot with the same yummy filling and chocolate frosting. Yum.

I scouted the area for Father John but gave up and sat outside on a bench. As I licked the chocolate from my fingers, I listened to a guy play a guitar, beautifully. The weather was perfect.

I called my sister. "Kim, guess where I am?"

"At a baseball game?"

"No! I'm in Boston, exploring on my own. I had my very first Uber ride and just ate a Boston cream donut. It was delish."

"Aren't you fancy? So, are you so sick of baseball?"

"Yes, but you won't believe how many problems our tour has had." I filled her in on everything.

"Don't tell me you are going to try to solve another murder mystery. I thought you swore those off when we left Rome."

"Kim, I wasn't planning on it, but after the guy died today, I can't help but get involved. I'm convinced none of the problems on the trip were accidental."

"Do you have any idea who may have locked him in there? Was there anyone lurking around the bus?"

I hadn't thought of that and said, "Well, last night I went downstairs for snacks in the lobby and our tour guide was there, the priest, and the Hanson fan, so I guess I'll keep an eye on them all."

"BE CAREFUL. I need my sister back here safe and sound."

"Don't worry about me. Hey, can I ask R.A. something?"

She hesitated before answering. "Uh. Sure. Hey, do you mind calling his cell phone? I'm not sure where he is right now."

She sounded a bit odd, almost like she was lying. But R.A. was always out somewhere fixing something for his older sister or a friend, so Kim often didn't know where he was.

I said, "Sure. I'll call him."

When R.A. answered the phone, he sounded out of breath. "Hey! How's the reluctant fan?"

"Well, I'd be better if Mike were here. Believe me. You would have gotten a lot more out of this trip than me."

"Hey, you might learn something. Just enjoy the fresh air and as much of the trip as you can."

"Speaking of fresh air. I have a question. Can someone accidentally get locked inside the luggage compartment under a bus?"

There was a pause as he considered my question. "Well…I would think there would be a latch inside that they could pull to release it in case of an emergency. But of course, if it was dark, maybe a person couldn't see that. Why do you ask?"

"Well, this morning a guy was found dead in the luggage area underneath our bus. I just wondered how it could have happened."

"Oh no. That's awful. Was it a friend of yours?"

"Not hardly, but still…"

"How was the weather? Was it really hot or super cold?"

"No."

"And police checked it out, right?"

"Yes, of course. It's all a big, sad mess."

"I really have no idea why he wasn't able to get out, but you be careful and stay out of trouble until Mike gets there."

I heard laughing in the background and wondered where R.A. was, but figured he was probably fixing the sound system in a restaurant if I knew him.

I said, "Hey, I gotta go. I'm heading into the oldest shopping center in America!"

"I hope you find some Pity-worthy bargains."

I moved into the iconic Faneuil Hall, built 280 years ago, so I figured I'd better shop in earnest. I found a big bag of Boston Baked Beans that cost ten times as much as a movie candy box of them. But, they were from Boston, so I had to buy them.

There were so many T-shirts for sale making fun of the Boston accent; 'Wicked Smaht.' 'Lobstah, Chowdah and Beeah.' And one that said, 'Bahston - Spilling the Tea since 1773.' They were all so great I wanted to get them all, but restrained myself. I did buy a keychain that said Green Monstah and asked several people where I could buy red socks, but nobody even carried them. Why wouldn't a team called the Boston Red Sox, market the heck out of special red socks? That was just one more dumb thing to add to my sports list.

As I waited in line to buy a pack of Tea Party tea, my ears perked up when the woman in front of me asked the cashier, "Where do I catch the train to Fenway Park?"

The clerk explained that a station was just across the street and a train left from there every 15 minutes! Cool.

When it was my turn, I asked how much the train ride cost and the man said, "$3 and it takes you to just a block from the stadium."

I had paid $25 for the Uber ride, but wouldn't make that mistake again.

I was so glad I hadn't wasted my afternoon riding a bus just to sit in a hotel room. I hated for my glorious outing in beautiful Boston to end but needed to head back to meet the crew at the ballpark.

The crowded train was chock full of Red Sox fans, and it only took 25 minutes to get to Fenway Park. I arrived in plenty of time for the game and had no problem getting through security with my souvenirs since I had them in my trusty clear bag. I found my seat, surprised to discover it was in the super old section with the original wooden seats from 1912! So cool! Well, it was cool until I realized how small and uncomfortable the chair was. With such long legs, my knees touched the seat in front of me and I worried about someone having to get by.

I called Mike. "Are you ever coming back? There are only two more games after today." I knew I was whining, but seriously…

"I will be there tomorrow. Not sure when, but Mom and Dad are flying in today. I'm bound and determined to watch my Yankees with my beautiful girlfriend."

A chill moved down my spine. 'Watch my Yankees with my beautiful girlfriend.' Gross Hair Guy had said the same words only yesterday, just before the Kiss Cam incident.

I shuddered at the memory, and said, "Well, I'm not so sure you'll think I'm beautiful when you see me. I'm probably too old and wrinkled to be your girlfriend now."

"What are you talking about?"

"Oh, never mind." I told Mike the whole story about Gross Hair Guy which ended with his death.

"And they didn't stop the tour right away?"

That hadn't occurred to me. "I imagine the tour company considered doing that, thinking it was just a horrible accident. We have only three games left, so they probably decided to let the tour finish. However, I'm not so sure it was an accident. Maybe we'll learn more tonight."

He sounded concerned. "I'll get there as soon as I can, Pity."

Where was everyone else? Had I beaten the bus back? There was no point in just sitting there alone, so I ventured out to take more pictures and see if they had buttons for first-timers like some other stadiums.

Yay! The worker at Fan Services gave me a cute button. I pinned it on my shirt, made a quick trip to the bathroom, and then went back to my seat.

I stood when a man dressed in an army uniform performed the "Star-Spangled Banner." He had an amazing voice and sang it just the way I liked–with no frills.

It was worrisome that our tour group still hadn't arrived. Was I at the wrong game? In the wrong seat? Had I misunderstood Crystal, and they were waiting for me at the hotel? I started to panic. Then I remembered I had Ava's phone number. As soon as the National Anthem ended, I called her. She picked up right away.

"Hi, Ava. Where are you guys? I'm sitting in the stands all alone and the game is starting!"

"Oh Pity. I couldn't find your number. You won't believe this, but our bus broke down, so we're waiting for another one to pick us up."

I almost choked at the news of more bus trouble. Note to self–stop taking long bus rides. Poor people. "How awful. I sure hope you get here soon."

She said, "Yeah, we should have gone with you. This is just crazy."

"Well, good luck! Let me know if there's anything I can do."

What were the odds that out of 48 baseball fans, the non-fan would be the only one at a baseball game? It was also weird to sit in a packed stadium with so many empty chairs around me. Where was that Grant dude and the priest? They should be here by now. I felt conspicuous sitting alone and opted to walk around some more.

A big green furry creature walked by me with people calling out, "Wally, can we take your photo?"

I was starting to catch on. This must be the Red Sox mascot, Wally. Ha! Wall-E for the green wall? Kinda dumb, but kinda cute, so I snapped some photos while he stood there.

As I took pictures from the side, a familiar voice called out, "Kitty!"

Who on the tour knew me by that name? Wait, they weren't even here yet. I closed my eyes. There was only one person who ever called me Kitty instead of Pity but that was impossible. I dreaded turning to see who it was, but slowly swiveled, and Lord have Mercy, it was Kenny! How in the world had my stalker found me in Fenway Park?

Kenny walked toward me wearing a red, Boston Red Sox t-shirt over an orange, plaid, long-sleeved, collared shirt buttoned up to his neck. In his annoying voice, he said, "I finally found you. I've been looking for hours."

Once I got over the shock of seeing him, I said, "Kenny, what are you doing here?"

"Oh, silly. You invited me."

I most certainly had not invited him and said, "When? How? What are you talking about?"

"Don't you remember? On your Facebook post from the Philadelphia game, you said, 'Wish you were here!' So, I checked the Ballparks and More website and found the itinerary. I booked a flight and here I am! I would have come earlier, but I had to go get my allergy shots and pick up a new prescription bug repellant in case the mosquitos were bad here."

I cocked my head at his logic. I mean, who in the world would take the proverbial 'wish you were here' from a public Facebook post as a personal invitation? And who would actually fly across the country to answer the call? Kenny. That's who.

What was I going to do? I had no real way to get rid of him. I looked at the strange man with the high-water pants and rolled my eyes. From what I knew, Kenny was harmless. Aside from two very boring dates 18 months ago, and him popping up at different times since then to proclaim his never-ending love for me, we had no relationship. I never encouraged the man, but he was my biggest fan and borderline stalker.

Kenny beamed. "I got us box seats in the air-conditioned section with all the food and drinks we want. Would you do me the honor of joining me?"

It was time to be honest. "Kenny, that's very nice, but I'm supposed to be meeting my tour group. They are just running late. And remember, I have a boyfriend now. He's stuck in Tulsa until tonight or tomorrow, but he will be back."

"I know." He chuckled. "You say that policeman is your boyfriend, but I believe it's only a matter of time before you see who was really meant for you."

"Kenny?" I gave him my sternest teacher voice and expression.

He held up his hands in surrender. "Okay, okay. He's your boyfriend. But you can still sit with me until your tour group gets here, right? Come have some food and watch a little of the game with a great view."

He gave me that puppy dog look that usually made me roll my eyes. That was the problem with Kenny—I tended to feel sorry for him, even though he had more money than anybody I knew. He took the time to fly all this way. Plus, the free food and drinks were tempting. My stomach had started growling an hour ago when I passed the concession stands. Maybe I could throw Kenny a bone and have a small meal with him since I was still waiting for everyone. I relented, "Well, maybe just for a little while."

He practically bounced in his shoes with excitement. "Come this way, m' lady."

Oh brother, what had I gotten myself into? Everyone at home says I'm too nice to Kenny. Even Mom, who never says anything bad about anyone, said I needed to cut him off and be firm. I thought I was being firm, but it never worked. He kept showing up and refusing to get the hint that I wasn't interested in him like that. And now, I was stuck with him again because I gave in.

Mike had met Kenny, and wasn't jealous of him, but I couldn't help but wonder what he would think of his latest stunt.

I followed the awkward guy to a door that said '521 Overlook'. Kenny knocked on the door and a big man opened it. He looked at the Red Sox lanyard hanging around Kenny's neck. Then the man reached over and slipped one just like it around my neck. I looked down at the card. Oh, wow this was an even cooler souvenir than my first-timer button.

We walked through another door and into a beautiful modern space surrounded by glass that looked out over the ballfield. The place was luxurious, but I was particularly impressed with the attached outdoor terrace. There were so many seats inside and out, and none of them were occupied. The fact it was empty was especially odd since the game had already started. Kenny pulled up a chair for me at a table beside the front window with a perfect view of the game, which was well into the first inning.

As soon as we sat down, waiters pounced, offering a variety of specialty drinks. They pointed out the full buffet at the side and named a few of the entrees. When one server mentioned Lobster Rolls, I said, "Yes please!" I wanted to run immediately to the buffet table, but instead, I asked her, "Is this a regular box seat?"

She chuckled and said, "No, Ma'am. This is the Bullpen Terrace."

I returned to Kenny, "Why aren't there any other people here?"

He gazed at me and folded his hands together. "It was easier to rent out the whole place. The suite I wanted was already taken."

He had rented the whole place? That must have cost a pretty penny.

From our incredible vantage point, I could see the entire stadium, including the empty section of seats where I should have been sitting. Would the bus ever get here?

Once I started sipping my first glass of wine, the calming warmth of the rich red drink relaxed me, and I went with the flow.

As we filled our plates, I was reminded of the buffet Kenny organized for our second date. What was it with him buying entire buffets?

There was no way the two of us could eat even ten percent of this spread, especially since Kenny was allergic to shellfish, gluten, and dairy. I did my darndest by taking two lobster rolls, but that didn't make a dent. I wished I could bag it all up and take it back to my family in Broken Arrow. But traveling with unrefrigerated seafood in a suitcase was a bad idea—especially for three days.

I forgot all about the game and the tour group as soon as I took a bite of the sandwich. It had been years since I'd had a lobster roll, and I melted as I ate the fresh rich, buttery seafood on a bun.

I pointed to the Green Monster and said, "Kenny, did you know that this is one of the only ballparks that still has a manual scoreboard? Look at that guy changing the numbers."

He watched and then gazed at me. "That's what I love about you, Kitty. You know so much about everything."

I snorted. "I just learned about that this morning when I took a tour of the stadium."

"Well, you know a lot more than I do. This is the first baseball game I've ever seen."

My head whipped around. "Seriously?"

He nodded. "My father never let us have a television, so I didn't see one there. And my mom was afraid we would get sunburned or be hit by a ball if we went to a live game."

Wow. He had no television growing up. I finally realized the poor guy had good reason for being so clueless. It also explained why he had so many allergies and feared the outdoors. He hadn't been introduced to the world of dirt, heat, sun, and bugs as a child like I was. But then again, maybe I could have avoided my apparent *wrinkles* had I stayed out of the sun.

I sighed and asked the strangest question I ever thought I would ask, "Would you like me to tell you about baseball?"

He looked as though he would cry and said, "That would be wonderful."

I started slowly as if I was teaching my kindergartners how to sing in a group for the first time. "Do you see how the two teams wear different uniforms? The guys out on the field are playing for…" I had to look at the giant screen to read the names, "the Boston Red Sox. They are wearing white with red socks on their uniforms. The guy out in the center is the pitcher. He's on their team, too."

Kenny gave me a serious look as he tried to absorb it all.

"The other team is in dark blue. They are from Atlanta and are called the Braves—but the only one you can see right now is one of their batters."

"Where are the others?"

"They are sitting on a bench in a little shelter underground called a dugout. The players will come out one at a time to bat."

The funniest thing about me teaching him was that I started feeling confident. How did I become a baseball expert?

I proceeded to tell what I knew, and Kenny asked a few questions. I did have to google to get answers to his trickier questions.

All the while, I kept my eye on our empty area. Where was that tour group?

In the middle of the third inning, I spotted Grant sitting in the first row of our empty section. Had he been there the whole time? He stood and cheered when Atlanta scored. Oh, yeah. That was his favorite team. I looked to see if he had that bag with him—one that might contain a knife. But how could he have gone through security with it? And where was that priest?

My phone rang and I was happy to see it was Ava. She said, "We're about ten minutes away, finally."

"You, poor things. I've been so worried. See you soon."

I turned to Kenny, "Well, my group is on their way, so I should go down to meet them. Thank you for the amazing meal."

He shook his head with that adoring look that always made me uncomfortable. "You just made the whole trip worth it by teaching me so much and letting me be with you."

I stood. "So, are you going back home today?"

"Yes. I ordered a private jet to take me home after the game. I just didn't feel comfortable on the big plane with so many strangers. Thank you again for everything, Kitty. You are amazing."

I blinked. Why was he thanking me? I said, "Well, have a safe flight home, and thank you again for dinner." I gave him a wave as I left the luxurious, modern area to go back a century to the 1912 wooden seats.

## Sports Joke #10
What is the hardest thing about skateboarding?
*The concrete.*

As I climbed down the steps, I waved to Grant. He yelled loud enough to be heard over the fan noise, "Is the bus back?"

"I don't think so. I've been out on my own."

"Me too. Boston is a great place. But still, you know where I want to go." He winked.

"Yes, I sure do." My eyes grew big at the thought that he was still fixed on going to Tulsa. As I entered my row, I asked him, "Did you see Father John while out and about?"

He nodded. "Yeah. I talked to him. He was with his sister. There. He's coming down the steps now."

Sister? I turned around to see Father John decked out from head to toe in Boston Red Sox garb. As I questioned whether the kiss I saw the priest give the girl was sisterly or not, the crowd grew louder. I turned back around. Ahh, finally. I watched the rest of our group ascend the steps. Crystal looked frazzled as they began to fill the empty seats.

I hugged Ava. "Was that just awful?"

"Sitting by the side of the road in a broken-down bus was not my idea of a good time. We never even made it to the hotel."

"I'm so sorry. That sounds awful." I had planned to tell her about my wonderful day of sightseeing and the special place I got to eat here but figured it would be like rubbing salt in her wound.

Vince said, "We kept tabs on the score and are glad the Sox are ahead."

"Yes. It's been a good game." I wished there was something else I could say.

When Vince sat down, he squirmed. "I forgot how uncomfortable these tiny wooden seats are." He turned to his wife. "Ava, I'm starving. Wanna go get us hot dogs?"

How sad that Kenny had that whole place to himself, and everyone here was so miserable. That's when I had a brilliant idea. I said, "Wait. Don't get food yet."

They paused while I texted Kenny. 'Hey, do you know how many people the Bullpen Terrace holds?'

He wrote back immediately. 'Hi Kitty! How are you? I'm already so lonely here without you. But I think there is room for about 50.'

I hesitated before making my big ask, then typed, 'Would you have to pay more if I brought my busload of people up to eat at your buffet?'

'No. The whole place is mine for the night. I certainly cannot eat all this food. I would love to have their company if you come back with them.'

I realized I would be in his debt, but didn't care. I replied, 'Oh, thank you so much! Please tell the servers to get ready 'cause I'm bringing a busload.'

I called as many sitting near me to listen up. I told them we were invited by my friend to enjoy a free meal and drinks in comfortable seats in the Bullpen Terrace.

Father John shook his head. "That's impossible. The Bullpen Terrace costs $20,000 to rent per game." He scoffed. "I'm pretty sure it's already booked by a corporation and wouldn't hold all of us anyway."

When the price tag hit me, I about choked. But then again, we're talking about Kenny, who has all the money in the world. I turned to the priest and said a little more curtly than I meant to, "Well, it is true. My friend rented it and he believes you all deserve to join him after your crazy day."

Word spread through the seats like a fast pitch. Our huge group followed me to the special entrance where they were each given a special lanyard. I smiled, knowing they were about to have the best meal they had eaten on the entire trip.

Once everyone entered the space, Crystal counted. I pulled one of the workers aside. "I hope you don't mind all these additional people, but they had an extremely bad day. Will it be too much extra work for you?"

He held up his hands. "Oh no. It was very unusual to only have two people tonight, and this…" He pointed to the group, "is what we're used to. There is plenty of food. We already added everything we were supposed to set out for the pre-game meal that your friend didn't need."

"Wow. Thank you. I'll make sure people tip you well."

He snorted. "No need. Mr. Dicks already gave us each a hefty bonus."

I looked at Kenny with his combover and pasty skin. He stood off to the side with an extreme smile fixated on me. As bizarre and annoying as he was, today I was rather glad he was my friend.

After everyone found seats, they ate the amazing food and ordered fancy drinks. I sat down beside Kenny and said, "Thank you so much for doing this. They needed the meal way more than I did."

"Why let the food go to waste? I'm glad they can enjoy it and I'm glad to have you back here too."

Between innings, I stood and shouted, "Everyone, can I have your attention?"

The guests, some of which I had met and most of whom I still hadn't, turned to me. A group including the brothers, and the tall woman/short man stepped inside from the outdoor terrace to listen.

I announced, "I want you to meet my friend, Kenny Dicks. He's from the Tulsa area too. He flew out here to see me but graciously paid for your seating, food, and drinks tonight, so please take a moment to thank Kenny."

He blinked at me, holding back tears. His voice cracked as he said, "Thank you, Kitty."

I held my breath, worrying that he would speak up and announce his undying love for me, or worse yet, recite another of his sappy love poems about me. Thankfully, people started approaching him to say thanks, so I was spared.

I stepped back and watched as Kenny acted almost normally around the baseball fans. He even shook some hands, which was difficult for him, since he was such a germaphobe.

I walked to the outdoor balcony and took a deep breath. The smell of popcorn filled the air, and I smiled knowing the horrible day had a nice ending. I soaked in the scene as children laughed, guys joked, and people sang happily. Somehow, the lights, the sights, and especially the sounds of the stadium made me happy. Even the crack of the bat against a ball and the announcer's excited voices were comforting. What was happening to me? Was I enjoying a game of baseball?

Back inside, I perused the dessert table and served myself a piece of Boston Crème Pie. Since Kenny's new fan club had dispersed, I sat in the chair next to him, eating and watching the rest of the game.

Every few seconds, I'd hear a loud, "Let's Go Red Sox!" or "Cowboy Up," coming from behind me. I recognized the voice as Father John's. At one point he yelled, "Braves Suck!" I couldn't believe how loud he was. Why didn't he go outside, so my ears could have a rest? So much for the comforting sounds of baseball.

After about an hour, Vince came inside and announced in an excited, sing-songy voice, "It's the bottom of the eighth inning!" He hadn't pointed that out in any other game, so why did he care this time? Even weirder, he and Ava motioned for me to stand up.

Just as I did, the loudspeakers blared the Neil Diamond song, *Sweet Caroline*. Then, the strangest thing happened–Every fan in the ballpark sang along when they got to the "Bom, Bom, Bom." Then after "Good times never seemed so good," everyone yelled, "So good, So good, So good!"

I was having such fun joining in, that I didn't even bother asking why they sang that song. I tried to get Kenny to sing, too, but of course, the clueless guy said he wasn't familiar with the song.

When the game ended and Boston won, "Love that Dirty Water" blasted, prompting the crowd to sing along again. I understood the connection when the final lyrics were, "Boston, you're my home." Now that made sense.

It was a festive walk back to the bus. Father John was especially obnoxious, bragging about his Boston team winning. I rolled my eyes at the blowhard. Poor Grant, however, looked so sad I was worried that he might use his new knife on himself or someone else, like the braggadocious priest. That was if he had indeed bought it.

I walked up to him and asked, "Are you OK, Grant?"

He let out a sad sigh. "Yeah. Just really wanted Braves to win."

"Well, was the rest of the day, okay? I mean after this morning's horrific find."

He smirked. "Yeah. I got some killer stuff at the market today."

I made a face at his choice of words and sputtered, "Oh. Well, that's good, huh?"

Grant let me enter the bus in front of him and I rushed up the steps to get to my seat. The bus must have been repaired rather than replaced because my jacket and backpack were right where I had left them on my seat. I covered Mike's seat with my stuff in case Grant decided to sit by me again and tout all the wonderful virtues of Hanson.

As the four brothers walked by, Barry said, "That dinner was awesome. Can you arrange that for the next two games?"

"Sorry, Charlie. That was a one-off."

I twisted my mouth. At least I was pretty sure Kenny was on a private plane heading to Tulsa now. But who knew, with him?

Despite the short ride and the worry of possible danger on the bus, I fell asleep against the window. It had been a long day and I'd had a few glasses of wine to boot.

When we arrived at the hotel, Crystal said, "Line up for your room keys and T-shirts!"

Oh boy! Finally, we'd get our T-shirts. I stood patiently behind an older couple who both wore red, Ballparks and More tees. I said, "So you've been on these tours before?"

The man answered in a deep Texas accent. "Yes, we're doing three tours back-to-back; the West Coast tour last month, the Great Lakes tour last week, and now this."

Wow. This couple had to have a lot of money since the regular price of each trip costs over two thousand dollars per person. They both wore cowboy boots, so maybe they were cattle barons or something. I said, "You must really love baseball and bus rides." I crinkled my nose at the thought of more tours but straightened my face before they could notice.

He said, "Oh, we do. We aren't nickel and dimed for travel to and from the games, tickets, parking, or even hotels. It's perfect." He paused and said to his wife, "Darlin, it looks like our shirts are blue this time."

I looked around the line and sure enough, Deb and Diana each carried a powder blue shirt while wheeling luggage onto the elevator.

The cowboy's wife, with an even thicker accent, spoke to me. "Your boyfriend sure is crazy about you."

I smiled. My boyfriend sure did like me. But when had they talked to Mike?

She added, "Thank you again for last night."

Oh. They weren't talking about Mike. They meant Kenny! What had he told them? Before I could dispute him being my boyfriend, they had moved up the line and were getting their shirts.

Once in my hotel room, I put Mike's new Ballparks and More shirt on his bed just in case he showed up. I laid mine on my suitcase, then ran to the bathroom mirror, looking for wrinkles. Yep, there was one next to my mouth—and another on my cheek. Dang. But it didn't seem so bad that I needed to erase them right away. Whew!

I called my girls. "What have you two been up to?"

Together, they said a brief, "Not much."

That sounded a little suspicious, but I didn't push it. "Well, I hope you're behaving yourselves with your dad and Shelly."

"We are." What was with the short, unison answers? They were surely up to something, but I went ahead and gave them an abbreviated version of the day.

Ren said, "Wait. Someone died?"

I nodded, then realized they couldn't see me. "Yes. It was awful."

Ree said, "That's horrible. And Kenny flew all the way to Boston because you said, 'Wish you were here' on Facebook?"

I said, "I know. I was shocked too, but really, Kenny's not that bad. He rented out this huge luxury suite that overlooked the ball field. It included a full buffet and drinks for fifty. Apparently, renting that place for just one evening cost him almost as much as a new car."

"You're kidding!"

"No. But the cool thing was that he let my whole tour group enjoy it and after the day they had, they sure appreciated it. Honestly, I'm beginning to understand him better after hearing more about his weird childhood."

Ree said with a shaky voice, "Mom, please tell me you're not gonna ditch Mike for Kenny. We can't handle having both Smelly Shelly and Kenny as stepparents."

The ludicrous idea almost made me choke. I said, "I assure you. I will never like Kenny in that way. But don't start getting ideas about Mike and me either. We are not that serious and I'm not sure I ever want to get married again. Only time will tell."

"Speaking of weddings," Ren said, "have you told Shelly that we can't wear those hideous red, white, and blue bridesmaid dresses?"

"No, but we'll come up with a plan of some sort." Dang, I knew there was something else I was supposed to be worried about.

After we hung up, I called my mom to fill her in on the trip. She said exactly what I expected, "You need to be firm with that Kenny, or he'll never leave you alone."

"I know, Mom."

When we finished our conversation, I thought about calling Mike, but didn't want to bug him again. He would be here when he could.

Sleep didn't come easy for me, even after such a busy day. I kept thinking about Howard. How in the world did he end up in the luggage compartment? Wouldn't he have yelled and pounded on the baggage door? I sure would have. And why did he die? It wasn't extremely cold or hot. But on the other hand, the guy was overweight and did a lot of huffing and puffing when he walked. Maybe he passed out before the door shut and with his dark clothes Mac didn't see him.

This theory would have been plausible if it weren't for the three other problems that had plagued our tour. It was all just too fishy.

I considered the other incidents. 1. Jason's drink was poisoned. 2. Marcia fell onto the stadium seats from the platform. 3. Grandpa Herrera tripped or was pushed down the steps.

What did they all have in common? I was pretty sure they didn't know each other. The Herrera man was a Yankees fan, as was the redhead, Jason. Was Marcia too? If so, that could be a connection. But how ridiculous was that? Why would anyone go after Yankees fans? Besides, more than half of our group rooted for the Yankees.

As I finally drifted off to sleep, I remembered overhearing Rob on his phone call. He indicated that there were accidents on the previous trip too. What kind of accidents?

I woke up thinking, 'Another day, another ball game.' Ha! That could be a new slogan for the tour company. I considered wearing my new Ballparks and More T-shirt, but there was another match-up between the Mets and the Yankees tonight. I held my Yankees shirt up to my nose. It smelled fine, so I put it on since it went well with Dad's lucky hat.

While lugging my suitcase onto the elevator, I realized I wasn't feeling any pain from either side of my body, or maybe I was just getting stronger or getting used to the pain. I was relieved that there would be only two more hotels before I could finally go home. I was ready to set up our swimming pool, so I could relax in it.

I walked into the breakfast bar and most of our group smiled at me like I was a celebrity. I quickly realized it was because I had taken them to the special suite for a meal and apparently to meet my "boyfriend." Oh, brother!

Natasha and Boris didn't smile at me, though. They stayed to themselves as usual. I was glad to see they were not drinking beer with breakfast, at least.

I sat at the table with the Herrera family, all wearing their usual Yankees attire. I told Joey, "So you get to see your team today."

He nodded as he took a bite of his breakfast-bar waffle.

"I'm sure they'll do better with you there."

I turned to his mom. "Would you mind sharing the photo you took of us standing at the top of the Rocky steps?"

She pulled up her phone. "What is your number?" I told her and she sent it to me.

When the grandpa rose to get himself more coffee, I asked her, "Is he doing better?"

She nodded. "Yes. It's a bad sprain." She leaned into me and said, "He says he was pushed, but I can't think of why someone would do that. He's so sweet."

There it was. Mike was right. Empujado *did* mean pushed. I frowned and said, "That's terrible. I'm glad he's doing better though."

When I saw the cowboy couple I had spoken with last night, I excused myself from the Herreras.

I sat beside the couple, who now wore their new blue Ballparks and More shirts. I said, "Hi. I thought I could get to know you a bit better. Where did you get those gorgeous southern accents?"

The woman looked straight out of an ad for active senior living. Her pure white hair was styled in a bob that matched her subtle classy make-up. Speaking in a soft southern voice, she said politely, "We live in Abilene, Texas. My Travis here owns the Cadillac dealership, and I handle the books."

Oh my gosh. Not another Cadillac dealership. I couldn't let that go. "Have you ever heard of Big Jack's Cadillacs in Tulsa?"

The man guffawed. "Why of course, we have. Jack is our biggest competitor. Every year, it's a battle to see who has more cars leave the lot. It's a friendly competition though."

I nodded. "Well, my ex-husband is marrying Big Jack's daughter."

The woman brightened. "Well, we've known little Shelly since she was born, and we have plans to go to her wedding."

I almost choked at the 'little Shelly.' She was anything but *little* anymore. Her fake boobs, fake eyelashes, big hair, and loud whiny voice made her seem huge to me.

I said, "That's so nice. Well then, you'll see my daughters since they'll be her bridesmaids."

A flash of brilliance hit me. Probably the only thing that would entice Shelly to change from the gaudy red, white, and blue dresses was worrying about what someone on her level would think of her. I said, "So, now what are your names, Travis and ?"

"I'm Odette."

I smiled. "Nice to meet you both. My name is Pity Kole." I sighed. "I won't be attending the wedding because…well, I'll be out of town that weekend." I didn't lie. I would be at our cabin in Missouri the very next day.

I leaned forward and asked, "So, what are you planning to wear to the wedding, Odette? Lots of lace?"

"Oh, no. I never liked lace. I always say understated is the way to go. I'm going to wear a simple dress. No bling for me."

Oh, that was too good to be true. I now had some ammo to use on Shelly. Then I got down to business on another issue. I leaned back and took a drink of my coffee. "So, since you two have been on several Ballparks and More trips, do you remember any strange accidents on either trip? Anyone get sick or have a fall, like this time?"

They looked at each other and Travis said in his Texas accent, "Well, that last goll-derned tour was nearly shut down because five people got food poisoning."

Odette added, "And a gal was locked in her hotel room and missed one whole game."

I tried not to look horrified and said, "That's pretty weird." I thought of another question for the two and leaned forward. "Hey, just wondering…on those other trips, did the guide take time to let people introduce themselves?"

Travis said, "Oh yes. Crystal was our guide both times. She let us go around and talk about ourselves. It helped so much to know where people were from and what they did. We were surprised Rob didn't do that this time."

I shrugged. "Me too. I have one more question before we get on the bus. Were any other people from this trip on your last tour?"

They both nodded and looked around. Travis pointed. "Yep. He was there." I followed his gaze to Grant, the Hanson fan.

Odette said, "Father John was on the tour and Rob of course, since he was learning how to be a tour guide."

That was interesting information. So, this was Rob's first tour as a guide. I should give him slack for being a newbie.

Odette said, "Oh, and the red-headed cousins. There might have been others, but I can't remember right now. Why do you want to know?"

"No real reason. Just wanted to know more about my fellow passengers." I stood. "Thank you so much. Oh, and what's the name of your dealership?"

In unison, they said the name as if they were starring in a commercial together, "Lone Star Caddy Corral."

What was up with all the kitschy names of Cadillac retailers? I said, "That's fun."

I wondered if they had an annoying slogan like Shelly's, 'You'll get the Max at Big Jack's Cadillacs.' I was so sick of hearing her spout that phrase in her dad's commercials, that I muted the TV when I saw her appear on screen.

We threw our trash away and got in line for the bus. Standing behind the twins, I tapped Barry on the shoulder so I could read today's shirt. He turned around. The black shirts with white lettering read, 'Best Brother Ever.'

I chuckled, and said, "Hey, tomorrow can you guys wear your blue, Ballparks and More tees so I can finally match you?"

Harry said, "That's the plan."

Barry winked, "Just for you, Pity."

Once on the bus, I texted Shelly. 'Hi Shelly, I hope your wedding plans are going well. I just wanted to tell you I just met Odette and Travis from Lone Star Caddy Corral on my bus tour of the baseball parks. Super nice people and they're excited to go to your wedding.'

Shelly wrote right back. 'Oh, they are my parents' good friends. I've known them all my life. When I was a little girl, I called Travis 'Wavis.' He used to let me push the button on his Cadillac so I could hear the song play. It was so loud."

That was one of the longest conversations I'd ever had with Shelly and it was only a text. I replied, 'That's a nice memory. Since I won't get to see Odette there, I asked her if she would be wearing a fancy, lacy dress to your wedding. She said she would probably wear something simple and understated. She thinks too much lace is tacky. I'll bet she will love your dress. The girls say it's gorgeous with sequins, right?'

There was a pause before the three dots appeared and she wrote back. 'My dress was custom made. It is white with little red and blue rings around the arms, waist, and hem.'

For some reason, I pictured the Olympic rings and hoped that wasn't what she meant. I wrote, 'Oh, well your dress sounds lovely and understated as I'm sure your whole wedding party will be.' I winced as I wrote that leading statement, but sometimes ya gotta do what ya gotta do for your kids.

After a bit she wrote, 'Of course they are. Tell Odette we have gift bags for everyone who attends.'

'That's so nice of you. I'll be sure to tell her. I guess I can't wait to see the gift bags my girls will get.'

I threw that in to give her a reason to gloat. Shelly loves nothing more than to make me jealous. Sadly, I *was* jealous. What was in those gift bags?

I knew it was kind of devious for me to make Shelly rethink the bridesmaid's outfits, but I'd do anything to save my girls from humiliation. At least her wedding dress wasn't lacey, so she wouldn't consider changing hers.

Mere moments later, Todd called. He huffed, "Thanks a lot, Pity."

"What?"

"Shelly's in a tizzy. She's all nervous about Odette and Travis coming to the wedding. Now she wants to change a bunch of stuff."

I rolled my eyes and said, "That was my plan, Todd. To have her change the girls' dresses."

There was silence while what I said hit him. He finally said, "Ah. I see. I did ask for help, huh? If it works, do ya mind if I tell Ree and Ren that I got her to change the dresses?"

"Knock yourself out, Todd. You need the girls to be happy with you on your big day."

He said, "I'll try to encourage Shelly to choose dresses that are less frilly or patriotic. I'll let you know if it works."

"Good luck! Please make sure the photographer takes lots of photos of Ree and Ren. And if you can, snag me a goodie bag since I'm not invited."

He chuckled. "I'll see what I can do. You still like free stuff, huh?"

"Yep."

He did know me well.

## Sports Joke #11

A gymnast walked into a bar...
*and was deducted five points.*

Crystal stood at the helm of the bus wearing a hat that looked like a baseball and a shirt covered with bats. Her green pants with bases covering them took the prize though.

She turned on the microphone and said, "Good morning, folks! It looks like it's goodbye for me. I'll hand you back over to Rob for the last two games."

Rob climbed the steps and put his hand on Crystal's shoulder. The movement was a little more familiar than what you would expect from two coworkers. Oh my gosh! Was it Crystal I had seen in an embrace with Rob at the Mets game? She was blond. That made sense since they were on the last trip together. How interesting.

Rob spoke into the microphone, "Crystal. We couldn't have gotten by without you." He turned to us. "Let's give her a big thank you for jumping in at the last minute."

We all cheered and shouted "Thanks, Crystal!"

Before she left, I stood up and scooted up the aisle past Rob and handed her a little keychain. "It's not much, but I appreciate you being so helpful and such fun."

"Oh, thanks." She studied it. "I love the little Oklahoma cowboy! It will remind me of you, Pity. I hope you have learned to like baseball a little bit on this trip."

I pointed to her hat. "I'd like it more if I could dress like you."

She laughed, made a final wave to our group, and left the bus. I was sad to see the peppy girl go. Rob probably was too.

Once I was back in my seat, Don, the new driver, started the bus and Rob picked up the microphone. "I'm sure you want to hear what we learned about Howard's death. The coroner deemed his death a medical episode. Apparently, he had a heart condition, and being trapped in a confined space was just too stressful for him. We hope he didn't suffer long."

My stomach turned.

He added, "The police have yet to determine how he got locked in the luggage compartment, but I'm confident it wasn't Mac's fault. He should be able to join us again tomorrow to finish the tour. I do have other good news. Marcia awoke from her coma and is doing great. She has two broken arms and the fibula in her left leg was fractured. But…since she's back home in New York City, she and her husband might make an appearance at the game today."

That was good news and my mind whirred. I wanted to ask her if she, too, was pushed. And if so, was she a Yankees fan? It still seemed far-fetched for someone to go after people who loved the Yankees clothes, and I scoffed at the idea. I repeated my concern in my head and started to worry for Ava and Vince who were die-hard Yankees fans. Then it hit me. Today, I looked like one too!

I took my hat off so it wasn't so obvious and scanned the bus, looking for anyone who might look suspicious. Everyone acted normally as they read, talked, and relaxed. Stop making everything into a mystery, Pity. You are just paranoid. I put my hat back on and tried to think of something else.

Leaning back in my seat, I imagined Mike meeting me at the game. I was counting on him showing up and needed to be prepared. I practiced the surprised look I would give him and then pictured myself running up, jumping into his arms, and kissing him.

"And just what are we thinking about with those lips all puckered?"

I left my daydream and opened my eyes to find Rob standing over me with an eyebrow raised.

I sputtered "Um. Well…" I cleared my throat. "Oh, nothing. Did you need something, Rob?"

He didn't look at me when he spoke. "Will Mike be able to arrive before the tour is over?"

I didn't want to admit that the odd expression on my face was me prepping for Mike's return. I quickly said, "He's going to try, but I haven't heard anything from him today, so I don't know for sure."

Rob's face relaxed and he smiled at me. "Well, if he doesn't make it, we'll take good care of you."

He turned to go back up front. Hmm. Like I needed special care.

As we rode the rest of the way toward the Big Apple again, I typed Baseball Suspects in a new note on my phone. I had to clarify this because I already had a note called Italian Suspects on my phone from my recent crazy investigation.

I listed the people who were on the last Ballparks and More tour who could be suspects. There was Rob, Crystal, Father John, Grant, the red-headed cousins, and of course, Travis and Odette. I deleted the cousins since they had been victims themselves but had trouble believing any of the others were involved in wrongdoing either.

Wait! I never looked at the photo the Herrera gal texted me. If the grandpa truly was pushed, it would have been someone near him who did it. Maybe one of my suspects was standing on the top step along with the older man.

My heart started pounding when I found the picture of our group standing at the top of the Rocky steps. I spotted myself first, standing with my arms up in a silly pose like Rocky. Next to me were the young teen, Isaiah, then Boris, and Natasha. It was surprising that the shady couple had even walked up those steps. Then there was Grant, Father John, the Herrera family, and finally, Rob.

I still doubted any of them caused all the problems including the death of Gross Hair Guy. But I put an x next to people on my phone list who had been on the last trip and who also stood atop the steps.

Just before reaching Yankee Stadium, I laid my phone on my seat and ran to the bathroom. Better safe than sorry. After all, I drank a lot of coffee this morning.

When I returned, my phone was gone. I looked under the seat and asked the guys behind me if they had seen it.

Harry said, "No. Sorry, I was asleep—had a little too much whiskey in our rooms last night."

Rob's voice came over the microphone and asked if anyone had lost their phone. I jumped up and ran to him. Like everyone else nowadays, I felt lost without it. I thanked him as I took it and asked where it had been. He said, "Joey found it and brought it to me."

On my way back to my seat I thanked little Joey and sat back down to let my heart slow to a normal pace. How in the world did we ever survive before cell phones?

As we waited for a guide to take us on the tour of the iconic Yankee Stadium, I kept a close eye on my possible suspects. Neither Rob, Father John nor Grant did anything unusual, so I gave up and looked around, hoping Mike would miraculously appear, but of course, he didn't.

The tour was nice, I guess. Father John grumbled every time the guide bragged about the Yankees. I leaned over to Vince and said, "What is his problem?"

"Oh, he's just a rabid Red Sox fan. Boston has hated the Yankees ever since they lured Babe Ruth from Boston back in 1919! They call it 'The curse of the Bambino.' It's all a big thing."

"So, they've had a rivalry for over a hundred years?"

"Yeah. Boston fans root for two teams —The Red Sox and anyone who is playing against the Yankees."

Wow. Being a fanatic could get way out of hand – but did Father John hate the Yankees enough to kill one? But seriously, a priest killing anyone was a ridiculous thought.

We continued, and I snapped photos everywhere to show Mike. My favorite part of the tour was seeing all the World Series rings from years past. I walked around the tall glass case several times to gawk at them before the guide said it was time to go to the game.

## Game 5
### New York Mets vs New York Yankees

As I followed Ava and Vince to our seats, my mind was scattered thinking about my list of suspects. I scanned the area as we walked. Father John was talking on a phone with his hand cupped around it like he didn't want anyone listening in. When I spotted Grant, he just waved and gave me a goofy smile.

While my head was still turned, I missed a step and stumbled down a few rows with my arms flailing about. I landed right in the lap of a big guy with a giant cup of beer.

Fortunately, the man caught me, so I wasn't hurt, but unfortunately, his 24-ounce can of cold beer gushed all over me. I gasped as the icy liquid seeped onto my skin. When I caught my breath, I sputtered, "I'm so sorry!"

Try as I might, I couldn't get my feet underneath me. I was like a wet turtle lying on my back. The big fella was now laughing hysterically but helped me up. He said, "You good?"

I nodded as Vince turned around and cocked his head at me. He ran back up the steps. "We can't let you out of our sight for a second, can we?"

Ava followed him up to me, grabbed napkins from her bag, and handed them over. I wiped my shirt and hands, but it wasn't much help since I was drenched and smelled like a brewery.

His buddies chided him in NY slang, "Wait 'til your gal finds out about this," and "I'm dead. Wish I got that on camera."

One guy snapped a photo of me standing there like I was in a wet T-shirt contest. I crossed my arms across my chest.

Humiliated, I blurted to the man, "I'm so very sorry. What kind of beer were you drinking? I'll buy you another."

One of his drunk friends, said, "Just lick it oaff heh shuert."

My eyes opened wide in horror, but the beer owner shook his head. In a thick New York accent he said, "NBD. You good, Ma."

I thanked him and followed my friends to our seats but stopped before sitting down and I asked Ava, "Why did he call me Ma? Am I that old?"

She chuckled. "No. It's just a casual way guys here refer to a woman."

"That's weird. All I know is I can't stand this cold shirt. I have to get something dry to wear. I'll be back."

Ava stood. "Want me to go with you?"

"No. I'll be fine. Just enjoy the day." I headed up to the team shop, turning my head away from the drunken guys as I passed.

It was easy to find a new Yankees T-shirt, but wow, they were expensive, so I headed to the clearance section and picked out one that would work. Father John walked by me tossing a baseball in the air. Hmm. That reminded me I should buy something Yankees for Dad, R.A., and Mike.

I looked at the baseballs but figured they probably already had one. I knew they had Yankees hats and T-shirts, but the jerseys here were super expensive. I couldn't find anything perfect until I found something they would never buy for themselves—little packaged guys called reaction figures. They were dressed in pinstriped baseball uniforms. So cute! There were four of them - Babe Ruth, Mickey Mantle, Yogi Berra, and Joe DiMaggio. Since even *I* had heard of all those players, I was sure the guys had too. Luckily, the baseball figures were on clearance, so I bought them all for $40!

After I checked out and was headed for the exit, I passed Natasha, the tall woman from our tour. She faced a wall of jerseys as she talked on her phone. Strangely, she was without her diminutive sidekick.

I stopped walking. I didn't know if she had been on the last trip, but I had proof she had been standing atop the Rocky steps, so I needed to check her out. With her back to me, I sidled up to listen in while inconspicuously looking through a rack of XXXL Yankees pants. I wasn't sure what man wore clothes that big but knew I wouldn't want to meet that giant in a dark alley.

I heard Natasha say, "We're getting close to finding out who it is. I'll report back soon."

She started to turn around, so I snuck out of the store, hoping she wouldn't see me, and headed to the bathroom to change. Once I had stashed the soggy shirt in my clear bag and put on the new dry shirt, I felt much better and had to smell better too.

As I exited the bathroom, I was swallowed up in the throng of loud New Yorkers excited for another subway series game. I was hell-bent on learning more about the odd couple, so I swam, well, walked upstream, and spotted the odd couple sitting in their usual seats at the top of the stairs.

After escaping the mob, I stood to the side of a pretzel trolley and watched them. Wait a minute. This place was jam-packed. There was no way those seats just happened to be empty this time. The odd couple must have bought special tickets to sit there.

Instead of beer, Natasha held binoculars. She lifted them and pointed them at our group rather than at the field.

I pondered the situation. The strange couple's odd behavior, aloofness, and her statement on the phone rendered me curious. Since I had never noticed what they wore, I studied their outfits to see what team they liked. Weird. Neither one of them wore a ball cap. They were wearing non-descript T-shirts and jeans. It was as if they were dressed incognito as undercover cops.

I froze. Maybe they really *were* undercover cops–or perhaps FBI agents! That would explain it all, including her comment "getting close to finding out who it is," on the phone. Maybe they were on the trip to investigate who caused the problems on the last tour.

Should I ask them? I could help their investigation by telling them what I knew. It sure couldn't hurt.

I sidled up next to Natasha since she was the only one of the two, I had heard speak. Maybe they were like Penn and Teller, with Penn doing all the talking and Teller staying silent.

I leaned in and said, "Hi."

She jumped back and put the binoculars in her lap.

"Oh sorry. I finally figured out why you two are acting so secretive. You're investigating the problems on the bus, right?"

Her green eyes flicked to me, then back to her partner. Wow. Those were pretty eyes. She said nothing, so I continued, "Well, I've been doing my own investigation and have the suspects narrowed down to three people."

I pulled up my phone note. "All of these were on the last Ballparks and More trip, where, as you know, several other unusual incidents occurred. These three suspects were also standing atop the Rocky steps just before Mr. Herrera was pushed. So right place, right time, if you know what I mean."

I noticed the two operatives glancing at each other and continued in a hushed voice. "Am I right that the person is after Yankees fans? Is that the motive?"

Natasha cleared her throat but said nothing and Boris shifted in his seat. I wished they weren't so hard to read. I could always tell what children were thinking after just a minute of being with them, but an actual spy or detective was another thing. They were probably trained not to give anything away. They sure were good at it.

I continued. "Okay, so here are my suspects, if it's truly someone on our bus. Number one: Grant from Tupelo Mississippi – He's a big

Hanson and Atlanta Braves fan, but I witnessed him buying a big knife in Boston. Suspicious, huh?"

The woman's eyebrows raised as she stared at me.

I went on. "Number two: Father John – I know he's a priest, but he's from Boston, and of course, they hate the Yankees, but he's overly grumpy about them. And I saw him kiss a girl on the lips, which seems very strange if he's supposed to be celibate. In fact, I'm wondering if he's a priest at all."

I wasn't sure why I made that last statement. I was probably way off base since the duo both crinkled their noses.

"Then there's number three – Rob, our tour guide."

Boris leaned forward and Natasha looked confused. I said, "He acted reluctant to have my boyfriend come back–maybe because Mike's a policeman? And this is odd; he was sneaking around at Mets Stadium, so I followed him to a lower level and found him standing in a corridor kissing some woman."

Having gained their rapt attention, I figured I was on the right track, but what did they know about this case?

I rested my mouth for a second, hoping they would thank me for the information, but the woman only said, "Who did he kiss?"

I lifted my shoulder. "Who knows? Grant said it was his sister."

Natasha said, "Grant's sister was kissing Rob?"

I shook my head. "No. Grant said that Father John said he was kissing his own sister." This conversation started sounding as ridiculous as Abbot and Costello's famous, 'Who's on First' routine Dad used to show us on an old videotape. Hmm. I should watch that again now that I know more about baseball.

She tilted her head, confused. "Then who was Rob kissing?"

Why did these two care who kissed who? I said, "Well, I'm not sure. She was blonde. Could have been one of the gals on the bus or I'm thinking maybe our other guide, Crystal. Now that I think about it, maybe Rob didn't have anything to do with the accidents. He was probably just sneaking around because well, I heard he's married."

I urged, "So…tell me who you suspect in the two falls, the poisoning, and maybe even Howard's death. And how are we going to prove it?" I lifted my eyebrows in anticipation.

Natasha whispered something lengthy to Boris and then turned back to me. "We can't divulge any information at this time."

My face fell. I had told them everything and they couldn't give me even a morsel of information? Oh well, they were on official business, and I wasn't. I sighed. "You know where I am if you want to talk. And I promise I won't tell anyone who you really are." I winked and left them sitting in their spot on top of the steps.

As I made my way back to my seat, I felt relieved that someone else was looking into the crimes. I joined Ava, dying to tell her about the odd couple but didn't, for it would break their confidence. The ballgame was just about to begin, so I focused on that instead.

A group of fans started chanting a name, Michael something. I watched to see what was happening. When a player turned and bowed, the crowd went wild. Then, they yelled another name, Aa-ron Judge! Aa-ron Judge! until another guy turned around and waved. They yelled a few more names until I had to ask Ava about it.

"Oh. The Bleacher Creatures are doing the Yankee roll call. They do it every game."

Hmm. What an interesting tradition. I watched the rest of the roll call, then stood for the National Anthem, after which the game began.

When the Mets scored a run, I yelled at the pitcher, "Come on, Martinez, get with the program!"

Ava turned to me in shock. "Wow Pity, you know the pitcher's name?"

I shrugged. "I learned it during the roll call."

"But are you actually watching the game?"

I looked at her in surprise. "Well, I guess I am!" I grimaced. "What is happening to me?"

A vendor came by yelling, "Get-cha Yankees pinstriped bea hea!"

I ordered one but found myself straining to see around his large body. Would the next batter get a hit, a ball, or a strike? Oh my. Was I not only watching a ballgame but interested in it?

As the game progressed, I was so sucked into it, I hated to leave to get a pretzel, so when another guy came by, I bought one to go with my pinstriped can of beer. I was nervous that Mike would miss seeing Yankee Stadium altogether, but I saved part of the delicious pretzel in case he showed up.

I heard a whack, and a ball flew overhead. Just like before, all kinds of hands reached up but this time the ball landed just behind me. I turned in time to see Grant jump up and catch it with his bare hand. Wow! That was cool. People patted him on the back and for the first time in days, he looked really happy.

Eventually, the beer got the better of me and I had to use the bathroom. Ava insisted on going along to keep me out of trouble. At the top of the steps, Marcia, the gal who had fallen onto the seats in Philadelphia was being pushed towards us in a wheelchair. We rushed over.

Ava greeted her first. "Welcome back! How are you doing?"

"Not good, but better." She nodded her super-tanned head at her broken arms and leg. She said, "I just wanted to see part of the game."

One of my questions was answered when I saw her Yankees hat. I pointed to it and said, "I see you are a Yankees fan, so you wouldn't want to miss this game."

Her husband said, "We love them so much we bought a house down the street from the stadium."

As surprising as that was, it answered an earlier question; The couple did not get their dark tans working on a farm. So, maybe they owned their own tanning bed.

I needed to find out if she had been pushed, and just came right out and asked, "So, Marcia, I'm curious…did you trip over something before falling? I mean, nobody saw what happened." I held my breath waiting for her answer.

Her husband frowned at me. "Please. She doesn't want to be reminded of that awful day."

I looked at the woman in the wheelchair who was just released from the hospital. How stupid of me to bring it up. She was wearing three casts for heaven's sake. I said, "Oh, of course. I shouldn't have said anything. I really hope you both enjoy the game."

As we turned to leave, Marcia spoke up, "It's okay."

I faced her again and she said, "So, I was probably standing too close to the edge, but then someone bumped into me, and I lost my balance and fell. That's the last thing I remember until I woke up in the hospital."

Ava made a face. "That's awful. And nobody fessed up? I sure would have if I had caused you to fall."

Marcia shook her head. "Not yet anyway." She paused then looked at her husband apologetically and said, "I may have imagined it, but just before I fell, I could swear a guy said something like, "This is payback. Hell is waiting for you.""

Oh my gosh! If a guy said that to her, then it *was* a deliberate push, but what did that mean? Payback for what? For being a Yankees fan?

I said, "Did you have beef with someone? Why would anyone say that?"

She shrugged, then winced in pain from lifting her shoulders. "Not that I know of."

I cleared my throat and patted her shoulder lightly. "I'm going to look into this for you. Thanks for being so strong. I'm not sure I would have come back with some nut job out there."

Ava said, "We hope you get better soon."

Now I had even more information. On our way back from the bathroom, I winked confidently at the FBI agent/detectives. Surprisingly, the woman nodded this time, which put a spring in my step.

I tried to focus on the game again, but since the Yankees were way ahead, it wasn't that important, and I started snacking on the Payday candy bar I had pulled from my bag. I typed the new quote Marcia had heard into my phone note, adding that she too was a Yankees fan. This whole thing was getting crazier and crazier.

Father John interrupted my thoughts by yelling, "Yankees go home!" I stared at him. They *were* home, you jerk. We were in their stadium. I studied him sitting in the row behind me and still couldn't believe he was a priest.

I checked on my other suspects. Grant was looking at something in his lap, but I couldn't see what it was. Beyond him, Rob was on his phone, smiling as he talked.

Oh, how I wanted to be a fly so I could flit over and listen to what he was saying. Then I could zip over to Grant and Father John, too. I imagined being the bug until Rob swatted at a real bug. Almost like being stuck with a pin in a voodoo doll, I jerked, imagining the pain the bug must have felt as it was smashed dead. Why did I have to have such a vivid imagination?

I took another bite of my Payday. Suddenly, something hit my head, and everything went black.

# Sports Joke #12

Where does the football player go for a new uniform?
*New Jersey*

"Pity? Wake up."

The voice sounded like Mike's. What a nice dream. Or was he actually here beside me? Or was I dead?

I opened my eyes, but it was too bright. I shut them again, but not before I thought I saw the outline of a man's face.

"Pity, are you alright?"

It sure sounded like his voice. I opened my eyes again. It truly was Mike's handsome face in front of me. Where was I? I looked past him to see a man dressed in white standing by Ava, Vince, and Rob. I was in a hospital!

I croaked, "Am I dying? Where am I?"

Mike smiled and said, "You are at Yankees Stadium in the medical room. You were hit in the head by a baseball. It's a good thing you woke up, we were about to take you to Bronx General Hospital."

I held out my hand and touched Mike's face. "You are really here?"

"Yes. I am here. I'm sorry I took so long."

I blinked a few times and then realized how thirsty I was. "Can I have some water?"

While the man in white brought me a water bottle, I rubbed my hand alongside my head. I felt a new lump growing on the opposite side of my Liberty Bell knot. How many bumps could someone get in a week without getting brain damage? I didn't ask the medic about it since I hadn't told anyone my Philadelphia story.

Mike helped me to sit up. After taking a sip of the water, my head still pounded, but otherwise, I felt OK. I asked, "Did you get to see the game? Is it over? How long have I been out?"

Ava moved closer. "It's still going on."

Vince said, "You've only been here a few minutes. We were all praying for you."

I said, "Mike, you need to go watch the game! Let's go."

They all held out their hands as Mike said, "Hold on. We need to make sure you are ok."

I lay back for a minute and said, "So, who hit the foul ball? Was it Johnson? Or how about Judge?"

Mike looked at me, then the others. "She must have been hit hard. She doesn't know those players' names." He turned to the medic. "Is this like those people who wake up from a coma and can speak a new language? But Pity suddenly knows ball players' names?"

Ava said with a little laugh, "No. She paid attention to the Yankee roll call today."

Mike looked at me in amazement. I tried to shrug but it hurt to move.

A man wearing a golf shirt with the Yankees logo embroidered on his chest stepped forward and answered my question. "That's what we are checking on now. It seems that the ball that hit you didn't come from the field. It came from elsewhere."

I squinted. "Wait. Someone threw the ball at me?"

He gave a little nod. "It looks that way."

"Did anyone see where it came from?"

Rob said, "I missed it because I was getting food."

Ava said, "No. I was busy eyeing your Payday, and wishing I had one when it hit you. But the ball came from behind us, so there was no warning."

Mike said, "I came bounding down the steps to surprise you, only to find you slumped over and surrounded by a big group of people."

I nodded, which hurt my head. "So, did anyone retrieve the ball?"

Mike said, "Don't tell me you want it as a souvenir?"

I wrinkled my nose. "Maybe? But I wonder if it has any fingerprints on it."

The Yankees employee said, "The security team has the ball now. They are interviewing people, hoping to find witnesses."

I understood. "Well, while they look, we should go let Mike watch the game."

Mike leaned into me and said gently, "Are you sure you're okay?"

"Yes. It's your last time to see the Yankees play in this stadium. Let's go."

Mike helped me stand up and the group nervously watched me take my first steps as if I was a toddler learning to walk. I half expected them to clap and say, "Good girl!"

The medical dude told Mike, "Keep an eye on her and make sure she doesn't fall asleep."

Mike nodded, and we made our way slowly back to our seats. People who had been sitting around me clapped as I returned. How embarrassing. As I sat down, I spotted the rest of my Payday lying beside my shoe. Dang. I never even finished it. A fleeting thought crossed my mind, but I told myself, don't Pity. It's been on the disgusting ground.

As we watched the game, I hung on to Mike as if he might leave again. At one point, I motioned for him to lean over. I gave him the kisses I had been practicing, but the real kisses were so much better than the imagined ones.

My mind, although a bit muddled after my newest injury, focused on who threw the ball at me. Seriously, had nobody seen it happen? And why me?

I took my phone from my back pocket, glad to see it was there, and pulled up my suspects list. It could have been one of them. Maybe since I was wearing Yankees stuff, I was a target. Or maybe the ball just slipped out of someone's hand, but I found that very hard to believe.

The Yankees won the game and Mike helped me walk back toward the bus. I asked, Ava and Vince who walked next to us, "Aren't you glad you don't have to babysit me anymore?"

Vince smirked. "Well, despite being a handful, you were sure entertaining."

Everyone was in a pretty cheerful mood, except Father John, who had a permanent scowl on his face. I leaned over to Mike and said, "Does he act like a priest to you?"

"Not really, but then again, I don't know very many priests."

I whispered, "He's one of the people I suspect might have thrown the ball at me. Either him or the Hanson freak."

"Why?"

"Well, for one thing, I saw each of them holding a baseball today. I'll tell you my theory on the bus."

Once in our seats, I quietly started to explain. "Remember all the weird incidents I told you about? Well, I think someone on this bus is trying to do away with Yankees fans."

He huffed, his brows knitted, and his lips even twisted—all signs of extreme skepticism.

I said, "I know. It sounds insane, but it's the only connection I can think of among all the victims, so I'm checking it out."

Mike took a deep breath and pushed his head back against the headrest. He looked as if he was speaking to the overhead compartment inches from his face when he said, "And nothing I say will keep you from investigating, right?"

I smiled. "You do know me. But guess what? Boris and Natasha are investigating too!"

He said, "Who?"

"Oh. Remember that tall gal and short guy on the tour? Well, I gave them nicknames, because they remind me of…"

He laughed and finished my sentence. "Boris Badenov and Natasha Fatale from Pottsylvania." He nodded. "Yeah, I can see why you thought that."

I stared at Mike, surprised he knew the names of the characters. I said, "Well, they didn't tell me whether they are FBI or police detectives, but they are trying to find out who is causing all the problems." I gave a happy sigh and continued, "So, now that I know someone else is investigating, I can back off a little."

I snuggled up closer and looked up into his blue/gray/green eyes. "And I bet you can find ways to make me forget the mystery for a while." I winked at him.

Mike gave a sly smile and kissed me. But just before we became hot and heavy like two teens on a school bus trip, he pushed me away mid-kiss, leaving me wanting more. "Wait a minute. If those two are investigating, why aren't they interviewing people too? They could have stopped you from getting hurt. And why didn't they come to check on you when you were hit?"

I waved him off. "Oh. They're undercover and probably didn't want to blow their cover."

He tilted his head. "Pity, I'm not so sure that's how it works. Did they intervene after the guy died?"

I lifted my palms. "Well, I don't know their protocol. But anyway, I told them everything I knew and who I suspected, and they seemed very interested. But now I have a new worry. For a short time, my phone went missing."

"Seriously?"

"Yeah. It happened a few hours before I was beaned by the ball. And dummy me, I left it on my seat so whoever read it would know what I was up to." I started to get excited. "What if someone read my list of suspects and tried to stop my investigation with a ball to my head? Or, if they were going after Yankees fans, I was wearing my new Yankees shirt and Dad's lucky Yankees hat. In other words, I was a perfect target."

At that, I lifted my hand to my head and sucked in a breath. "Oh no! Where's Dad's hat?"

"Maybe it got knocked off when you were hit. You weren't wearing it when we carried you to the medical room."

I said, "Hold on. I'll be right back." I stepped over Mike's legs and rushed up to Ava and Vince's seat, glad to see they were still awake.

"Hey, you two. I have a question. Do you know what happened to the hat I was wearing when I was hit by the ball?"

Ava said, "It might have fallen to the ground, but we were so freaked out, all I thought about was tending to your wound and calling for help."

Vince nodded. "I don't remember seeing it."

I thanked them and rushed up to Rob and asked him the same question.

"I have no idea. It wasn't there when you returned?"

"No. And it's my dad's lucky hat," I pouted.

"Hmm. That's sad. Hey, I have something for you." He rummaged through his bag and handed me a baseball.

"Is that *the* baseball?"

"Sure is."

I took it and rushed back to my seat.

I held the ball behind my back, so Mike couldn't see it. He said, "You look happier. Did you find your dad's cap?"

As I shook my head, I frowned. "No. And I feel awful about it. I promised him I would guard it with my life. But I got something else." I handed the ball to Mike.

He raised his eyebrows. "Is that the one that hit you?"

"Yep. Rob just gave it to me."

"Well, it's something at least."

I sat down by the window again and worried about Dad's hat as I rubbed the baseball. It felt good in my hand. I wasn't sure I'd ever held one before. It was smooth and the red stitches were nice and even and made a pretty pattern, just like the shirt I had designed. I said, "Is this made of leather?"

When Mike nodded, I held the ball to my nose and took a whiff of the leather. This was a pretty good prize to counter the bump on my head.

Exhausted, I leaned my head on Mike's shoulder and closed my eyes.

He said, "Don't go to sleep just yet. I need to check your pupils when we get to the hotel."

"Ok, then keep me awake by telling me all about your brand-new niece."

When we pulled into Trenton, New Jersey, Rob made an announcement, "Due to the late night, you can sleep in tomorrow. We won't leave for Baltimore until 9:00 a.m."

I'd say 2 a.m. was a late night. I said to Mike, "30 extra minutes isn't my kind of sleeping in."

Mike frowned. "This trip hasn't been much of a vacation for you, huh? Late nights, early mornings, and too many games and bus rides."

"It's actually been pretty good, but I will be happy to get home and relax."

"Well, I'll take good care of you until then."

Just as we started to stand up, Rob said, "Let's all wear our new blue Ballparks and More shirts for a group photo tomorrow morning. Oh, and if anyone happened to pick up the Yankees cap Pity was wearing when she was hit, she would sure like to have it back. It belongs to her father."

I smiled and told Mike, "I'll thank Rob for that when we debus."

He said, "Is debus a word?"

I shrugged. "I don't know, but they call it deplaning when you get off an airplane, so I'm going with it."

As we "debussed," I thanked Rob, even though nobody had miraculously turned in the hat.

Once in our room, Ava stopped by in nurse mode and checked out my head and pupils.

"You look good to go. Now get some sleep."

Nothing made me happier than to hear that. After she left, I snuggled up next to Mike and shut my eyes for the night.

A mere six hours later, my phone alarm rang. What a headache. I felt like I had been hit in the head with a baseball. Oh, yeah.

Mike was true to his word. He took extra good care of me by surprising me with breakfast in bed. It even included a side of ibuprofen.

We dressed in our matchy-match blue shirts and took a selfie in our room. Before leaving, he donned his orange Baltimore cap with the Oriole on the front and hauled our bags downstairs.

Rob had us all gather in front of the bus and took several photos.

Since I was standing right beside Natasha, I looked up and whispered, "Are we any closer to knowing who the culprit is?"

She looked at me as if she'd never seen me before. That was probably another skill they learned in spy school. Finally, she said, "You need to leave us alone and let us do our job."

It was like I'd been splashed with cold water. I turned away before she could see the disappointment on my face.

Mike said, "Rob you need to be in a picture. I'll take it since I missed half the tour." He took the next one, but I may have been caught on film giving the photographer a seductive smile.

I ran to Mike and handed him my phone. "I need you to take one more photo, please." I rushed away, leaving him confused. I grabbed, Harry and Barry and said, "I'm ready for my photo with the four T-shirt brothers."

They laughed and summoned the other two brothers and posed with me. Mike was a good sport and took several photos of us.

As we boarded the bus for our last long ride, I was happy to see Mac sitting behind the wheel again.

"Hey, you. Good to see you back in the driver's seat, Mac!"

"Yeah, just like you said, I was cleared of wrongdoing…for now anyway. They are looking into other possibilities."

While settling into our seats, Grant passed by us. I never had asked him about the baseball he caught. Duh! If he had it with him, that would exonerate him at least from throwing the ball. I stood and held up a finger to Mike, so he knew I'd be right back. Then I followed the guy to his seat. "Hey, Grant, can I see that baseball you caught? It's so exciting that you caught a foul ball."

"Better than having one clock you in the head, huh?" He laughed.

"Right." My head hurt at the reminder, but I wasn't distracted and raised my eyebrows. "So, can I see it?"

"Nope. I gave it to a kid who was bummed that he missed catching a foul ball earlier. Besides, I have a bunch, and sure didn't need one hit by a Yankee."

I frowned and wondered if he had told me the truth. I brightened. "Well, that was very nice of you."

I moved back to my seat and soon we were off and running to the final game of the tour. I pondered Grant's remark and wondered if fingerprints had been found on the ball. And what about Father John? Had he bought that ball he was tossing around in the gift shop? Did he still have it? Should I ask him about it?

Since the ride was long, Rob surprised us by playing a videotape of the movie *Sandlot* on the bus. The video quality was terrible, and the volume fluctuated, but Mike and I both love movies so we enjoyed it anyway. Why hadn't they let us watch movies on all the other rides?

If I had ever noticed the little TVs hanging up front, I would have asked earlier.

Upon arrival in Baltimore, Mac drove us to the Babe Ruth Museum so we could take a tour. I asked Mike, "Why is there a Babe Ruth Museum in Baltimore instead of New York?"

He said, "It's his birthplace."

I nodded but my stomach soured at the thought of experiencing anything else baseball-related. I turned and said, "You know, I truly believe Babe Ruth was a great player, but I don't think I can stand another baseball tour. Would you mind if I took an Uber to the Edgar Allan Poe Museum instead? I looked it up and it's not far from here and I kind of want to see it." I perked up. "When we're done, we could meet down at Baltimore Harbor and have crab cakes and a romantic late lunch before heading to the game. Please?"

His face looked incredulous. "I don't like the idea of you going off on your own, especially after yesterday. I'll come with you."

"No! Absolutely not. You are not missing Babe Ruth. He's the best. It was just an idea. It's fine. I'll go with you." I wanted to kick myself for even bringing it up.

He took a deep breath and blew it out while eyeing me sideways. "Are you sure you'll be ok if you go?"

"Of course! I'm getting good at this Uber thing. I haven't been murdered even once yet."

"Yet?"

I punched him in the arm and pulled up my Uber app. "Look! Larry can be here in just three minutes! It's supposed to be a tiny museum, so it won't take me long unless they have a really good gift shop." I winked. "I'll text you when I get a ride to the harbor, and then we can plan on where to meet."

When we de-bussed (my new favorite word,) we approached Rob and I said, "I'm taking an Uber to the Edgar Allan Poe Museum, so please take me off your roll call list for now. I'll meet you all back at the game tonight."

Moments later, Larry drove up to the curb in his green Subaru. I made him confirm my name before getting in then turned to Mike. "See, all is good! I'll miss you terribly, but for only a little while until I see you again."

I hopped into the car and rode away with Larry, hoping Mike didn't think I was horrible for leaving him.

When I arrived at the tiny, two-and-a-half-story row house turned museum where Edgar Allan Poe had lived with his aunt, I jumped out and thanked Larry. I walked inside the small living room which also served as a gift shop. Even with only a few bookshelves of goodies, I could already see I'd be spending time browsing the Poe-related souvenirs.

The gal behind the desk wore a nose ring, dark clothes, and black lipstick. It was a fitting look for welcoming guests to a gothic author's museum.

I showed her the ticket on my app, and she said with absolutely no inflection, "Here's the brochure." She handed me a printed sheet called 'The Telltale.'

"Do you take me on the tour?"

"No tours today. I'm the only one here. But there is just three rooms. One on each floor. You can't get lost."

Despite her poor grammar, I was intrigued by the goth girl's style. I felt goofy smiling so much around her. I ventured into the next room and learned that Poe had moved to the home in 1833 as a 23-year-old.

The 2nd floor bedroom featured a wall of quotations by authors and filmmakers, including Stephen King and Alfred Hitchcock, all crediting Poe for inspiring their works. That was cool!

I climbed the extremely narrow stairway to the attic bedroom where Edgar began his career as a writer. My sleeve caught on some rough wood on the wall, and I stopped to pull myself free. Dang it. My new T-shirt was snagged. At least it didn't rip.

The attic room was tiny and dim. Maybe only 8 feet wide by 10 feet long but it seemed even smaller with the slanted roof. It was roped off to keep people from touching the furnishings which consisted of a small wooden bed, a trunk, and a wooden chair. What caught my attention first was the bizarre shadow of a raven on the floor. There in the dormer window stood a stuffed bird staring at me from where it perched on the sill. The bird, so befitting to be in the Master of Macabre's room, gave me the willies.

I stood wondering how the young author had come up with such creepy characters and bizarre situations so many years ago.

Then, the door slammed shut behind me.

# Sports Joke #13

Why can't basketball players go on vacation?
*They aren't allowed to travel.*

When the door banged shut, my heart nearly leaped out of my chest. After all, here I was in the home of the man who wrote "The Tell-tale Heart."

I laughed at my paranoia. The wind had probably just blown or maybe the old home had uneven doors which caused it to shut on its own. Silly me.

I tried the doorknob, but it didn't turn. How odd. I knocked to let the girl downstairs know I was stuck. After waiting a minute with no response, I knocked again, louder. Then I pounded.

It dawned on me. Duh. Maybe the museum was interactive. Maybe the management wanted their guests to be scared, so they rigged the door to slam shut by itself. Then, at a specified time, the lock would release again on its own, like in a haunted house at a theme park. That girl downstairs was probably just laughing so hard–well, at least maybe she cracked a smile.

One thing didn't make sense. What if someone had a heart condition? Wouldn't that be a liability if they didn't warn guests of a closing door? The museum staff should ask people to give their medical history before climbing the steep stairs and getting fake-trapped inside.

I scanned the brochure to see if it mentioned some mechanical door, but instead, it bragged that everything was authentic. Nothing had been altered since Poe lived there almost 200 years earlier.

Yikes. Was I really stuck here?

I took my phone out and was happy to see I had cell service. I found the number for the museum and dialed it, but nobody answered. I left a message, then called again. This time, I held my phone down and distinctly heard the faint sound of the phone ringing downstairs. Why didn't the goth girl pick it up? And why didn't she come up after I pounded?

I considered trying to break the door down but hated the idea of damaging the historic site. Surely it was just a faulty doorknob, and someone would figure it out soon. Be patient, Pity. The only thing I could think of doing was to call Mike.

He answered after the first ring. "Are you already finished?"

I relaxed at the sound of his voice. "Not exactly. I'm trapped in Edgar Allan Poe's bedroom."

"What?"

After explaining my situation and giving him the address, he said he would be there as soon as he could.


With no room to sit on my side of the velvet rope, I shifted on my feet and then took photos of the room. I snapped the bird's shadow, the bed, and the stupid door that kept me from my freedom.

It wasn't long before feet stomped up the stairs and there was the sweet voice of Mike. "Pity, are you in there?"

"Yes. Just me and the raven."

I heard a little clunking around and then his muffled voice said, "There's something jammed in the lock. I'll go get something to get it out."

"Ask the girl downstairs."

He said, "Nobody's there," and then I heard him jog back down the narrow stairway.

Where was the goth girl? Ooh, that question, 'Where was the Goth Girl?' sounded like a good mystery book title, almost as good as 'Death by Liberty Bell.' Her absence did explain why she didn't answer the phone.

Mike came back up and managed to open the door. There was my knight in shining armor, or my policeman in a Ballparks and More T-shirt anyway.

I hugged him and said, "You are sure a sight for sore eyes."

He surveyed the room. "This is a little creepy. Were you scared?"

"Not really. I had faith that a tall, handsome man would save me. I just don't understand how the door shut and got locked."

"Something was jammed into the latch. I had to use scissors I found on the desk downstairs to pry it open. Kinda weird."

Kinda weird was an understatement. As we descended the steep narrow steps, I growled, "Again?" This time, my other shirt sleeve was caught on the broken piece of wood sticking out from the wall. When I pulled it loose, there was a piece of the same blue fabric stuck beneath it.

"Mike, did you rip your shirt on this piece of wood?" I pointed to the small swatch of light blue fabric stuck on the shard.

He turned back to see where I pointed. "I don't think so. When I realized how narrow the stairwell was, I turned sideways to go up and down each time."

"Well, you are smarter than me. It bit me twice." I grabbed the little strip of cloth and took it downstairs with me. Once in the bright light of the lobby, I held up the piece of fabric. "Look! This torn piece is in the shape of Oklahoma. Can you see if I have a hole this shape?"

He turned me around in a circle looking up and down. "I don't see any holes—just the rip here and a snag on the other side. Check me, in case I was in such a hurry that I didn't feel it."

Repeating the process on him, I checked all over, even standing on my tiptoes to see his shoulders. "Nope. Your shirt looks brand new."

"Maybe the other piece of fabric was there before you went up to the attic."

"It wasn't. I was snagged here on the way up, and I'm sure this wasn't there." I held up the fabric." I gasped. "What if whoever came in after me was wearing a Ballparks and More shirt and locked me inside?"

Mike let that sink in and narrowed his eyes. "Who was around us when you told Rob you were coming here?"

I shrugged. "I wasn't paying attention, but now I'm concerned for the gal who works here. What happened to her? And why aren't there any other visitors?"

"You know, I was in such a hurry to get to you that I just ran inside. I think there was a note on the door, but I didn't read it."

We rushed to the door and found a note that read, 'Closed for a family emergency.'

Mike said, "She must have been really worried to have run off without telling you or at least locking the door."

I nodded and said, "I'm glad she didn't lock it, or you wouldn't have been able to get in and save me. You know, I'm not sure it was a real emergency. What if it was a scam cooked up by the guy who came in after me so that she would leave."

Mike said, "Why would they lock you in here? Surely, they knew you would get out eventually."

I considered this. "Maybe just to scare me? At any rate, I'm glad to be free." I brushed my hand along my forehead. "Whew."

Mike sighed. "Now that you're safe, do you still want to go to the harbor?"

I said, "Absolutely, those crab cakes won't eat themselves."

"Let's go then…" He turned and then did a double take. "Pity, what are you doing?"

"Uh. I want to look at the little souvenirs."

"Are you kidding? Why would you want anything to do with this place after being locked in that scary room?"

I picked up a small flowerpot with the head of Edgar Allan Poe. "But this is so cool. And here's a wine stopper with one of his quotes on it. You know a souvenir is worth a thousand words."

"I believe that's a picture. And besides, who would you pay?"

"I'll just leave cash on the desk with a note."

He rolled his eyes. "I want no part of this. I'll wait outside."

As I held a glass raven Christmas Ornament up to the window to see the colors, I smiled to see my strapping boyfriend leaning against the wall.

Just as I "bought" my goodies, he bolted inside. "Get out now!"

I scoffed. "Seriously, Mike? I'm not doing anything illegal. I paid for my stuff."

"No! I smell gasoline!"

I grabbed my bag of goodies and ran out the door, instantly getting a whiff of the familiar smell. There was no car around that may have made the gasoline odor. "I said, where is it?"

Mike didn't answer but pushed me back away from the tiny museum while dialing 9-1-1. He pointed to the side of the house while giving directions to dispatch. I kept my distance but walked to the side so that I could see what he pointed at.

There, tucked in a corner of the old house, was a rag poking out of a wooden slat. The other end of the rag was inside a gas can. I felt like someone punched me in the gut when I realized someone had planned to set the Edgar Allan Poe Museum on fire–with me trapped inside it!


Within mere minutes, emergency vehicles arrived and removed the hazardous materials. I could hardly breathe, thinking of how close I came to possibly burning to death. Thankfully, Mike kept his arm around me as we spoke with officials.

The investigating officer suggested Mike may have scared off the arsonist when he arrived. He asked Mike, "Did you happen to see anyone leave?"

"No. My mind was only on getting Pity out of the attic."

The officer took in a breath and said, "Well, the city of Baltimore thanks you for saving this historic site. It would have gone up like matchsticks."

I shuddered at the thought and held on even tighter to Mike.

A car screeched to a stop behind the firetruck and out popped the Goth Girl. She ran to us. "What happened? Is there a fire?"

The officer said, "I'm sorry, but you need to stay back. This is official business."

I put my hand on her shoulder and explained, "This is the girl who works here."

He frowned and said, "We've got questions for you."

She ditched her drab style and bubbled. "I'm so sorry. I panicked when I got the call about my mom. I wrote a note and left, forgetting there was anyone in the building."

I said, "Who called you?"

"I don't know. A guy said Mom was having heart pain and needed me to go home. When I got there, she was just enjoying a cooking show on TV."

So, I was right. It had been a ruse. I asked her, "Can I see the number he called from?" I held out my hand for her phone, figuring the area code would tell us where the caller was from, narrowing down my suspect list quickly.

She said, "I'm sorry, but he called on the museum phone and it doesn't have caller I.D."

The investigator asked, "Does the museum have security cameras?"

Goth Girl rolled her eyes. "It doesn't even have WIFI."

The officer thanked the two of us and said we were free to go. Before he could question the Goth Girl further, I told her, "I bought some souvenirs and left cash on the counter."

She nodded as if that was fine. I raised my eyebrows at Mike.

"Okay. Okay." He shook his head.

I took Mike's hand and said, "I'm too wound up to go to the harbor."

He looked at his watch. "I don't think we have time anyway. Shall we call an Uber to go to the ballpark?"

I looked at my map app. "It's only a mile to Camden Yards. How about we walk?"

"Good idea. It will be good for us to get some exercise and clear our heads after that mess."

As we walked, I fumed, "Now I'm even more determined to find the culprit! I'm gonna check out every shirt on our tour until I find a hole that's just this shape." I pulled the blue fabric from my pocket and showed it to Mike. "I'm so lucky it's such a recognizable shape."

"Yes. So lucky." He smirked. "Are you going to tell your special investigators what just happened?"

I frowned. "Well, today Natasha told me to leave her alone."

He gave me a sarcastic pout. "Poor Pity. I still think there is something fishy about two FBI agents who just sit there and aren't asking questions." He turned to me. "You don't think they are involved, do you?"

I laughed. "I did consider them at the start, but I'm pretty sure they are on the right side of the law."

He perked up and said, "Hey, Rob should know who else left the group today. He took roll. You could ask him."

"Good idea, smartie pants." I locked arms with him. "There are so many reasons to keep you around."

I was happy to enter the last ballpark and watch an entire game with Mike, even though I was still on a mission.

## Game 6 – The last one!
### Washington Nationals vs Baltimore Orioles

We found our section easily when we saw the sea of light blue Ballpark and More T-shirts. As I scoured the group for my suspects,

Father John stood out like a sore thumb. It wasn't because he had an Oklahoma-shaped patch of skin showing through a hole in his blue shirt. But rather, it was because he was wearing a bright red shirt.

I grabbed Mike's arm. "May I see the group photo you took of everyone standing beside the bus this morning?"

Poor Mike. He was trying to get to his seat so he could watch the beginning of his first whole game of the tour. But he managed to dig the phone from his pocket and hand it to me. When I held it up to his face, he nearly stumbled down the steps, but the phone recognized him and turned on.

We sat down and I found the picture. Everyone in the photo wore identical blue shirts, including Father John. Why had he changed clothes? I nodded. Maybe it was because he tore his shirt?

I quickly found my other suspect in the photo. Grant stood on the other side of the bus driver. He wore his Ballparks and More shirt and a big smile. I scanned our seats to find Grant and confirm that he was still wearing his blue shirt, but I couldn't spot him anywhere. Oh, duh. He was probably getting food or drinks.

I would have talked to Mike about my suspicions, but he needed to enjoy at least one full game, so I left him alone.


Rob was sitting on the opposite end of our row. I wanted to talk to him but didn't want to crawl over 15 people. I told Mike I'd be right back and climbed the stairs only to find Boris and Natasha sitting atop, in their usual fancy seats, drinking their beer.

Mike was right. Why weren't they doing anything? They were the worst investigators ever.

I waved and rushed to the next entry and ran down the steps to Rob. I sat in an empty chair behind him. "Rob, can you tell me how many other people skipped the Babe Ruth Museum?"

He looked back at me and gave me a surprised look. "Uh. Well, I'd have to look at my list, but I know some people left before and others left after the tour to go to the harbor instead of stopping by the hotel."

"Oh. Thanks." I whispered to him, "Do you happen to remember if Father John was one of them?"

"Yes. He loves to explore. I learned that on the last trip."

Aha. So, maybe he did lock me in the room. "What about Grant? Did he ride to the hotel on the bus?"

"Well actually, Grant had a flight out of town today. He left from the Babe Ruth Museum to fly to Houston for some concert."

I chuckled inwardly, figuring it was a Hanson concert. But he, too, could have followed me to the museum. I was back at square one.

Rob shrugged. "Why do you ask?"

"Well, to be honest, I've been investigating all the accidents, including Howard's death. I have a few suspects but need more evidence before I know anything for sure." I paused for a minute and said, "And in addition to getting hit by a ball yesterday, I was locked in an attic at the Edgar Allan Poe Museum, and then someone almost set the building on fire with me locked upstairs. I think that someone was from our tour."

His mouth dropped open. "Really? That's terrible. How did you get out?"

"I called Mike, and he saved me. Then there was a whole big thing with the Fire department and Police coming to investigate."

Even though I had taken Rob off my suspects list early on, I scanned both sides of his shirt for a hole, just in case.

After finding a smooth blue shirt, I said, "Thanks, Rob. Gotta go, I'm on a mission." I ran up the steps again but couldn't resist stopping by the investigators.

Making sure nobody else was around, I said, "So, when are you going to arrest someone?" They gave no indication they even heard me, so I said with more force, "In case you didn't notice, I was beaned by a baseball yesterday and it wasn't a foul ball. You need to help me figure this out. I mean, someone just tried to set me on fire in Edgar Allan Poe's bedroom. Are you ever going to do anything?"

The two raised their eyebrows and glanced at each other as if I was insane, but still said nothing.

In a snarky tone, I said, "Oh, and while you were here drinking beer and looking like cartoon characters, one of my suspects, Grant, flew the coop. He is gone." I raised my hands in frustration. "You might want to check out the priest before he disappears too. After all, he's not even wearing a blue shirt today."

I waited for them to respond, but when I looked at them, I realized neither of them was wearing a Ballparks and More shirt. In a huff, I blurted, "And you two would seem a lot less conspicuous if you wore your shirts like the rest of us. I mean, if you really are undercover agents, you might want to play the part."

I clenched my jaw, disgusted that they had done nothing to capture the culprit, and stomped down the stairs where I sat, fuming.

When the teams switched positions between innings, I filled Mike in on the newest news.

He squinted, "So, Grant is gone?" He turned his head back and looked at the priest in his red shirt. "And yeah, that's weird that Father John changed shirts, but you know he's an odd guy. He probably didn't want to be wearing anything but his Boston Red Sox shirt."

"Yeah, true. Maybe I shouldn't worry about it. The two FBI, or Police, or detectives…whoever they are, sure don't seem to care. Why should I?"

Mike took my hand. "Pity, I believe you are on to something, but I hate for you to get so worked up. You know we fly home tomorrow morning, and it will all be over. Let's just hope nothing else happens today and we get home safely."

I gave a big sigh and decided to watch the game with my boyfriend. I mean, that was why I was here.

At one point, I stood and yelled, "N.A.T.S. Nats, Nats, Nats! Woo!"

Mike turned to me with his mouth open. "Did you just yell a Washington Nationals cheer?"

"Yeah, that's what you do when the Nationals score."

His eyes widened. "Wow. I have been gone a long time."

I raised my eyebrows playfully. It wasn't five minutes later when I joined the Orioles fans in their chant "O.R.I.O.L.E.S!  O!"

He said, "What have you done with my sport-hating girlfriend?"

"Well, she's still here. Maybe she's slowly and reluctantly becoming a bit of a baseball fan." I snuggled into him. "Hey, Mike, would you ever consider playing in that Broken Arrow adult baseball league I heard about?"

"Maybe. I played as a kid. Might be fun. Why? You want to see more games?" He scrunched his nose and squinted at me.

"No. I was just hoping to see you wearing some of those sexy baseball pants someday." I gave him a wink.


When Father John started yelling profanities at the players, I couldn't stand it anymore. What kind of priest did that? Why hadn't I done some real investigation on him yet? I remembered him saying his church or cathedral was called The Body of Christ something or other, so I pulled up my phone. Maybe there were bad reviews about the crass man. Or did people even review the clergy?

I googled churches with similar names in Boston and found a chapel that fit. On the landing page of the website, it indeed said Father John O'Neil was the priest. Okay, so he was a priest, even if he didn't act like it. I clicked on the staff page and found his name, but the photograph was that of an older bald man.

Wait. That was not our Father John! Maybe there are two priests by the same name at the chapel like our John was his son? But priests don't have children. I scrolled down but saw no other priest on the site. I was sure I had the name of his church. Maybe they hadn't updated the photo on the website, so I checked the date. But it had been taken after Saturday's Mass.

I could hardly contain my excitement and almost nudged Mike, but instead, said, "I have to tell Rob something."

This time, I chose the short way to get to him, by climbing over everyone in our row. "Excuse me. Pardon. Oops. Sorry."

When I finally reached Rob, I asked him to go up the stairs with me. "It's important."

Once we stood at the top of our section, I explained the whole thing to him.

His eyes grew round as he scanned the chapel website and said, "I need to confirm this." He found the phone number of the chapel and called from his phone. Even though I could only hear one side of the conversation, it was clear that I was right. The real Father John O'Neil was talking on the phone to Rob!

When he hung up, the flustered tour guide said, "I guess I'll call the police."

I brightened. "Or you could just tell the secret agents on our tour?"

He looked confused and said, "What secret agents?"

Surely, he was aware of them, but I pointed to the two who happened to be watching us. Boris had his phone up as if he was taking a picture of us. It was weird that he pulled his hand down so quickly. As we walked over to the odd couple, I said, "They wouldn't confirm that they were FBI to me, but that's what I assume."

I stopped in front of the two and said, "We think we have our man. Father John is an imposter!"

Before they could speak, Rob said, "Are you two FBI agents?"

Natasha said, "No. We are not."

My mouth dropped open. "Well, then, tell Rob that you're police detectives."

She shook her head.

I stammered. "But you led me to believe you were."

With a snotty tone of voice, she said, "I can't help what you believed. We never said we were police or FBI."

I wasn't sure which shocked me more - that I was right in thinking Father John wasn't a priest, or that I was wrong in thinking these two were with law enforcement. I shook my baffled head.

Rob had walked away and was on the phone. When he returned, he said, "The police officer I spoke with said not to alert him or tell anyone else what we know."

My heart started racing. "Did you tell them about all the other accidents and the death on our trip?"

"I did. Once they do some checking with the chapel and Boston police, they may apprehend him here."

I rushed over to Boris and Natasha. "Forget everything we just told you. We have an order from the *real* police." I emphasized real out of spite. How had I read them so wrong?

My bigger worry was how to keep the whole thing quiet. I had never been good at lying or keeping secrets and my face was an open book. The only way I could think of to keep from spilling the beans to Mike or Ava, was to stuff food in my mouth, so off to the concession stand I went.

I texted Mike and asked him what he wanted to eat. He wrote back. 'I'd love to have a real ballpark hotdog. And a beer if you have enough hands.'

My reply was four hand emojis. Score one for me—I hadn't blabbed anything important in my text.

I finagled the hotdogs and beer down the steps to my seat and gave Mike his. Even though I was nervous about the whole thing, I was able to joke, "So, if you had been here on Tuesday, you could have seen *me* as a hotdog."

Mike turned to me with his mouth full of bun. "What?"

I said, "Ava, tell him that I really was a hotdog at Mets stadium."

She grinned. "Pity was indeed a hotdog." While Mike chewed and swallowed, she found the video and showed it to him.

He watched it and almost choked on his hotdog. He looked at me in amazement. "What the…How? And why?"

I was glad to have another topic to expound on besides what was whirring around my mind, and I described the incident in detail. "The only good thing that came out of my stint as a wiener was this." I pulled the $200 check from my wallet. "I got paid!"

He closed his eyes and laughed. "Only you!"

By the seventh-inning stretch, I still hadn't divulged any information, but I kept turning around to watch the loudmouth. What in the world did he gain from pretending to be a priest? And why did he want to hurt Yankees fans? I couldn't stand the man now, but I also couldn't keep my eyes off the dangerous weirdo.

Mike had just handed me some peanuts when he was distracted by something beyond me. I turned to see a couple of Baltimore policemen rush down the steps. They stopped at the row where Father John sat. Oh My Gosh! This was it! I gulped and kept my eyes open wide so I wouldn't miss anything.

When the jerk saw the officers, he stared too, but then his eyes darted around like a scared rabbit searching for an escape route.

One officer asked Odette and Travis to stand and move into the aisle so they could reach John, or whoever the heck he was. While making their way toward the fake priest, one of the policemen pulled a set of handcuffs from his belt.

Our entire tour group gawked at the scene, stunned. I was close enough to hear a plain-clothed officer say, "Jacob Goldschmidt, you are under arrest for impersonating a priest in four states. You are also suspected of five other felonies."

Father John's mouth dropped open, and he yelled, "That's not true and you have no proof."

The uniformed man said, "Oh yes, we do. You need to come with us."

My eyes opened wider. We actually got the guy, and his name was Jacob Goldschmidt?

John/Jacob's face turned from beet-red to white. He suddenly bolted to the right, climbing over people just as I had done an hour earlier, but he did it without apologizing.

The immediate problem for the suspect was the four brothers sitting at the other end of his row. I was surprised to see Mike had joined them. The five big men grabbed Jacob rather roughly and held onto him until the officers made their way up the steps and around to cuff him.

In the kerfuffle, the priest's large cross clattered to the ground and bounced down to the row right behind me. I picked it up, noting its heavy weight. As a common courtesy, I started to hand it back to him. But why? Even if he needed it to pray for a lenient sentence, he didn't deserve it. I would give the cross to the authorities.

When the perpetrator was escorted up the steps, Mike followed them, and I ran to catch up with the arresting officer. I handed him the cross. "I'm not sure this is evidence of anything, but he wore it all the time."

He stopped and asked me, "Are you the one who determined that he was an imposter and was responsible for hurting other people?"

I nodded. "He just didn't act like a holy man to me, so I checked it out. I discovered he was not the real Father John."

Mike stared at me since he wasn't privy to that information. I had kept my secret just as I was told.

I said, "I highly suggest you contact the police in these cities for information." I listed them off along with the strange accidents that took place on our tour:

" #1. Washington Nationals Park, where a man was poisoned.

#2. Citizens National Park and the Rocky Steps in Philadelphia, where two people were pushed.

#3. New Haven, Connecticut, where a man died after being locked in the luggage compartment of a bus.

#4. Yankee Stadium, where I was clocked in the head by a baseball."

"Father John, I mean Jacob, was in the vicinity each time and was likely responsible." I took a breath and said, "And talk to this investigator…" I handed him the card, "about the attempted arson here in Baltimore this morning."

When Mike and the officer stared at me. I said, "If you have any questions, I'll be happy to answer them."

The man took my name and phone number. "Well, I'm Detective McDonald. That's valuable information, but maybe you could text it to me." He handed me his card. "And if you think of anything else, let me know."

As Mike and I walked back to our seats, he asked, "How did you do that? Rattle all that off so fast?"

"Well, it's been on my mind every day. Guess I just stored it away in a little pocket of my brain."

Once in our seats, I showed Mike, Ava, and Vince the photo of the real John O'Neil. I rapped ala Eminem, "Will the real Father John please stand up? Please stand up. Please stand up."

Mike said, "He was a rather crass priest, but never would have guessed he was a fake."

Vince said, "For him to be such a rude know-it-all did seem odd."

Ava opened and closed her mouth like a fish and said, "And to think I confessed to him just last week."

I cringed. How many others had done the same thing?

Vince asked, "And you think he was the one who caused all the problems? And even murdered Howard?"

I shrugged.

As we stared at the field, none of us focused on the game.

Back on the bus, everyone was a buzz, speculating on the arrest.

Mike said, "That's just so strange. Why would he impersonate a priest?"

"Beats me."

"And why did you believe that couple was FBI?"

I closed my eyes in embarrassment. "Well, I overheard her say, 'We're getting close to finding out who it is,' into a phone. What else could I surmise from that comment?"

He chuckled. "Could be anything, Sherlock. Just don't give up your day job. And for heaven's sake, don't try to become a rapper."

## **Sports Joke #14**

Why should you never fall in love with a tennis player?
*To them, "Love" means nothing.*

When we pulled up to our final hotel, I was surprised to find it was the same one we stayed at the very first night. The cute, tiny Shamika stood by the door to welcome us back. "Did y'all have a nice trip?"

"Well, sort of." In my head, I added, if you don't count people being poisoned, pushed down steps or off a platform, murdered, slammed with a ball, or locked in an attic by a fake priest. Now that was a movie plot nobody would believe. Or maybe it would become a hit.

Mike and I got to our room at a decent hour. Neither of us was exhausted nor had a concussion, so we were finally able to enjoy a romantic evening together. I was so glad to have him back.

The next morning, I was rejuvenated. The murderer had been caught and he would get his due process. I could go home knowing I had helped capture a criminal.

We took our time getting up and around since our flight wasn't until noon. I looked through my souvenirs. Seeing one in particular gave me a great idea. I just hoped it wasn't too late.

When we entered the breakfast room, I made a beeline for the Herrera family who were putting their dishes away. "Joey, I have something for you."

The little boy looked up. "You do?"

I held out one of the small, packaged action figures I had bought at Yankee Stadium.

His dark brown eyes lit up. "It's Joe DiMaggio? For me?"

"Yes sir. I thought you needed it since your name is Joey and he's your favorite player."

His Mother said, "That's so kind of you."

I smiled and said, "He's a sweet boy. It was nice to meet you. I hope you have safe travels back home."

Mike stood to the side with an eyebrow raised. I said, "I'll tell you later."

When I saw Odette and Travis, I grabbed Mike's hand, pulled him over, and introduced them. "This is crazy, but these two are going to Todd and Shelly's wedding on the fourth. They own a Cadillac dealership in Texas and know Shelly's parents. It's a small world!"

We visited with them for a while, then Mike went to get his breakfast. I made my way to say goodbye to the Dodger Divas.

"Hey girls, sorry, I haven't hung out with you much lately, but we'll always have Philadelphia." I held my hands together in reverence.

We all laughed when Diana said, "Bongggggg."

I gave them each an Oklahoma keychain and made my way to Ava and Vince.

Vince joked, "What are we going to do without our pitiful friend?"

Ava nudged him. "Vince, that wasn't nice."

I laughed. "Believe me, I've heard that one before. Listen, I can't tell you how much I appreciate you befriending me while Mike was gone. I will cherish our time together, even if it was a bizarre week. Please know that my house is always open to you if you want to visit Tulsa."

She smirked, "Only if that Hanson lover isn't staying with you. Hey, where is he anyway?"

"He left yesterday morning to go to a concert." I laughed. "I'm pretty sure I know who he's seeing. He was sure a strange one."

"Keep in touch, Pity. You have our numbers, right?"

"I sure do."

After giving them big hugs, and two keychains, I started to join Mike but spotted the four brothers handing in their keys at the desk. I rushed over to them. "I'm going to miss you all–and your shirts."

Harry said, "Well, we'll miss you and your antics. You were pretty entertaining."

Barry smirked. "So, did you end up liking baseball at all?"

I cocked my head, "Ya know? I kind of did and it's hard to believe, but I think I finally get the appeal. But it will be a long time before I go to another game after seeing so many this week."

I gave them each a keychain and said goodbye. Then I finally grabbed a cup of coffee and muffin and sat with Mike.

"You are sure a busy bee."

"I had to say goodbye to my new friends."

He gave me a smirk. "I knew you would get something out of this trip."

"I really did."

My mouth was full of a dry packaged blueberry muffin when Rob walked to our table and sat down. He shook his head. "I want to thank you for investigating the injuries and discovering who was at fault. It was all just too much for me. I'm not sure I'm cut out for this job."

I put my hand on his and said, "You did fine. There were a lot of strange problems you had to deal with."

I started to say my pat answer, "and nobody died," but that wasn't exactly true. I did say, "My only suggestion is to have people introduce themselves at the meet and greet."

Mike nudged my knee, but I couldn't help it. I was being honest.

Rob said, "Yeah, I had several people tell me that in the last few days."

I added, "But otherwise, you handled everything like a pro."

Someone behind me spoke in a deep, commanding voice, "Robert Braydon, I have a phone call for you."

We turned to find the short, silent non-FBI agent holding a phone out to Rob. Wait, Boris could actually speak? Behind him stood Natasha, with arms folded, looking smug.

Rob took the phone warily and said, "Hello?" His face brightened. "Oh, Hi honey. I'll be home later today. I can't wait to see you."

I took another bite of my muffin and tried not to eavesdrop, but it was hard not to, since he was sitting only a foot from me. Rob's forehead wrinkled. "What? Why do I need to get a hotel room?"

I wondered the same thing. Had they had a flood in their house? Was there a fire? I stopped chewing and listened.

Rob's face turned white, and he gave an audible gulp. "You hired Natalie and Brad to investigate me?" Rob stared at Natasha and Boris and said, "Oh." He closed his eyes.

So the two fake agents were here to watch Rob! And they had names—Natalie and Brad.

Rob let out a breath. "I see. Yes, we'll talk about it tomorrow."

Looking as if he might get sick, Rob handed the phone back to Boris/Brad, who then turned to me and said, "Thank you for the information about him kissing a blond woman at Citi Park. That helped discover the truth about his affair with Crystal."

I winced. It wasn't my intention to get Rob in trouble. I couldn't care less who had an affair with whom. I shrank back, trying to disappear, but peeked up in time to watch Rob's defeated look change to a disappointed one—directed at me.

I straightened my back and tried to explain. "I'm so sorry, Rob. I was investigating the accidents and Howard's death, so I watched anyone who acted suspiciously. When you snuck off, I followed you and jumped into a room so you wouldn't see me. That's when I accidentally stepped into a hotdog costume." I shrugged.

"Then later, when I thought those two were FBI," I glared at Natalie and Brad, "I told them about each of my suspects and mentioned how you acted strangely that day. You weren't on my suspects list for more than a few minutes. I scratched you off when I saw you with the blond woman. And I only mentioned Crystal's name because she's blond."

Rob sat twisting his wedding ring round and round on his finger as I continued, "Of course, you had nothing to do with the murder or other problems. I didn't mean to interfere with your personal life." I took a breath after my long-winded and redundant explanation.

He shut his eyes. "It's okay, Pity. I was the one at fault. This day was bound to come. My marriage was over long before I met Crystal. We met on another baseball tour and then, well…" He took a deep breath "I just had trouble telling my wife I wanted a divorce. I guess it will happen now and I'll have to start over with nothing since my wife is the one with all the money."

Rob said goodbye and slowly entered the elevator. I felt bad for him but turned to Brad and Natalie. With a smug expression I said, "So, I wasn't completely off base. You *were* investigating someone."

Natalie shrugged. "So? But you were annoying."

Mike chuckled as they left the hotel, their job complete.

I said, "I sure won't miss those two."

He took my hand. "Let's go home, Nancy Drew."

After landing in Tulsa, Mike drove me to my house where the girls met us out front. They were bright and happy and somehow, very tanned. How long had I been gone? Oh, yeah. A whole week.

I ran to Lauren first. Holding her shoulders out at arm's length, I said, "Are you really 18? How can that be? I remember bringing you home from the hospital through that very door." I pointed to the front porch. "You were so tiny and had that mop of dark hair. And now look at you! You're old enough to vote, serve on a jury, and sign a legally binding document."

"Yeah. And I can enlist in the service and die for my country but can't buy a beer for three more years. Kinda crazy how that works."

I pulled Marie into a hug and said, "What have you two been doing while I was gone?"

They looked at each other and Ree said, "We have a surprise for you!"

I raised my eyebrows. "You do?"

Ree took my hand and pulled me around to the side gate of the house. I said, "Can I put my suitcase away first?"

Mike smiled and said, "I'll take it in. Go with the girls."

Ren grabbed my arm. "We were sorta busy while you were gone."

"Oh yeah?" I kneeled to hug Harriet, who wagged her big fluffy tail uncontrollably at me. "Hey baby, were you busy too?"

I followed the girls around to the backyard where they yelled, "Surprise!"

I froze. There was a full-blown above-ground swimming pool in my yard! With water in it! I sputtered, "What? How? When?"

Ree stripped off her shorts and shirt, uncovering a bikini. She climbed the steps and hopped in, making a big splash.

She yelled, "The water is still really cold, but we love it!"

I turned to Ren with my mouth open. "Who did this?"

"We did! Well, it was mostly R.A. and his friend. Mike came over twice to help while his sister was resting." She beamed.

I approached the big round pool and marveled at how nice it looked nestled under the tall pine trees. Tears filled my eyes as I realized how much work had gone into this. They even had to bring in a load of sand and level it before setting up the pool. And I hadn't lifted a finger. I reached out and hugged Ren. "You guys are something else. I can't believe it's already done!"

Ree popped her head up above the rim and said, "But we left the deck for you to do."

"Is the pump working and everything?" I walked around the pool and heard a motor running. Just then I noticed the pond was missing. "And you filled in the pond?"

Ren nodded. "Yep. It wasn't easy, but we got it done.

While facing the dirt patch that used to be our pond, freezing arms grabbed me. I squealed. "Ooh! That's cold!"

I turned to find my youngest daughter clinging to me. Ree said, "It was so hard not to tell you on the phone. Are you surprised?"

"Yes, and now I know why you sounded so suspicious on the phone. It's a great surprise, and I can't wait to get in."

Ren said, "Well, you might want to wait a few days until the water warms up. We know how much you hate cold water."

Mike made his way out the back door. "You like?"

"I do." I turned and hugged him. "Thanks for your help with this. I can't believe you didn't spill the beans."

"I'm pretty good at keeping secrets."

"You got any more?"

He raised his eyebrows with tightly closed lips. "Maybe?"

"Ooh. Well, I'll get it out of you somehow." I reached over and tickled him. "You know you can use this pool anytime you want."

He walked over to the edge and felt the water. "I will do that, but it's still a bit chilly for me. Look, I need to go get ready for work. Thanks so much for going on the trip for me."

"It was a crazy vacation." I took his hand and walked him to the front of the house. "I'm sorry you have to work on your first night back. Now when do I get to meet that precious baby niece of yours?"

"How's Saturday afternoon? Sally asked me to invite you. Scott will be back and my parents will still be here so you can meet them."

"Fantastic!"

He kissed me goodbye and left me to hear about the girls' adventures in setting up a pool.

It sounded like a heck of a lot of work. I said, "I still can't believe I didn't have to help at all."

Ren smiled. "Uncle R.A. said it would be a fun surprise to just 'git 'er done.' Plus, we had time, and were anxious to swim so…"

I nodded. "I'm calling him right now."

After I repeatedly gushed thanks to my brother-in-law, I joined my girls on the porch to tell them about the trip.

Marie's blue eyes were huge. "So, what's this about a Hanson fan?"

I described the odd Grant guy. "I wouldn't be surprised if he knocked on our door someday to have me introduce him to them." I grimaced. "I should never have told him my full name."

Ren said, "And how, exactly, did you become a hotdog?" She scrunched up her face, ready for another one of my wacky stories.

I showed the video Ava had texted to my phone. After laughing Ren said, "Keep that to yourself. I'd be mortified if it got out."

Ree watched over my shoulder. "I kinda love it. None of my friends have a hotdog for a mom."

I punched her arm playfully. "Hey, the wedding is Sunday. Are you two excited? And more importantly, did you get new dresses?"

Ren closed her eyes. "Yes. They are so much better. We can't show them to you because they are at Dad and Shelly's house."

Twisting her hair around her finger, Ree said, "I still don't know how he talked her into changing them. I'm just thrilled we won't look like creamsicles or walking American flags."

I grinned inwardly about Shelly's change of heart but kept the secret for Todd. "You know your dad would do anything for you."

Ree snuggled up to me. "Sorry you can't come to the wedding."

"It's alright. The only reason I want to be there is to see you girls." That was true. I didn't particularly want to see my ex-husband get remarried, especially in a cow pasture.

I invited the family and Mike over for pizza the next night to tell them about the trip. The first thing I did was to hug R.A. "How did you manage it all? I came home and boom! There was a pool in my backyard. You are amazing."

He blushed and said, "Believe me. I had lots of help. Mike and these girls were workhorses."

Kim said, "Well, I wasn't much help since I had to work, but I did make sandwiches for the workers."

I hugged her. "Thanks, sis."

When Mom and Dad arrived, we headed out to show off the new backyard feature. I held my father back before he could go out the door. "Dad, I'm so sorry, but somehow in the confusion of getting hit by a baseball, I lost your favorite Yankee's hat. I'm so very sorry."

"All that matters is that you weren't seriously injured." He hugged me. "I can always get a new ball cap, but I can't get another Pity."

I gave a big sigh.

We joined the gang outside, and Dad looked over the new setup. "Well, that swimming pool is a fine addition to your yard. I'm sure you'll get a lot of use out of it."

"Grandpa, you and Grandma can swim too!" Ree beamed.

How cute. I grinned. The pool had been a good decision.

Mom said, "Thanks, Marie. Next time, I'll bring my bathing suit."

Dad joked. "You think I can get in it without breaking my neck?"

We all agreed the ladder was easy to climb and he would be fine.

While eating pizza on the back patio, I said, "I bought something for my favorite Yankees fans." From a bag I'd brought out, I removed the three remaining reaction figures, handing Babe Ruth to Dad, Yogi Berra to R.A., and Mickey Mantle to Mike.

Mom looked at Dad's miniature Yankee. "Isn't that cute?"

Kim leaned over and said, "So adorable."

When my girls also ooh and ahhed over the toys, I worried that they were terrible gifts for men. But Dad held his little Babe Ruth up. "I love this. He'll go on my Yankees shelf next to his signed ball."

I forgot Dad owned a ball signed by the "Sultan of Swat." Maybe I shouldn't mention to him that I skipped going to the Babe Ruth Museum.

R.A. turned his package over, inspecting it. "I can't decide whether I should open it or keep Yogi in pristine condition in his container."

Mike leaned over and kissed me. "How did you know I liked Mickey Mantle?"

"I didn't. I've always thought his name was cute and hoped you liked him. Oh, remember when I gave something to that little boy before we left? His name is Joey, and his favorite player is Joe DiMaggio. He'd had a rough week, so I gave it to him."

This made me think of how Grant had given his ball to the kid who had missed catching a foul ball. I'll bet that boy was as excited as Joey was about his toy.

I turned to the girls. "I wasn't sure what to get for all my gals, so I got you these." I handed them each an 'I Heart New York' bag, a little liberty bell ornament, a "Wicked Smaht" key chain, and a bookmark from the Edgar Allan Poe Museum. Then, I pulled out my bag of Boston baked beans and passed them around.

R.A. popped a red candy-coated peanut in his mouth and said, "So, did you really get locked in Edgar Allan Poe's bedroom?"

"Yes." Everyone's eyes widened as I told them how I too, had been a victim of the fake priest and how he had locked me in the attic. Then I reluctantly told them the 'rest of the story.'

"Mom! You could have died in the fire!" Ren's eyes had filled with tears.

"Well, I didn't. Mike came along at just the right time." I leaned over and patted his shoulder.

Ree asked, "What was his motive? What did you do to him?"

"I guess the guy wanted me to stop investigating. Or maybe he hated me because he thought I was a Yankees fan."

Ree said, "Well, whatever his motive, being locked in that place sounds creepy especially if the guy wanted to start a fire."

I shook my head. "Poe's bedroom wasn't so bad, but there was a fake raven in the window and the shadow on the floor scared me at first. I didn't know about the gas can until I had been freed by this guy." I looked up adoringly at Mike. I hoped he didn't hate me giving him that look as much as I disliked it when Kenny did it.

Kim shook her head at me. "It's like everywhere you go, you find trouble. Why?"

I winked. "Talent. Pure talent." I ate another piece of candy.

Harriet barked and Ren said, "That must be the doorbell. I forgot to tell you I invited Chris over. Is that, OK?"

"Sure, we have plenty of pizza, so why not?"

Ren escorted her boyfriend outside to join us. The handsome teen made polite hellos, then brightened, "Mrs. Kole! Did you know your reel has gone viral?"

I squinted. "I have no idea what you are talking about, Chris."

Ren gasped. "Mom! Tell me you didn't post your hotdog video on social media."

I shook my head emphatically. "I did not."

When Chris pulled his phone from his pocket, Ren and Ree jumped up and crowded around him. "Let us see."

He played it for them and with the volume turned up high, I heard the unmistakable sound of a big bell clanging. Oh No! Don't tell me someone recorded my embarrassing fall! The Liberty Bell incident was far worse than the hotdog video and hearing the bell ring made my head pound.

Dad said, "What is a reel?"

I closed my eyes, wanting to disappear as R.A. explained to my father about the short videos people post online.

Mom put her hand on my arm and said, "Pity, are you alright? Your face is white."

Ren scoffed. "Well, she should turn white after that stunt."

Kim held out her hand for Chris' phone. "Okay, now you have to show us."

Chris said, "I thought you all would have seen it. Everyone's showing it around."

After the entire family had seen the video, Mike finally took the phone. I watched it with him. Luckily, there wasn't a good shot of my face, but it was clear enough so my friends could recognize me. Dang.

Mike gave me a side-eye. "And you kept this from me?"

I shrugged. "Guess I have secrets too."

Ree, who sat in stunned silence, read a posted comment aloud. "The Liberty Bell hadn't rung for 185 years until this woman came to Philadelphia."

I cringed while the others laughed.

Mom said, "That must have been painful when you hit it."

Kim laughed. "We all know how hard Pity's head is."

I defended myself. "It did hurt and I had a bump on my head for a while, but I'm okay now. I was kind of hoping nobody would find out. But as long as the cat is out of the bag, you might as well see it from a different point of view." I pulled up the photos the Dodger Divas had taken and passed my phone around.

"Oh, these are even better!" Chris chuckled.

I turned to him. "No. You may not post them."

When everything died down, Mom changed the topic. "Pity, are you sad that you don't get to go to the wedding? The girls brought over the new dresses to show us. They're pretty and fit perfectly."

Ren and Ree smiled at that.

I said, "It's OK. I'll just have to see the photos."

Chris cocked his head. "Wait a minute. Why don't you get to go? My whole family was invited."

"The bride doesn't want me there. But, it's fine."

Mike sat up straighter and said with a twinkle in his eyes, "Well, maybe you can attend the wedding, after all."

Everyone stared at him. What did he mean by that?

He waggled his eyebrows playfully at me. "Last night I answered a break-in call at Big Jack's Cadillacs. I caught some punks rummaging around stealing stuff and preparing to paint the side of his dealership.

They were drunk and could have done some real damage, but I stopped them just in time." Sometimes I forgot what a good policeman Mike was. I liked how he wasn't bragging, just humbly stating a fact.

He continued, "When Jack arrived, he was so happy that I prevented further damage, that he gave me an invitation to the wedding. He said to bring a guest. I told him who I wanted to bring, and he said, 'Go ahead! Pity should get to see her daughters in the wedding, anyway.'"

My mouth dropped open. "So, I can go with you, for real?"

Mike pulled a paper from his pocket. I finally saw what Big Jack had been handing out to everyone. It looked more like a flyer than a wedding invitation.

I looked at the girls. "What do you think?"

Ree said, "Yes, Mom! Go! Please!"

I wrinkled my nose. "But I don't want to upset Shelly."

"You will be the last thing on her mind," said Ren.

I twisted my mouth, thinking it might be a really bad idea to show up uninvited, but then again…

Kim nudged her husband and said, "R.A., now you can tell her."

I cocked my head. "Tell me what? Is there another viral video of me doing something ridiculous?"

He raised an eyebrow and said, "Probably. But we didn't know how to tell you that Kim and I are also going to the wedding."

My mouth dropped open. "Why? How? Did you buy a Cadillac?"

"No. Todd called me last night and said they needed an extra soundman for the band that's playing at the reception. He asked me to do it and said I could bring Kim. And I get paid, too!"

It made sense that Todd would call R.A. Those guys always got along. I said, "That's so cool!"

I turned to my parents. "Are you two going to the wedding too?"

Dad laughed. "I'm sad to say we didn't buy a Cadillac or thwart any vandalism. And we certainly don't know how to set up a sound system. But we will be at the cabin waiting for all of you to join us for the annual ping pong tournament.”

I laughed but felt uneasy. Everyone else was legitimately invited, but I was not. I excused myself. “I’ll be right back.”

I took my phone into the bedroom and made a call. “Hey Todd, can you talk a sec?” I filled him in on the situation and said, “What do you think?”

“Hmm. Shelly might get bent outta shape, but if Jack said you can come, do it. He’s paying.”

“Can you warn her maybe? I don’t want a problem at the wedding.”

“She’s gonna be on cloud nine that day – she probably won’t even notice.”

## Sports Joke #15

Why did the golfer wear two pairs of pants?
*In case he got a hole in one.*

The next day was relaxing. It felt good to be home and sleep in the same bed two nights in a row. Even though the girls had stopped by the house a few times a day while I was gone, our pets were overjoyed to have us home again. Harriet was a Velcro dog, refusing to let me out of her sight. Edgar talked more than usual and enjoyed getting out of his cage to walk on the coffee table. I had to scold him when he started to chew the corner of the wood, though. Silly parrot! Even Iggy, the iguana, was more active in his aquarium since our return.

While waiting impatiently for the pool water to warm up, I did laundry and tried to find a place for my baseball shirts that I would probably never wear again. While in the closet, I looked for something appropriate to wear to the wedding, but I was still apprehensive about going and decided to wait to pick out something later.

As I put my souvenirs away, I picked up the baseball that hit me on the head. Had they found Father John's/Jacob's fingerprints on it? I guessed I could call the detective to get an update.

That evening, I drove my VW over and picked up my bestie, Lin, to go to the romcom my girls had seen on Ren's birthday. I handed her a New York visor. I said, "I got us matching ones from a street vendor in the Big Apple."

"Cool." Lin popped it on her head.

On the drive, I told her about "Father John" and all he had done, including the arson attempt. "The worst thing was that every time I turned around, the hypocrite was counseling or taking confessions from someone on our tour."

"I'm sure glad you helped get him arrested." She smirked. "And yet another mystery solved by a wacky music teacher-turned-investigator."

I chuckled. How ridiculous was it that I had been involved in so many mysteries over the past year and a half?

Lin asked, "Have you heard anything from the Baltimore police officer since you got back?"

"No. I may call him though. I want an update on the imposter and find out what his motive was."

She turned to me. "Do you really think he was trying to rid the world of Yankees fans? Seems like a mighty big project."

"I know. It's preposterous, but I can't think of any other connection between him and his victims."

"Well, maybe he's just crazy. I mean what did he get out of impersonating a priest besides hearing confessions?" She turned to me. "Hey, you didn't confess to him about that weekend we spent in Arkansas and changed our names to Grace and Kelly, did you?"

I laughed as I pulled onto the busy 71st street. "No, *Grace*. But we didn't do anything bad—well except get tattoos." I added, "Oh, yeah. We did sneak beer into the theater, but that was your idea."

With a serious face she said, "Well, *Kelly,* for your information, I've grown up since then." As I drove along, she dug around in her purse and then gave me a playful grin. "I bought this to put in my movie theater Coke." She giggled and held up a tiny bottle of rum.

I laughed so hard when I saw what was in her hand that I almost hit the car in front of us. "Oh yeah, real mature, Lin."

She whispered, "I know. And I have one for you too. Speaking of movies, when is the film starring you and your "Hollywood boyfriend," coming out?"

I chuckled at the thought of the megastar, Aaron Winston, being my boyfriend. I did like to think that for a brief moment in time, we were at least friends. I said, "For one thing, I will not show up in any of the movie scenes. And again, he is not my boyfriend. But gosh it's been a year and a half since it was filmed so I hope it premieres soon."

"Well, if you hadn't gotten involved in the mystery on the set, the movie might have had a different ending."

I nodded. Maybe.

We made it to the theater unscathed and bought popcorn and drinks before enjoying the cute movie. To be honest, I couldn't even taste the tiny amount of rum in the big theater Coke. Sometimes it's fun to be a little bit crazy, but I might not mention this stunt to my daughters or my policeman boyfriend.

By Saturday the temperature outside was hot, but the pool water was still too cool for me. I sat on the patio glider petting Harriet and watched Ree and Caitlyn goof around in the water. Ahh, to be young again and not even care about the water temperature. But come to think of it, I didn't like cold water, even at their age.

While I sat planning how and where to build the deck, Ree's head popped up above the rim of the pool. "Mom, don't forget Ren and I are going to the rehearsal dinner and spending tonight at Dad's."

"Oh, that's right. And the wedding is tomorrow. Are you excited?"

"Kinda."

"I sure am!" Caitlyn stood on the step of the ladder and said, "My mom bought me a new sundress to wear."

I said, "Oh, that's cool. Good idea. I might wear one too."

When the girls started splashing again, I called Kim. "What are you wearing tomorrow? Should we dress like cowgirls? I mean we'll be outdoors at a ranch."

"Well, let me look at the invitation." I heard rustling as she found the flyer. "It says Business Casual. I might wear that dress I got in Rome."

"Oooh. That will be perfect. I would wear mine too, but it's supposed to be hot, so I may wear a sundress with a wrap instead."

"Are you going to wear dark sunglasses too, so Shelly doesn't recognize you?"

"Good idea! Hey, wanna ride together?"

"Probably not. We need to go early so R.A. can help set up the stage."

"Oh, sure. Well, let's sit together during the ceremony—maybe somewhere in the back since I want to keep a low profile."

"OK."

Knowing that the next day would be busy, I started collecting all the things we needed to take to the cabin for our annual 4th of July weekend.

Ren and Ree had already showered and were packing to take things to their dad's house. I hollered, "Girls, bring me everything you want to take to the cabin. Don't forget your swimsuits, flip-flops, books, towels, and anything else you need."

"OK, Mom." They scurried around packing separate bags for our trip to Missouri.

I wrapped birthday presents for Eli and Lauren, then packed my swimsuit, towels, sunscreen, bug spray, and wading shoes. I put the non-perishables in Trader Joe's bags and got my big cooler out so it was ready to load the morning after the wedding reception.

I called E.J. to remind her to please feed and check on our fur, feather, and scale babies while we were out of town.

Once the girls were dressed and ready for their evening, I had them check and recheck their bags. "I can't wait to see my girls all dressed up tomorrow."

Ren said, "I'm really glad you get to go."

I twisted my mouth. "I just hope there isn't a blowout when Shelly sees me."

She said, "You know her. She only cares about how she looks."

I sure hoped so and said, "Mike will drop us back here after the reception, and in the morning we'll head directly to the cabin to meet Mom and Dad. Then we'll jump in the creek. I kissed the girls and said, "You both look so pretty. See ya'll tomorrow out in the pasture."

They laughed and left for the rehearsal and dinner.


Mike picked me up at three so we could go see Sally and the new baby. As we drove, I said, "I hope they like the sayings I put on the onesies."

"Which are?"

"You'll see."

When Scott answered the door, I said, "Welcome home, Scott! And congratulations on the new baby!"

"She's a dream come true. I'm just so glad Mike stepped up to help out while I was overseas." He shook his brother-in-law's hand.

He led us into the living room where a handsome older man and a striking tall woman stood. Mike said, "These are my parents, Sam and Melinda. Mom and Dad, this is my girlfriend, Pity Kole."

I stepped toward Melinda, studying her wrinkle-free face and lovely blonde hair. She had to be seventy but didn't look old enough to be Mike's mother. I wondered if she used that special wrinkle cream the gal was peddling in Boston.

I gave her a hug. "Sorry, I'm a hugger."

She gave me a sweet smile. "That's fine. I am too. We certainly have heard a lot about you from Michael."

I raised my eyebrows at him. "Michael?"

He shrugged and I stared at the older version of Mike and held out my hand. "I'm so happy to meet you, Sam."

"The pleasure is mine." He had the same twinkle in his eyes, but they were steel blue. He said, "We sure appreciate you letting him leave the baseball tour to be here with Sally."

I said, "Family always comes first, especially before baseball."

"Did you enjoy the games?"

"Um. Not what I expected, but the trip turned out to be very interesting."

He raised an eyebrow, but Mike stepped in. "So, where's Sal?"

"Here I am."

I looked up when Sally entered the room looking radiant and carrying a pink bundle. Before I could say anything, in zoomed little Jesse, holding an airplane above his head.

He froze when he saw me. "Did you bwing Wee and Wen?"

"No, I'm sorry, Jesse. They are at their father's house tonight. They told me to say hi, though."

 I stepped forward. "May I hold her?"

Sally said, "Sure, have a seat."

I sat immediately and when the soft warm blanket full of baby was deposited in my arms, I could smell that familiar sweet smell. Her tiny nose, face, and fingers were adorable. I said, "She's just perfect. Does she have a name yet? Mike wouldn't tell me."

"Yes. Meet Ivy Jade. We are pretty sure she will have green eyes since all three of us do. We hope her name will clinch it."

I leaned over to the gorgeous baby. "Hello Ivy, nice to meet you."

I asked Mike to hand them my gift bags. Jesse promptly dumped the dinosaur puzzle on the floor and started putting it together.

Sally opened the gift bag and pulled out a onesie. She smiled and read aloud, "I fought the nap, but the nap won."

Jesse jumped up, stuck his hand in the bag, and pulled out another outfit. "What does this say?"

Scott read, "And then there were four." He told Jesse to count the people in his family to explain the shirt.

Sally said, "Those are so cute. Thank you, but you already gave me gifts at the shower."

"Pity made them with her new vinyl cutting machine," Mike bragged. I smiled.

On our way home, Mike pulled up to the local hardware store and parked in the back. I raised my eyebrows. "You know, we're not 16, we can make out in a house instead of behind a store."

He chuckled and leaned over, but instead of giving me the kiss I expected, he opened the glove box and grabbed a measuring tape and two pairs of gloves. "Let's go get your supplies for your deck."

"Ooh, fun! And now I know why it's called a glovebox."

We started by picking out the best pallets from the free stack. It wasn't hard to lift them into the truck with Mike's help, but I was very glad we wore gloves.

Inside the store, I bought the required wood and screws necessary to build my deck. As I paid, a rack of gift cards caught my eye. "Oh my. We need to get a wedding gift for Todd and Shelly!"

He said, "Not to worry. I already purchased something from their gift registry."

I stared at him. Who was this amazing man who looked up a registry on his own? He was sure unlike any other men I knew.

Mike mistook my surprise for me waiting to hear what he bought, and he said, "They wanted a gold-plated gravy boat, so I bought it. I did not, however, get the Tiffany ice bucket or the Kayak."

"That's a good thing."

I figured the kayak was Todd's idea. He used to be very outdoorsy until he met Miss Priss, who probably wouldn't be caught dead in a boat unless it was equipped with a full bathroom.

At home, once everything was unloaded into my backyard, I said, "Thank you so much for helping me—and for having a truck. I'm excited to build the deck all by myself. This is where I'm going to put it." I walked off the area that I had carefully measured out.

He nodded with a skeptical look.

I raised an eyebrow at him. "Oh. So, you don't think I can do it?" I waggled my head. "Challenge accepted, Mister!"

"Well, it's not that. I believe you can assemble a deck. But have you considered the fact that this is a round pool, and the boards and pallets are all straight? If you want it to curve around and be snug up to the side, you'll have to cut the pallets with a circular saw. Do you think you can do that?"

I looked at the pool and the location of the future deck. He was right. I hadn't thought about rounding the wood and frowned. "Yeah, I don't have that kind of electric saw. What do you suggest?"

"Just let me help you with that part, and then you do all the rest on your own. I'll never tell anyone that I helped a tiny bit."

How could I reject his offer? "Okay. Thank you. And for your help today, I'll buy your dinner tonight. I mean you did line up a fancy date for us tomorrow at my ex-husband's wedding."

"I sure did." He winked and said, "I'm in the mood for Egg Roll Express take-out. What do you think?"

Within thirty minutes, we had picked up fried rice and beef cho chos and were eating in front of the TV watching a movie. Then, since my girls were gone, Mike spent the night at my house for the very first time.

Even though we had dated for more than a year, I had never invited him to stay over while the girls were home. I know…I'm old fashioned but I didn't want to set a bad example. Of course, they didn't seem to care that their dad lived with Shelly, so maybe it didn't even matter to them. But it mattered to me.

In the morning, I watched Mike while he slept. His salt and pepper hair was messed up and he looked so darned cute. I could get used to waking up to this.

Maybe it was all the talk about weddings during the past few months, but I wondered if I would ever want to tie the knot again. If I did, I would surely want it to be with this kind and handsome man. I didn't need to worry about it for a while, so I pushed the thought aside and went into the kitchen.

I brought Mike a cup of coffee and said, "Are you ready to witness the ex and the bridezilla tie the knot?"

He sat up in bed, rubbed his face, and smiled making his blue/green eyes twinkle. "Come here, you."

I snuggled up carefully, hoping he wouldn't spill hot coffee on me. But, I had forgotten to shut the door and Harriet leaped on the bed, nearly causing a coffee disaster, but Mike was a pro and didn't spill.

He said, "Well, good morning, Miss Harriet."

After a snuggle session with the furball, Mike said, "I'd better head home to shower, wrap the present, and change. It's gonna be a hot afternoon. Do you think they will mind if I wear a swimsuit?"

I snickered. "If you want something cool, I have an extra sundress you can borrow."

"Thanks, but I don't think it would fit. I'll find something."

And he sure did. When he picked me up at four thirty, he looked amazing in his white linen shirt and slim-fit tan pants. What a hunk.

He looked me up and down. "You look gorgeous. I hope Todd doesn't decide he wants you back instead of marrying Shelly."

"Too bad, so sad. I'm not interested."

We drove five miles south of Broken Arrow and finally came to the giant wooden ranch gate looming over the entrance to their long drive. The cutout metal sign overhead read "Big Jack's Ranch." What about his poor wife? Wasn't her name on anything? I picked up Mike's tacky flyer/wedding invitation from the front seat. Printed at the top were the words, Big Jack and Joanne Jones invite you to the wedding of their daughter, Michelle "Shelly" Jones to Theodore "Todd" Peterson.

I had to stop reading when we drove over a bumpy cattleguard, or I would have gotten carsick. We joined a line of vehicles heading down the long, dusty driveway to their ranch house.

When the huge rustic home appeared, I said, "Hey Mike, doesn't this remind you of the Dutton Ranch in *Yellowstone*?"

He shrugged. "I think it looks like Southfork Ranch from *Dallas*."

"I guess we'll have to wait and see whether John Dutton or J.R. Ewing comes out to greet us."

Neither of the TV characters showed up, but workers wearing orange vests ushered Mike to park in a field where about 30 Cadillacs were already lined up. Were they all guests' vehicles or were they new cars Big Jack had for sale? No telling, with him. He might announce a special wedding price for today only!

When we exited the car, I was instantly glad I had put my hair up and dressed in a cool outfit. It was beastly hot.

Two giant tents: one with a sign reading, RECEPTION, and another labeled, WEDDING, had been erected on the property. We headed toward the WEDDING tent. My sandals were covered in dust by the time we made it inside. The only thing worse would be if it started to rain and all the dirt turned to mud. I looked up and was thankful to see a bright clear sky.

Inside the tent, hundreds of matching white folding chairs lined the area. Red, white, and blue flowers hung at the end of each aisle. As I neared the seats, I realized the flowers were fake. Shelly had bragged that she would only have imported flowers—did she mean imported from a factory in China?

Patriotic bunting and big American flags lined the stage giving the setting more of a presidential debate look rather than a wedding. I turned to Mike. "In case anyone forgot it was Independence Day, this should remind them."

Mike's eyes were huge as he said, "She sure went all out."

I said, "I have a hunch this ain't all of it. Let's sit here in the back so she won't see me."

Once seated, I scanned the people who had arrived to see if I recognized anyone. Ren's boyfriend, Chris, sat with his parents towards the front. I also recognized a teacher friend and a few other people.

When Kim arrived, I motioned for her to join us. She hugged me and nodded to Mike. "Ooh, you two look so fresh."

I said, "And you look so pretty in your Italian dress, Kim."

She rolled her eyes. "Thanks, but I'm a big sweat ball. Why in the world did I think coming early with R.A. would be fun? July is the worst time to have an outdoor wedding in Oklahoma. I just can't wait to get up to the cabin and dive into that cold creek."

"Better you than me."

Mike leaned over. "Is the water really so cold that you don't get in?"

Kim rolled her eyes. "No. I love it. Pity's just weird. She takes an hour to inch into the water."

I sat up straight. "But once I get in, I love it too. I just don't like the cold on my skin."

He asked Kim, "Is R.A. still setting up the sound system?"

"Yeah. It's a bigger deal than he expected. He should finish soon." She laid her purse on the next seat to save it for him.

I watched people arrive while keeping my eye out for Travis and Odette.

I jumped in surprise when someone hugged me from behind. I turned to see a mop of red hair. It was Caitlyn, my biggest fan. I hugged the sweet redhead and looked up to see her mom, Trish, standing in the aisle with her severe bun, giving me a tight smile. As always, Trish looked stiff and unfriendly, but her pursed lips were actually the best smile she could give.

"Hi, Trish. I love your dress."

She nodded without returning any niceties while her husband, the judge, smiled. They urged Caitlyn to join them in seats towards the front.

I watched others as they found their seats. Quite a few men wore cowboy boots and hats as part of their business casual attire. My mind returned to *Yellowstone* and *Dallas*. Any characters from those shows could have walked into this wedding and fit in just fine.

I had to wonder how many guests were friends, and how many had just purchased a Cadillac.

When a well-dressed man wearing a cowboy hat walked in with a woman with beautiful white hair, I said, "Hi Odette and Travis!"

Travis, being a Texas gentleman, tipped his hat to us. Her navy dress was truly beautiful and fit perfectly. The two of them looked so different from the t-shirt and ball cap-wearing couple I had met on my trip.

Odette gave a surprised smile. "Pity, I thought you were going to be out of town today."

"Yeah, we decided to leave first thing in the morning instead. You remember Mike. And this is my sister, Kim." They nodded and Mike stood to shake Travis' hand.

Odette raised her eyebrows excitedly, "We'll talk more at the reception."

The two found seats further down the aisle. I explained to Kim who they were and how they knew Shelly's parents. "Their Cadillac dealership is called, 'Lone Star Caddy Corral.'"

With my head turned to talk to Kim, a familiar-looking silhouette stood in the opening of the tent. As he entered, and the sunny glare was gone, I clearly recognized my overly friendly stalker. What was Kenny doing here? I ducked down. Oh, right. He probably bought a car and received an invitation. I elbowed both Mike and Kim and pointed toward where he stood.

We all watched the odd duck walk past us wearing a suit that looked a few sizes too big for him. It hung off his narrow shoulders, making him look like a little kid dressed in his dad's jacket. For all I knew, it *was* his dad's jacket. The whole thing was weird because

Kenny was so rich. He could have hired a tailor to come to his home and custom-create as many suits as he wanted.

Kenny sat a few rows up and across the aisle. Luckily, he hadn't seen me, or he would have made his way to my side. That was the last thing I needed.

Mike looked at me quizzically, so I shrugged. I didn't know why he was here.

While I stared at Kenny, another man came down the aisle and sat beside him. Something about his tousled hair was familiar. When he turned his head, I nearly choked on my own spit. It was Grant the Hanson fan, little round glasses and all!

## Sports Joke #16

What has 18 legs and catches flies?
*A baseball team.*

Now that was a plot twist! Why was Grant here? And why was he with Kenny?

I elbowed Mike so hard he said, "Ouch!"

I leaned in to him. "Look! It's Grant and he's sitting with Kenny."

He looked at the two sitting a few rows ahead and across from us. I could see Mike's wheels turning. "Well, that's not so shocking, is it? Didn't they meet when you took the whole group to Kenny's fancy feast in Fenway Park?"

I nodded slowly. "Of course. That's probably what happened. Grant heard Kenny was from Tulsa and since I had rebuffed his plea to stay with me, he glommed onto the unsuspecting Kenny."

Mike smirked. "Looks like a match made in heaven to me. Two lonely, weird guys hanging out together at some strangers' wedding."

I laughed at his statement but thought he might be right. Maybe I shouldn't feel sorry for Kenny. He may actually need a friend. But still, I'd have to talk to them at the reception and find out more, even if it meant Kenny trying to win me over yet again.

Kim leaned in and said, "What's going on? Who is that guy with Kenny?"

I was going to answer, but R.A. rushed in and sat down beside her. His blue eyes were open wide as he said, "You won't believe this…"

R.A.'s exciting news was cut off when music blared through the speakers. I was so surprised by the loud guitars that I put my fingers in my ears like a little kid. I'd never heard the song before, but it was definitely a country tune with a twangy guitar and an even twangier singer.

Todd walked out onto the small stage wearing a cowboy hat, boots and a white suit. It was an interesting look, but not too bad for a non-cowboy. He took his hat off and held it to his heart. His hair was combed back and even from this distance, I could see that his beard was neatly trimmed, which was unusual for him. He was flanked by his two brothers, dressed similarly. I really liked both Ted and Tom and was glad to see them again.

The scene took me back to my own wedding day when those brothers stood up for Todd along with two of his friends. Across from them, were my attendants, Kim, Kay, Lin, and Lis.

I looked at Todd and found myself comparing the way he looked today to the time of our wedding. Back then, his hair was longer and parted down the middle to embrace the Leonardo DiCaprio look. Of course, I had attempted the Jennifer Anniston hairdo—neither of which worked out so well. Things sure had changed over the years.

I took my fingers from my ears so I could listen to the lyrics.

*I took one look at you, my love, and knew you had to be...*
*The gal of my future, the woman of my dreams.*
*And since I get to make the choice, I know what I will say;*
*Darlin' I will marry you on this very day.*

*Yes, today is my destiny, I'm standing here in wait*
*For my beautiful bride who is comin' out the gate.*
*I know she is a beauty — the apple of my eye,*
*And today I am so lucky to call you my own wife."*

My face contorted as I absorbed the lyrics. Did he actually sing, *she's comin' out the gate*, like a bucking bronco might? It was an odd song for Shelly to choose for the procession, but whatever.

I was still listening when Kim nudged me. I turned to see Marie walking carefully down the aisle in low heels and carrying a bouquet. My eyes teared up to see how beautiful she looked in the light blue dress. Her long blond hair was loose around her shoulders, and she wore light makeup that made her look a little older than her 14 years. When she spotted me, she smiled and raised her eyebrows in excitement. I could tell she was nervous but having fun.

Behind her, Lauren made her way in gracefully. She was wearing a pink dress that fit her 18-year-old figure beautifully. Wow! I sure had some pretty girls. I quickly lifted my phone and managed to get a few photos before they passed by us.

Their dad beamed as the girls approached the stage, looking as proud as I felt. Both Ren and Ree positioned themselves across from Todd and his brothers. Their dress colors, although thankfully not Red and Blue, somehow fit the theme in an understated way.

As I studied the scene, I was surprised Shelly didn't have a multitude of attendants. Stranger yet, all the people standing up for the couple were from Todd's family. Why didn't she have any of her friends as attendants? Did she even have any friends? Hmm. It made me a little sad for her, but knowing her personality, not *that* surprised. I was just glad I could attend to see my girls participate in a wedding for the first time.

That horrible song finally ended, and the traditional wedding march began. The congregation stood and turned to face the back of the tent.

Big Jack, with his large body and giant cowboy hat, strode in like he owned the world as he escorted the bride down the aisle. He, somehow, got all of the attention when it should have been Shelly. She was dwarfed by her larger-than-life father.

A sheer veil covered her face, so it was hard to get a good look at Shelly's hair or her face. Her dress was white and fairly simple except for the little red, white, and blue circles around the veil, neckline, and sleeves. I was glad that they didn't look as much like Olympic rings as I had feared.

The train of her dress extended a good six feet behind her. This was not surprising. She took up a lot of space in real life, so why not at her wedding?

Personally, I was happy that her own view was hindered by the veil, so she wouldn't notice me, but I held my hand over my face as she walked by, just in case.

Once they had made it to the stage, Big Jack helped his daughter up the steps and she took her place to stand beside Todd. Ren did her job and moved the train aside and took Shelly's bouquet from her. Big Jack joined his wife, Joanne, in the front row.

The officiant started the typical non-denominational service. After a while, a matronly woman walked to the microphone and sang John Legend's song, *All of Me.* She sounded nothing like Legend's smooth voice. It was loud, operatic, and with a schmaltzy wide vibrato that was anything but romantic. Once the woman finished her dramatic rendition, she returned to her seat.

The minister said, "And now Todd and Shelly's daughter, Lauren, will read a poem in honor of the union."

It bothered me that he had called her Todd and Shelly's daughter, but I needed to get used to it; since Shelly would be my girls' stepmother in a matter of minutes, whether I liked it or not.

Ren tentatively walked to the microphone and cleared her throat before speaking softly,

*"As most of you know, Todd is my dad.*
*I'm lucky to have him for he's really rad."*

Being her mother, I recognized Ren's discomfort in saying the outdated word, rad, but she continued,

*"Shelly will soon be my stepmother*

*She is more beautiful than any other."*

I almost choked and Ren's face turned pink with that line. Even through Shelly's veil, I could see her red lips mouthing the words from memory as poor Ren read the rest of Shelly's egotistical poem.

*"It will be very exciting to live with a star,*
*A local celebrity known wide and far.*
*So, let's give a cheer and thank our God*
*For the amazing couple, Shelly and Todd"*

The guests stayed silent. Were we really supposed to clap or cheer? Finally, there was a spattering of applause. I joined in for Ren's sake and watched my sweet girl dash back to her spot beside her sister. How embarrassing for her to have to read the ridiculous words Shelly wrote about herself.

It wasn't long before the officiant said, "You may now kiss the bride." When Todd finally lifted the veil, he gave a big smile, so I was glad for him.

Shelly puckered her lips for a kiss, but I had no interest in watching this ritual and turned my head away. I noticed Grant nodding his approval. Weird.

After the kiss, everyone clapped in earnest, and Shelly faced the front unveiled. I was taken aback by her heavier-than-usual coat of makeup. Her eyes were doubled in size. I could even see her enormous fake eyelashes from where I sat in the 17th row.

When the recession music began, Shelly stepped from the stage and marched down the aisle slowly with Todd trailing behind, trying not to step on her train. He looked as if he wasn't a part of the ceremony at all. Shelly waved to the guests as she passed each row like a beauty queen in a parade.

I gulped, realizing if she continued waving to each row, she would eventually notice me. I didn't want to cause a scene in front of everyone, so I snuck past Mike and whispered, "I've gotta go out before she sees me."

He said, "Come on Pity, you're being paranoid."

"Eh. I'm not so sure." I excused myself as I squeezed past people in our row and scooted outside by way of a tent flap.

When I made it outdoors, I stood at the side of the tent in the blazing heat and listened to music and applause coming from inside.

When Shelly squawked, "Come on, Todd. Stand over here," I peeked around the corner to see her pointing to where he should stand. My ex obediently moved next to her under a red, white, and blue flower-covered archway.

Once in position, the photographer snapped several photos of the two. Shelly smiled with her head tilted up, then down, and then to the side, while Todd stood stiffly beside her. She did not even look at her new husband. Poor Todd. At least when I married him, I loved him and acted like I did.

My girls, escorted by their uncles, exited the church next. That perked me up. I pulled out my phone and took a few candid photos of the sweet scene. I crouched in my odd position trying to stay hidden with my ear to the corner of the tent as I took pictures. Then, I swatted at a bee which was probably attracted to my sweat. I lost my balance and started to fall. I grabbed hold of the tent flap and pulled down a section of the canvas.

I didn't think anybody inside the tent saw me. But unfortunately, the entire wedding party did. I cringed from my awkward position squatting on the ground in my flowered sundress.

Todd squeezed his eyes shut. The girls stared in disbelief. Shelly instantly turned beet red and then practically screamed, "What is SHE doing here? SHE was not invited!"

Todd tried to calm her down, but Shelly would have none of it and shook him off. She left her position under the archway and marched toward me, her finger pointing at me the whole time.

She spat, "I knew you would try to ruin my wedding. There you are, lurking around the corner trying to cause problems like you always do. You just can't stay away from Todd, can you?" She thrust her giant diamond ring in my face, almost hitting my nose. "You can't have him. He's taken and is mine now!"

It was ludicrous to think after all these years that I would want Todd back, and worse yet, that I would try to sabotage their wedding to win him over. I almost laughed at her accusation and tried to stand up to tell her how wrong she was, but my heel was caught in the hem of my sundress. I took my shoe off my foot and stood with it still hanging from my dress.

She was now so close to me that her eyelashes looked like caterpillars ready to attack me. And on the word, "taken," her spit hit my eye. After wiping my eye clean, I opened my mouth for a rebuttal, but I caught sight of my girls with their hands over their mouths and I changed my tune.

I took a deep breath and said, "Shelly, I'm really sorry to have upset you. I was invited by someone and came to see my girls all dressed up. I will leave if you want me to."

"Who? Who?" Shelly shouted, sounding like a rabid owl, then finally screeched, "WHO. Invited. You?"

At this point, I was so humiliated I wanted to cry. My heart raced and I wasn't sure what to do.

Just then, a deep voice said, "I invited her."

It was not Mike, but Big Jack, himself, who spoke. His large body filled up the tent opening. He gave his daughter a stern look as if reprimanding a toddler and said, "Michelle Diane Jones, you are embarrassing me. This gal is with her boyfriend, who stopped vandalism at my dealership. They are my guests, not yours. Let her be and calm down before the other guests join us out here or I will cancel the entire honeymoon I paid for."

Shelly finally had nothing to say. Her mouth opened and then shut as she considered her options. She removed her finger from my face, and said, "Yes, Daddy." With her head lowered, she turned around and walked back to Todd.

Ren, being the considerate girl that she was, must have felt sorry for the bride because she dusted off Shelly's train and placed it nicely around her feet so the photo shoot could continue.

When the newlyweds and their families were in position, her father said, "Now let's smile for the camera, and then we'll all enjoy a party like no other."

My heart continued to pound in my ears as I watched the wedding party pose for pictures. I stood to the side afraid to even unhook my shoe from my dress, for fear I would cause another ruckus.

It was so hot, that sweat trickled down my back. A breeze would have been nice, but this day was the worst kind of heat. It was 98 degrees with relentless humidity and the air was stagnant. Why in heaven's name didn't they take photos inside after the guests moved to the reception tent? Everyone in the photos would undoubtedly look sweaty.

As if to illustrate the heat's capability, a lock of Shelly's hair fell from her fancy do, and her face turned beet red. The girls wiped their brows but somehow kept their adorable smiles. I could feel my own bangs frizz. Nobody felt or looked good.

Over the speaker, the minister directed the congregation to go outside for the receiving line before heading to the big tent for the dinner and reception.

Finally, the photographer finished, and the guests from the tent started moving outside to join the receiving line.


As soon as Mike, Kim, and R.A. exited, I unhooked my shoe from my dress hem and returned it to its rightful place on my dusty foot, then made a beeline for them. Unfortunately, I didn't quite make it there before Kenny bounded over like an excited puppy.

"My darling Kitty! I knew you were here as soon as I recognized your gorgeous daughters–Lauren and Marie, right? He pointed to Ren and Ree, who attempted to give smiles to an untold number of strangers in the receiving line.

My shoulders slumped and I said, "Hi, Kenny. Yes. This is their dad's wedding. What are you doing here?"

He squinted at the bright light and said, "I must get out of the sun. Come back inside, please?"

He took my hand in his sweaty palm and started pulling me back to the tent, past guests standing in line to get out.

I looked for Mike, but he was busy being patted on the back by Big Jack. Kim was hugging my girls, so I reluctantly followed Kenny inside the tent.

"Here we are together again." He gave me his adoring look that always made me uncomfortable.

I groaned. "Look Kenny, I need to go back. My boyfriend is waiting for me."

"But I haven't seen you since Philadelphia. It's been over a week."

I rolled my eyes thinking that was not nearly long enough. He said, "You'll never guess who I brought as my guest today. He just ran to the bathroom but should be back shortly."

I said, "Grant from Tupelo?"

Kenny's mouth opened wide. "Kitty Kole, you are the most amazing person I have ever met. You're so smart and look at how beautiful you are today!"

I doubted I looked beautiful, especially after standing in that heat. I wiped the sweat from my brow and said, "So, why are you here? Do you know the Joneses?"

"Oh, yes. I've known Jack and Joanne for years. My father always buys his Cadillacs from them, and they mailed him an invitation." He sighed, "But Dad is in China working to acquire a company that makes oil field parts, so he asked that I take his place. I never dreamed I'd see you here. I was going to bring my sister, but Grant is staying with us now and he wanted to come."

I felt a tap on my shoulder and turned to find Grant, himself, staring at me with a goofy grin. "Hi, Pity. See…you can run into people by accident in Tulsa."

I smiled. "Hi Grant." I looked from one man to the other. "So how did this all come about?"

Grant said, "Well, after you introduced us at Citizen's Bank Park, I explained to Ken how much I wanted to see Hanson and he said I could stay with him. He even offered to show me around. It's been awesome. I have ridden in his sports car, a Cadillac, and a limousine."

I had never known anyone to call Kenny, Ken, and realized I'd never heard anyone call him anything, except maybe Mr. Dicks. I smirked. "And have you run into Isaac, Tayor, and Zac yet?"

"No, but I'm not giving up."

"Mom, what are you doing?" I turned to see the silhouette of Ree standing in the opening of the tent. She urged, "The reception is about to start." Then she disappeared.

I told the guys, "Kenny, that's nice of you to show Grant around. Look, I should go. Guess I'll see you in the next tent."

When I made it back outside, the girls and Mike greeted me. He grimaced. "So, maybe you weren't paranoid after all. I heard what happened."

I rolled my eyes. "I know. I'm so embarrassed. Shelly was furious that I was here and get this, she accused me of trying to steal Todd back. As if." I scoffed, then remembered my girls were standing there. "No offense to your dad, but well, you know…"

They both nodded, knowing that would not work.

I put my arms around the girls and said, "I'm so glad I came, even if I did cause a scene while trying to stay out of sight. You two were so beautiful up there. And your dresses are really cool!"

Ree looked down at her dress. "It is nice but face it. Nothing is cool today." She fanned herself with her hand.

I looked at Ren. "Lauren, you even did a great job reading Shelly's love poem to herself."

We all chuckled, and she said, "I just hope nobody thought I was the one who wrote it."

Ree looked antsy. "Mom, can I go hang out with Caitlyn, please?"

"Of course. And Ren I'll bet you want to hang out with Chris?"

Both girls rushed off together. I took my empty arms and wrapped them around Mike. "Let's party!"

The interior of the big tent was an assault to my eyes. The tablecloths were explosions of red, white, and blue fireworks. The white walls were covered in matching garlands. The twirly red, white, and blue streamers hanging from the tent top hit me in the face as we walked. It was overkill and there was no place for my eyes to rest.

I whispered to Mike, "Shelly must have ordered every patriotic decoration ever made."

On the tables at each seat, there was a canvas drawstring bag with an American flag printed on the side. My eyes grew big. Finally, I would see what the goodie bags held. But as much as I wanted to snatch a bag off a table, I needed to wait until I found Kim and R.A. so we could sit with them.

On the left, there was a bar with bartenders wearing matching red, white, and blue vests over their white shirts. To the right was a gift table full of a crazy number of packages and cards. Wow. I pointed the table out to Mike, and he put his gift with the others.

Beyond the gift table stood the tallest, gaudiest cake I had ever seen. It had three huge layers, each one frosted with a solid color. The top was covered in red icing, which I knew from experience, always tasted bitter. The middle layer was a dark blue which would undoubtedly turn my teeth blue. I refused to eat from the top or middle sections but wasn't sure how to snag a slice from the bottom white section.

The worst thing was the cake topper. It was a big Uncle Sam, but instead of his typical stovetop hat, he wore a cowboy hat. Next to him stood a big Besty Ross holding a flag and wearing fake eyelashes and bouffant hair rather than her iconic mop cap. Oh, brother.

"Pity! Over here!"

Kim motioned for us to join them at a table off to the side. Good. No need to get in the bride's way again. Before we sat down, Mike said, "Do you want a drink?"

I smiled. "More than you know. Please get me something cold — anything with alcohol."

He laughed and left me to join Kim. I plunked down in the chair next to her. "So, you heard about my confrontation with Shelly?"

"Yes. The girls told us. We heard some of it from inside the wedding tent."

I hit my forehead with my palm. "Did I really ruin her wedding?"

She put her hand on my shoulder. "No. She was out of line. And nobody else knew who she was screaming at. Besides, check out this big to-do." She waved her hand around the room. "After dinner, drinks, and dancing, nobody will remember what happened."

"I sure hope so. Where's R.A.?"

"Doing some speaker stuff."

I looked at the stage set up at one end of the tent. "So, what did he want to tell us just before the wedding started?"

She smiled. "Oh, let's just let it be a surprise."

I didn't press Kim for more information. Sometimes R.A. was known for getting excited about little things, like he'd say, "Wow. I just saw a hummingbird!" or "A guy just gave me this really cool tool." Gotta love a guy who got as excited over everyday things as I did.

I almost salivated looking at the bags, wondering what was in them. "Have you checked the gift bags?"

"Not yet." Kim picked hers up. "Shall we?"

I grabbed my bag, surprised at how big and heavy it was. I had trouble pulling apart the drawstring, but found star-spangled tissue paper inside, of course. I pulled it out and looked up to see Kim already wearing American flag glasses. Cute. I pulled mine out and put them on too. The next thing I found was a red and white striped matchbook that said, "Match made in Heaven." That was kinda cute.

What surprised me most was what I pulled out next - a bundle of bottle rockets. My jaw dropped as I stared at Kim. She was equally shocked when she lifted a Roman candle from her bag. I said, "Seriously? They are giving out fireworks as wedding favors?"

She laughed. "That's the weirdest thing I've ever seen, but R.A. is gonna love it."

That was true. My brother-in-law and his boys were all pyromaniacs. Their favorite holiday was the 4th of July. I was sure they had already bought boxes filled with fireworks to take to the cabin tomorrow.

I held up my bottle rockets and scrunched up my face. "Do you think we're supposed to shoot these off here at the party?" Without waiting for an answer, I kept digging.

Next, I found a shot glass that said, 'Party in the USA. Todd and Shelly's wedding, July 4.' The last thing at the bottom of the bag was a $10 gift card to a local coffee shop with a funny note attached that read, 'You may want to use this tomorrow morning.'

I couldn't imagine Shelly being so creative and wondered who their wedding planner was. Everything was cool, except for the explosives.

Just when we had put everything back in our bags, an announcer said, "Presenting Mr. and Mrs. Peterson!" The Springsteen song, *Born in the USA* blared from the speakers.

All eyes turned to the tent opening. Just as Shelly and Todd entered, red, white, and blue confetti dropped from the ceiling. It was as if the couple had just won *America's Got Talent.* Shelly waved her hand like she was Miss America. Poor Todd lumbered along beside her, wiping away tiny bits of tissue paper that stuck to his sweaty face. I knew him well enough to know that this was not his idea of a good time. The funny thing is, that Todd used to be strong and loved being in charge, but he gave it all up when he started dating Shelly.

## Sports Joke #17

Why was Cinderella so bad at sports?
*She had a pumpkin for a coach.*

Once the procession passed, Todd and Shelly were seated at a table in the front. Mike returned and said, "Shelly sure does like her pomp and circumstance! I almost slipped on confetti coming back." He offered me a choice of two icy drinks, one blue and one white.

My eyes lit up. "What is that?" I pointed to the blue one.

"A Blue Hawaiian. All their drinks are red, white, or blue."

Kim held up her bright red cocktail. "Strawberry Margarita!"

I settled on the blue one and looked at Mike's white drink. "And let me guess, Pina Colada?"

He clinked my glass. "You got it."

While all three glasses were still mostly full, I grabbed them and lined them up on the bright tablecloth and snapped a pic. Wow. It could have been the cover of the July issue of *Southern Living* or *Food Network* magazine.

Having taken a sip of all three drinks, I discerned that Mike's was best. We made him open his bag so we could watch his expression. When he pulled out a cone-shaped fountain, he cocked his head and said, "Ok, so they are giving out both alcohol and fireworks freely? Sounds like a disaster waiting to happen."

"At least they gave us safety glasses?" I pointed to my wild, red, white, and blue glasses which had already slid down my sweaty nose.

He rolled his eyes as Kim said, "I'm going to go check on R.A. I have to tell him what's in the goody bags."

When she left, I looked for my girls. I spotted Ree sitting with Caitlyn and her parents, laughing and giggling about something.

Ren was at a table, talking to Chris and his folks. She looked so grown up in her dress. I guess that made sense since she was 18! Where had the time gone?

I couldn't see Odette or Travis and wasn't sure I wanted to know where Kenny and Grant's table was. I didn't have to wonder long though, because the two guys appeared right in front of us.

Kenny said, "Are these seats taken?"

Mike and I stammered, not knowing exactly what to say. But it didn't matter, because they sat down before waiting for us to answer. Oh well…

We tried to have a polite conversation, but it was awkward with the two strange men.

I asked, "So, Grant, what have you done since arriving in Tulsa? Have you been to the Gathering Place yet?"

"No. I wanted to check it out, but you know Ken here can't be outside because of bugs and sunshine."

"Oh, that's right. Of course."

Grant said, "But Ken's house is amazing. It has a swimming pool that he and his sister have never used. Only the pool guy ever uses it. And me, of course."

"The pool guy?" I cocked my head at Kenny.

Kenny explained. "I have a pool man who cleans it weekly, but nobody uses it, so I said he and his family could enjoy it. They come over almost every day in the summer."

That made sense—sort of. But talk of a pool reminded me that I had my own pool now! I was sure Kenny's was much nicer than my little above-ground pool, but I felt a tingle of excitement remembering I'd be building a deck when we came home from the cabin. And maybe by then, the water would be warm enough for me to get in. At least it would be warmer than the creek water.

Mike took a drink and asked, "So, Grant what was your favorite part of the baseball tour?"

"Oh, all of it, except when the Braves lost." His face twisted and turned dark.

Mike and I glanced at each other in the uncomfortable silence until a cheerful, Southern voice interrupted the moment with, "Well hello, old friends!"

I looked up to see Odette and Travis standing behind Kenny.

I said, "Hi! It's a Ballparks and More reunion! You remember Grant and Kenny? Do you want to sit with us?" I really hoped they would since they would be much more fun and interesting than our other two table mates.

Travis said, "I believe we will."

They sat in the empty seats, and we all discussed the wedding, the unusual gift bags, and the weather.

Changing the subject, I said, "I still can't believe Father John was a fake."

"I know! And I actually confessed to him." Odette shook her head.

Grant squinted. "What did you say?"

She said, "I said, I can't believe I made a confession to him."

"No. What do you mean he was a fake?" He looked at me, confused.

I furrowed my brow and then remembered. "Oh, that's right, Grant. You left a day early to go to a concert right after the Babe Ruth Museum. You missed it."

"Missed what, exactly?"

Grant fidgeted with his hands as I explained how we discovered that Father John was not a priest at all but was impersonating one from Boston.

Travis added, "And he was arrested in the stadium, in front of everyone during the Nationals/Orioles game."

Mike said, "You missed all the excitement."

Grant spat, "But why would he do that?"

For some reason, the man sounded angry instead of amazed at the weird news.

I said, "Who knows? But the best thing is that by arresting him, they were able to catch the guy responsible for the injuries and death on the trip. I'm pretty sure he is the one who threw the ball at my head and locked me in a museum. I'm so glad he's locked up now."

Grant stuttered, "Y-you think he did all those things?" Worry flickered in his eyes. "But…John told me all about him being a priest in Boston. We discussed his chapel and parishioners. I believed him."

I raised my eyebrows. "That's the problem. Everyone did."

"So, did he lie also about the girl he kissed in Boston? Was she not his sister?"

Poor, innocent Grant. I looked at the clueless guy and said, "Well, I saw them too. I doubt anyone kisses their sister on the lips like that - especially a priest. That was when I became suspicious."

Odette took a deep breath. "You know, he never acted very holy - except for when I spoke to him one on one. Then, he was very calm, comforting and forgiving. He listened carefully and always took notes. Then the next minute, he was using profanity. How bizarre of him to impersonate a man of the cloth."

Grant said, "So did you say there is a real Father John?"

"Yes. An older man. Rob even spoke to him."

"Well, what is the fake John's real name?" Grant was so riled up he almost spit the words.

Mike turned to me. "Didn't Detective McDonald call him Jacob Goldschmidt when he arrested him?"

I nodded. "Yeah, that's it." It reminded me of the children's song, *John Jacob Jingleheimer Schmidt,* I had my 3rd graders sing.

I chuckled then said, "I've been wanting to call that detective." I rummaged around in my purse and pulled out his card. "Since we're all together I can do it now and get an update."

Mike said, "But Pity, it's a holiday. He's probably at a barbeque or something. Maybe wait until tomorrow."

"Oh yeah. That's probably true." I put the card away.

R.A. and Kim showed up and forced a pleasant hello to Kenny. Then I introduced them to the Ballparks and More trio. Unfortunately, the whole story about Father John had put Grant in a major funk. He barely acknowledged my sister and R.A. He sat silently with a scowl while servers brought food and drinks.

The rest of us chatted as we ate an amazing meal of barbeque ribs, potato salad, and fried okra. But Grant barely took a bite and stared at his plate. He seemed to be mumbling something under his breath, but I couldn't hear what. Man, this news had really upset him. Maybe he had trusted the "priest" with some very personal information and felt betrayed. I could see how that would be devastating.

R.A., on the other hand, was stoked about the fireworks. Since he had gotten a box of sparklers in his bag, I traded him my bottle rockets. He said, "I just don't understand how this is going to work. Are they going to have us shoot these off right outside? Seems a bit unsafe with hundreds of people firing them off at the same time."

Once our plates had been taken away, the D.J.'s voice blasted over the speakers. "Everyone, gather around. The newlyweds are going to cut the cake!"

I turned to Mike. "Shall we?"

He said, "Sure. Should be interesting."

Everyone at our table stood, except Grant, who continued to mope.

We joined the huge crowd of guests surrounding the cake table to watch the event. It was pretty much the traditional cake-cutting ritual, except for when Shelly gave him a forkful of red iced cake, Todd frowned at the taste. I could tell he was dying to spit it out, but being a good sport, he chewed and swallowed. Then he picked up a piece covered with dark blue icing. I put my hand to my mouth remembering how he had smashed cake into my mouth at our wedding. I almost yelled, 'No! Not the blue!' But not wanting to cause another commotion, I bit my tongue and anticipated a catastrophe.

I watched the scene take place, as if in slow motion. Todd moved the forkful of cake with blue icing towards her. When he smooshed the giant piece into her mouth and he smeared it all around, I cringed.

Shelly smiled and giggled unaware her face was blue. I was happy she was having fun, but I feared what might come. Even after wiping her mouth with a napkin, her face was still dark blue. Todd's eyes grew large, but he wasn't about to say anything to his new bride.

Kim whispered to me. "Whose idea was it to have solid-colored icing on the cake?"

"Maybe the baker is as sick of her commercials as I am."

People snapped photos. I could only hope the official photographer was adept at Photoshop and could erase the indigo stain from her face.

The blue-faced bride announced, "All you single gals, come on over. I have a bouquet to toss!"

I watched as several young gals rushed in front of Shelly. Then I felt a shove. "Get up there, single gal!" Kim could be so pushy.

I swiveled to her. "No. I'm not going. Those girls are all in their 20's. I'm old enough to be their mother!"

Odette said, "Go on, Pity. It's just for fun."

Travis nodded and Kenny stood with a bewildered face, probably not even familiar with the tradition.

Then Mike said with a smirk, "I dare ya."

That did it. I was not one to turn down a dare and trudged that way. I stood behind the eager faces and slunk down so I didn't tower above the young beauties.

When Shelly spotted me, her nose wrinkled, and she made a big show of turning around and tossing the bouquet in the opposite direction. I was relieved, not wanting anything to do with the flowers, but strangely the bouquet flew back into the air. The girls were treating it like a volleyball. It was up again, never landing for more than a second as it bounced from one to another.

For some reason, when the bouquet came to me, it got caught on my barrette and I tried to loosen it without pulling out my hair.

Just as I freed myself from the bundle of fake red, white, and blue flowers, Shelly turned around to see who had caught them. Her eyes turned to slits and she fumed when she saw me holding her bouquet.

Her giant blue/purple lips pursed, and she huffed, "Figures."

Back in my seat, I sat with a piece of cake with white icing and holding the big ugly bouquet. I said, "Mike. I wasn't trying to catch it. It got caught in my hair clip."

He raised his eyebrows, "I think you dove for it."

I punched him in the arm.

The announcer said, "Get those dancing shoes on. The band is about ready to play." Kim and R.A. sat straighter and winked at each other.

I needed a cold Piña Colada before I could even think about dancing. I said, "Anyone want another drink?" I took orders from our group and Kim came along to help carry.

As we stood in line at the drink station, she said, "So what's up with that gloomy Grant guy?"

I said, "I don't know why he's so upset about Father John being arrested. Maybe they were friends. Oh yeah, I never told you. Grant is the Hanson freak from the baseball tour who wanted to stay with me. But then he met Kenny and voila, he's Kenny's problem, now."

Her eyes grew wide. "Seriously?"

"Yes. I know. So crazy to be that obsessed with a band, huh?"

Kim's lips were curled in as if she had something to tell me.

I held my hands up. "What?"

She giggled and whispered, "Hanson. Is. Playing. Here. Tonight!"

My breath caught. "What? No way! How?"

"I guess Big Jack has connections. That's what R.A. wanted to tell you earlier. Is your weird dude going to go crazy?"

"Well, if anything can bring him out of his bad mood, that'll do it. I'm excited, too! I've never seen them perform, live."

"Me neither."

We carried the drinks back to the table and handed them out to everyone except Kenny who drank water and Grant, who was in another world. I made a zipped lip motion to Kim, so we could watch Grant's reaction when he learned who the band was.

Even though the big tent was equipped with big standing fans which moved the air a bit, it was still sweltering inside. You would think this late in the day, it would cool off, but it didn't. My icy Pina Colada helped a little.

R.A. who was drinking a beer, which was not red, white or blue, said, "Duty calls. I need to go make sure all is set up on stage." He guzzled down the rest of his brew and took off.

When the ambient music stopped and the announcer put his mouth to the microphone, I grabbed my phone so I would be ready to catch either Grant's reaction to Hanson, or photograph Hanson themselves. I snapped a before-picture of grumpy Grant with his elbows on the table and head in his hands.

The voice came on loud and clear, "It's a once-in-a-lifetime wedding party! Please welcome Tulsa's own band. Give it up for...Hanson!"

The crowd clapped enthusiastically, but Grant continued to stare at his plate.

I aimed my phone at the stage and watched the three brothers run out waving. They sure had changed since their start as young boys in 1997. Hard to believe they were now in their 40s, and each had children of their own. Isaac carried his guitar; Taylor went to the keyboard and Zac sat down at the drum set. So cool!

Kim nudged me. "Look at him. It didn't work. Is he hard of hearing?"

Grant still sat in a stupor, facing his plate. I said, "Grant. Did you hear that? Hanson is here!"

He blinked as if he just woke up and looked at me. "What?"

"Turn around! Hanson is the band tonight."

He whipped around so fast he knocked his plate to the edge of the table. I snapped a photo as Grant finally realized his favorite band was standing only feet away. He jumped up and ran past the tables to the front of the stage where he started snapping photos of the group.

We all sat stunned. Odette, who was next to the empty chair, moved Grant's plate full of food back to the middle of the table and said, "Well, that was a quick emotional turnaround."

Mike's eyes were wide too. "I have never seen such an immediate transformation in my life."

A little late on the draw, Kenny said, "So, is that the group Grant came to Tulsa to meet?"

I said, "Yes. The very one."

Travis cocked his head. "I haven't heard anything about Hanson for probably 15 years."

Kim said, "Oh, they are a really big deal here in Tulsa and still tour around the country."

Travis shook his head. "Well, good for Grant to get to see his favorite band, but I wonder why he was so upset over the so- called priest's arrest?"

Odette said, "You know he kept mumbling something about payback and going to Hell."

I raised my eyebrows at her. "What was that? Do you happen to remember his exact words?"

She closed her eyes, trying to recall them, and said, "I think it was, 'He will get his payback. Hell is waiting for him.'"

That phrase sounded familiar and I pictured a wheelchair. That was it. Those were the same words Marcia said she heard a man murmur before he knocked her off the ledge. To confirm it, I found my Suspects note on my phone. Yep. Marcia had told me an almost identical phrase. 'This is your payback. Hell is waiting for you.'

My heart skipped a beat as I stared at the joyful man near the band. Why was he repeating those words here? I gasped. What if Father John wasn't the killer? What if it was Grant?

I started to have trouble breathing, but I needed more information before telling Mike and Kim my new suspicion. Think, Pity, think! Had any of the other victims been told something similar? I looked at my list on my phone.

Besides Marcia, the only other one who could have heard something from the culprit was Señor Herrera.

After all, whoever poisoned Jason did it when he was gone. Gross Hair Guy (Howard) sure couldn't tell anyone anything.

Wait. I got a text from the Herrera gal last week with the Rocky photo. I quickly found it on my phone and texted her back.

*'Hi, this is Pity from the ballpark tour. I have an odd question for you. Did your father mention if someone said something to him before pushing him down the Rocky steps?'*

Mike's reminder that it was a holiday stuck with me, so I figured I might not get a reply today, but I turned on my ringer and stared at my screen, nonetheless.

Kim said, "Aren't you watching the band?"

"Uh. Yeah. They sound great."

She said, "What are you up to? You're acting like you do when you are deep into an investigation." She paused and said, "No. Pity. Tell me you aren't up to something."

I looked at my sister and said, "Did you hear what Grant was mumbling?"

She waved me off as if it was no big deal, but I stared at her. "Those are the same words someone told the gal right before he pushed her onto the seats below."

I finally had Kim's attention, and she focused on the guy next to the stage.

Even with all the loud music, Mike somehow overheard our conversation. He said, "Pity, are you suggesting that Grant could be responsible for the problems on the trip?"

"I don't know. But just in case, I wrote the daughter of the old man who was also shoved to ask if he heard the pusher say anything." Just then my phone pinged with a reply.

*'Hi Pity. I am with my father now. He says he thought someone whispered, "This is revenge. Hell waits for you."*

I sucked in my breath and wrote back, *'Did your father tell the police that?'*

*'No. He didn't think about it until later.'*

*'Okay. Well, thanks. I'll let you know if I find out anything else. Tell Joey hi from me and Happy Independence Day!'*

She sent me an emoji of a firecracker.

I showed the thread to both Kim and Mike who sat on either side of me. Kim said, "That is pretty weird."

I stood and told them quietly, "I think I'll call that detective, but it's too loud in here." I motioned to the tent flap. "I'll go outside."

Kenny, Odette, and Travis had been watching us, so I said, "I'm sorry, I have to make a quick phone call. I'll be right back."

Mike followed me outdoors. The sun was low in the sky, but it was still beastly hot. I wiped the sweat from my forehead, wondering why I had even bothered putting on makeup.

I waited as the phone rang and went to voicemail. I left a message, reminding the detective of who I was, and then said, "I have questions about Father John, I mean Jacob, and have new information for you about another guy who was also on our tour. He is with me and has said some things that seem very suspicious. Please call me back as soon as you possibly can." As I hung up, I wished I could redo my message because I was sure I sounded stupid, but there were no takebacks. My words had already been released into space.

I leaned against Mike. "What do we do if Grant is a murderer?"

He wrapped his warm arms around me and said calmly, "Let's see what the detective says." Somehow, Mike still smelled good despite the heat.

I pulled away suddenly, surprising him. "Wait. If he has the torn Ballparks and More shirt in his suitcase, that would be proof that he was at the Poe house."

"Yeah. But do you even have the missing Oklahoma-shaped piece to prove it?"

"I actually do. It's in my coin purse."

"Well, that may be, but there is no evidence of any other crimes."

I frowned. Sometimes, it wasn't so great to have a level-headed police officer as a boyfriend. I said, "You're probably right."

"And how would we know what's in his suitcase anyway?"

I raised my eyebrow. "He's staying with Kenny, right? Well, he lives with his sister and she's probably at the house and could do some snooping, right?"

"Pity, I can't condone looking in someone's things without their permission. But it is her house and I'm not on duty, so..."

Since I had Mike's semi-consent, I ran in and asked Kenny to join us outside.

After assuring him that there were no offensive bugs and that the sun wasn't too bright, he followed me outside. I explained. "I'm probably wrong about this, but while we're waiting to hear from the detective on the fake priest case, I wonder if your sister wouldn't mind looking in Grant's stuff for evidence, so I can set my mind at ease."

Kenny twisted his mouth. "You think Grant is involved with something distasteful?"

I said, "Maybe, but maybe not. It's just a hunch."

He blinked repeatedly and said, "This is highly irregular, but Penny does like an adventure, so she may not mind taking a look."

It occurred to me that I'd never heard his sister's name. So, they were Kenny and Penny Dicks. Okay.

I used Kenny's phone to call her so that my line could stay open for the detective's call.

When she answered, I introduced myself and then immediately stopped speaking. I couldn't talk because Penny babbled on and on about how much Kenny loved me. Apparently she had been dying to meet me and just knew we would become best friends.

She continued with, "What hobbies do you like? How old are your girls? Do they like to shop? I could take them to Utica Square and buy them some fancy clothes. That would be such fun for me."

She sounded a little nutty, but fun - much more so than her stuffy brother. I tried to say something, but she kept going. I finally handed the phone to Kenny and pleaded for him to get her to listen. He spoke to her for a few seconds and handed the phone back to me.

This time, she said, "Go ahead. I understand you need my assistance. I'm very happy to help."

I started, "Penny, if you don't mind, would you go into the room where Grant is staying and look in his stuff? It's part of an important investigation." I winced at my semi-true words and then described the blue shirt with the hole in the side.

"Sure! I'll go in there right now."

There was a rustling sound on her end, and at the same time, my phone rang. Not sure what to do, I handed Kenny's phone to Mike so he could talk to Penny while I answered my own phone. "Hello?"

"Is this Kitty Kole?"

I smiled, "Yes, Detective McDonald?"

"Yes. So, you have more information for me?"

"I think so. But first I want to apologize for contacting you on a holiday."

"It's OK. I'm stuck at the station working on a case."

I said, "That's no fun. I wondered when you arrested John, I mean Jacob Goldschmidt, did he admit to injuring people who were on the tour?"

"No. He did not. He only admitted to impersonating Father John. He denied any involvement in the injuries and death, so with no proof, we released him right away."

"So, he's not in custody?"

"Right. There was nothing to tie him to the other crimes, so he was let go and is awaiting arraignment in Boston on fraud charges."

I felt stupid, believing that everything was wrapped up and that the killer had been caught. I said frantically, "Well, if he didn't cause the incidents on the tour, did he say who he thought did?

He said, "No. We asked him that very question numerous times."

"Did you happen to contact the other city police departments where the problems occurred?"

"Yes, I followed up on your information, but only one of them had any proof of anything. It was the incident at Yankees stadium."

I was so excited and interrupted. "The baseball that hit me. What did you learn?"

He rustled some papers and said, "Ah here it is. The fingerprints on the ball matched a…Grant Green of Tupelo Mississippi."

## Sports Joke 18

Why is swimming a confusing sport?
*Sometimes you do it for fun and other times you do it not to die.*

I sucked in my breath. "Grant Green? Seriously?" I sputtered into the phone. "He's the reason I called you! He's here now, and I believe he is the man we should have been looking for."

Just as I started to tell him why I suspected Grant, Mike caught my attention by holding up Kenny's phone.

I said, "Excuse me, I have some other information coming in."

I held my phone down and raised my eyebrows at Mike who said, "Penny found the shirt. You were right. It has sort of an Oklahoma-shaped tear in the side, and she said it smells like gasoline!"

I took the phone from Mike and said, "Penny, can you hold on a minute?"

"Sure."

I pulled up my phone again and told the detective about the shirt that was ripped at the Edgar Allan Poe house. "I actually have the missing piece, and Grant's shirt was just found at the house where he's staying. But that's not the only reason we suspect Grant." I took a breath and continued, "When he found out Father John was a fraud, he repeatedly mumbled the same phrase two of the victims had heard right before someone pushed them."

"And what was that?"

"'He will get his payback. Hell is waiting for him.'"

"Do you have an idea of his motive?"

"Yes. They were all Yankees fans."

He paused. "Yankees? Like he was after Yankee fans?"

I could tell he was finding that hard to believe but I went on, "I know it sounds crazy, but it's the only connection I could find. Every victim was wearing Yankees clothes – including me."

He said, "Motive or not, we'll check him out further."

"Okay, but he's here with us now. What do you think we should do? I'm at a wedding reception, and Grant is currently distracted by watching Hanson sing."

"Hanson, the MMMBop brothers?"

"Yes."

"Wow. That's pretty cool. My daughter loves those guys."

I said, "I expect him to be busy for a while because he's abnormally obsessed with them. Oh, and my boyfriend, Mike Potter, is a police officer here in Broken Arrow, Oklahoma. He has connections if we need to arrest the guy. So, tell me what we should do." I realized I was sounding desperate and added, "Please."

I could hear Penny's tiny voice coming from Kenny's cell, and I handed it back to Mike, so he could talk to her. Juggling two phones was confusing.

McDonald said, "While he's busy, let me check the records further. I'll get back to you as soon as I can. Just hold tight and stay clear of him if you can."

"Okay. I can do that. Thank you."

"Oh, and before I forget, Jacob said the reason he pretended to be Father John was for a novel he was writing. He was writing it from the viewpoint of a priest. Apparently, he kept detailed notes, but his notebook went missing during the tour. He described it as having a Red Sox logo on the front, if it happens to turn up."

"Okay, hold on while I ask the gal if it's in Grant's bag." I took the phone from Mike and said, "Penny, do you happen to see a notebook with either red socks or a B on the cover."

"Socks on a notebook? Ha. That's silly. No, but I found a Yankee's hat in his bag."

I wondered why a staunch Braves fan had a Yankees hat, especially if he hated the Yankees enough to kill a fan. Wait, maybe it was Dad's missing hat. Grant could have grabbed it after he threw the ball at me.

While I pondered this, Penny yelled, "Wait a minute! I found the notebook. It's right here."

I breathed faster with the new revelation and put both phones to my ear so I wouldn't get confused. "Detective McDonald, Grant does have Jacob's notebook."

After the detective hung up to check records, I relayed the information to Mike and Kenny. They both looked stunned. I asked Mike, "Should you send someone over to Kenny and Penny's house to get the evidence?"

He said, "Not without a warrant. We should wait to see what McDonald tells us to do."

I nodded and felt jittery. Grant could be extremely dangerous and there were a lot of innocent people here…including my daughters!

We went back to the tent where Kim told me I had missed the bride and groom's first dance, the father/daughter dance, and the toasts. Fine with me. I had more important information to tell her.

With the loud music, I leaned in and nearly shouted to explain everything to Kim, Travis, and Odette.

Once I had told the entire story, Travis gawked. "You mean to tell me that we not only were duped by a fake priest but were sitting with a possible murderer here?"

I was afraid Travis would get angry, stand up, and leave in a huff. Instead, he gave a firm nod. "We'll help you get this figured out, Pity. This whole mystery has been weighing you down for a while and we had no idea you were involved."

Odette said, "Just let us know what we can do to help. You may not know this, but Travis used to be a Texas Ranger, so he knows how to help."

I scoffed and asked, "How can an ex-major league baseball player help with this?" But, then again, I was a music teacher.

They laughed and Mike said, "Pity, I believe he was part of the Texas Department of Public Services—you know like Walker, Texas Ranger. But good try staying in baseball mode."

While I turned pink, Kim stared at the stage. She said, "Just look at that guy. He's having the time of his life."

I looked up and indeed, Grant the possible murderer was now dancing. If we didn't get him out of here, things could turn and there was a chance Shelly's wedding really could be ruined.

"Mom! Are you having fun?" I jumped when sweaty hands were wrapped around my neck.

I stammered, not sure how to answer Ree. "Hi, sweetie. It's a great party." I felt a little nervous as I hugged my baby girl. "Have you and Caitlyn been dancing?" My voice sounded squeaky, but I was nervous about her being close to Grant.

"No, but we're getting ready to. We've been blowing bubbles at each other. Dad will only let us light sparklers unless we have adults with us. Does he think we're babies? I've been shooting off fireworks for years." She pushed her hair behind her ears and added, "But, we'll make the best of it."

"Well, maybe he's more concerned about Caitlyn's safety."

She nodded. I introduced Ree to Travis and Odette and said, "And you remember Kenny?"

She smiled at the Texans and nodded to Kenny before saying, "Well, I've gotta get back before they sing *MMMBop*."

I caught her sweaty arm, not wanting her to go near Grant. "Stay over to the side of the stage because…um the speakers are too loud for your tender ears."

"Mom, now *you're* treating me like a baby."

I tried to detain her by asking, "Hey, do you know who arranged for Hanson to be here?"

She shrugged her narrow shoulders. "It was probably Grandpa Jack." Her eyes flew open wide, and she covered her mouth as if she was surprised at what had come out of her mouth. She apologized softly to me, "He told me to call him Grandpa. Is that, OK?" Her face was scrunched with worry.

I could see how Jack would seem fun to have as a grandpa, especially with her with all his money and local fame. Todd's parents had both died when Marie was too young to remember them, so having another set of grandparents would be a good thing. Aside from being overbearing, Jack was a kind man and a philanthropist. How could I object? I leaned in and said, "Of course Honey, as long as you don't call Shelly, Mom."

She looked horrified. "Never in a million years. You are my only mom. Ooh, that's the intro to *MMMBop*! See ya!"

I started to yell, 'Stay away from the man with the Harry Potter glasses,' but she was already gone.

We watched the girls dance to the song. I would have danced too but was far too nervous to enjoy anything.

During the next song, I jumped again when my phone rang. It was the detective. With all the noise in the tent, I was afraid I wouldn't be able to hear him. I pointed to my phone and hopped up to go outside where I was surprised to find it had grown dark.

"Hello?"

"Ms. Kole?"

"Did you find out anything about Grant?" I held my breath while awaiting his response.

"Well, yes. There is some disconcerting news. Ten years ago, Mr. Green was questioned about the disappearance of his wife. He had an alibi and there was no evidence to convict him of anything. Unfortunately, the wife has never been found."

I sucked in my breath, causing me to choke. After coughing a bit, I was able to say, "Oh my. I remember him saying his wife was no longer in the picture. I just assumed they had divorced."

"They did not."

I cringed. "He said he has children. Has anyone spoken to them?"

"He has three adult children, but they are all estranged from him, and none of them would take my call."

"Oh. I see." I couldn't help but wonder if the reason for their estrangement was due to him naming them after Isaac, Taylor and Zac Hanson, or maybe because their mother went missing.

"Do you think there is probable cause to get a warrant to confiscate his belongings?"

"It would be better if you had something that tied him to the murder of Howard Riley?"

"Well, I did see him in the lobby of the hotel late on the night before his body was found in the luggage compartment."

He said, "But then again if you were there too, that doesn't really prove anything."

"I guess. But what if he's dangerous? We have proof he threw the ball at me, locked me in an attic, and probably planned to burn the place down. Couldn't the local police at least come here and question him? Maybe he would confess. I'm starting to worry that Hanson will stop playing and it will be too late to arrest Grant."

Just as I spoke the words, I realized the music had already stopped. I had been so focused on talking to the detective that I hadn't noticed the silence. In fact, it was so quiet I could hear gravel crunching near the corner of the tent.

When I looked up, a figure rushed around the side. I followed the person, but by the time I got to the corner in my heeled sandals, the person was gone.

"Ms. Kole, are you still there?"

I said, "Yes. I'm sorry, but the music stopped and now I'm getting nervous."

"Why don't you have your friend's supervising officer call me right away? We'll discuss what to do and I'll keep you in the loop."

"Okay. Thank you!"

After hanging up, I rushed inside to talk to Mike but found Grant sitting at our table again. R.A. had also rejoined the group. I forced a smile and hoped my voice didn't waver, "Did you get to meet the guys, Grant? The Hanson brothers, I mean?"

With a straight face, he said, "Not yet." When his steely eyes didn't leave mine, I gulped, feeling uncomfortable.

I turned my head. "R.A., do you know of any way Grant could get an autograph?"

"Well, I don't know them personally, but I guess we could try. I've gotta tear down the set anyway. Let's go, Tupelo."

I felt a little bad sending R.A. out without telling him he was leaving with a possible murderer.

Grant still had his eyes fixed on me as he stood up. I looked away and he followed my brother-in-law.

As soon as they were out of sight, I filled the group in on what the detective had said. I turned to Mike. "Can you have your supervisor contact Detective McDonald right away? Here's his number." I jotted it down between the red stripes of the flag on my napkin. I grabbed his hand and said, "I think Grant knows I'm on to him. He may have listened in on my call to McDonald! Please have them hurry."

Mike stood and said, "Kenny, I'll need your address. Pity, if Grant comes back, play it cool."

While he wrote down the address, Kim said, "I'll keep an eye on her until you get back."

The five of us who remained at the table discussed the situation. Kenny said, "I just don't understand what he could gain from hurting people."

I raised my eyebrows. "I still say he didn't like Yankee fans."

Travis leaned his elbows on the colorful table. "I don't believe that's a good motive. He'd have to rid the world of millions of fans."

Kim and Odette rolled their eyes as though my theory was stupid. The more I thought about it, the dumber it sounded. Feeling like a dope, I scanned my brain for another motive.

I brightened. "Maybe once he read the fake priest's notebook of confessions, he took retribution on those who admitted to their sins?"

The others looked at me as if that was more plausible.

Kim squinted and said, "But taking the law into his own hands is pretty scary business."

I remembered something. "You know…Grant told me he liked Hanson because they were so wholesome and came from a good Christian family. Maybe he believed he was doing God's work."

Odette frowned, "But what about that young man, Jason, who was poisoned–what could he have done that was so bad? He was sweet; like an overgrown Boy Scout."

I thought of the quiet redhead. That was true. I added, "Or Marcia and Señor Herrera? They were both nice too."

Travis said, "People aren't always what they seem. They still could have done something heinous." He rubbed his chin. "However, I'll agree that the only one of the victims who acted shady was Howard, but even he didn't deserve to die at the hands of a zealot."

Mike came back to the table with a serious expression. He spoke quietly, "Police are on the way to your house, Kenny. Might want to let Penny know." He turned to all of us, "Then they'll send a unit here if they see a need. In the meantime, we should keep an eye on Grant."

We looked up to see if we could spot the man but just then the microphone squealed, causing us all to jump. The announcer said, "The sun has set. It's time to celebrate the newlyweds and Independence Day in style! The bride asks that you bring your fireworks and matches outside. We'll light sparklers and have Todd and Shelly walk underneath them. Let's get going!"

I lifted my hands in disbelief. "They are seriously doing this? You guys go on out. I'll watch for Grant."

Kim shook her head. "I'm waiting for R.A."

"I'll stay here too," Mike said.

Odette said, "We'll be right outside if you need us." She and Travis took their explosives outside. Kenny followed them, looking lost.

I caught Ren's eye as she and Chris jumped up, fireworks in hand, ready to join the throng of partygoers. I waved her over to me.

She was out of breath when she and Chris stood in front of us. "Hi, Mom. This is some party, huh? I'm so glad you were able to see Hanson. Let's go shoot some fireworks." She motioned for me to follow her.

I pulled her to me and whispered. "I'm sort of on a reconnaissance mission and can't go yet."

She rolled her eyes. "You are so dramatic. What is it this time? Did you notice someone with a gun in their belt? Remember, this is rural Oklahoma. Everyone has a gun."

I took her hand. "I'm not joking, Lauren. Whatever you do. Stay away from a man with Harry Potter glasses. He could be dangerous. And keep an eye on your sister."

She gave me a strange look, but said, "Okay. I will stay clear of Harry Potter." She pulled Chris outside to join the rest of the crowd.

Kim, Mike, and I searched for any signs of R.A. or Grant, but we didn't see them. I said, "Let's go find them."

The three of us moved to the stage area but they weren't there either. When Mike took off, we followed him outside and behind the stage where roadies were loading equipment.

The announcer was right. It was dark outside. The air was still stifling hot, but that was nothing new for summer in Oklahoma. I swatted at a mosquito and instantly hoped poor Kenny had brought his bug spray, or he would be miserable.

Mike spoke in a lively voice so as not to raise concern, "R.A., buddy. How's it going?"

Kim's eyes lit up when she followed Mike's gaze to her husband, who was halfway up a tall pole, unhooking a speaker. I was relieved to see him too.

"Hi, guys. I'm just finishing this up and then I'll come down and shoot off my bottle rockets."

Not wanting to get R.A. involved, I asked rather casually, "Hey, do you know where Grant is?"

He squinted. "Grant? Oh, the Mississippi guy who wanted to meet Hanson? Yeah, he's around here somewhere." He scoffed. "Once he got their autographs, he disappeared." From his perch up high, R.A. pointed. "I think he went that way."

Kim said, "You go. I'll stay with R.A. and fill him in when he gets back down to Earth."

Along with Mike, I headed through the darkness to find a murderer.

I grabbed Mike's hand. "What do we do if we find him?"

"Just act nonchalant and don't engage."

I gave a big sigh. "I'll go get our fireworks, so we blend in with the rest of the party."

"Okay, I look for Grant. Remember, I'm wearing a white shirt so should be easy to find in the dark."

"Okay." I entered the tent alone. When I got to the table, I sat and fiddled around with the drawstrings of our two bags and finally pulled out the matches, sparklers, and the fountain.

Suddenly someone grabbed me from behind with sweaty hands. I giggled. "Okay, Marie, I know what you want. You can have my sparklers, but I need to tell you…"

Before I could finish my sentence, a knife glinted in front of my face and a deep voice growled, "I want more than your sparklers. I want you to drive me to the airport."

# Sports Joke #19

Why did the Pickleball Paddle break up with the Tennis Racket?
*There were too many strings attached.*

The room felt small and the air stifling. I could hardly breathe but turned my head and stared at Grant. I gulped. "I can explain the phone call. We just want to ask you some questions." I stammered, "And I can't drive you to the airport. I don't have a car here or even any keys. Let's just sit and talk about it. Here. Have a seat." I hoped he would sit down, so I could have time to think of an escape plan.

Instead of sitting, he pulled the drawstring out of my swag bag and tied my hands behind my back. Despite not being much bigger than me, he yanked me up to a standing position and wrapped his arm around my neck, cutting off the circulation in my throat. When he started pulling me toward the back entrance of the tent, I gulped some air and said, "You don't have to do this."

"You stuck your nose into things that weren't your business. That's why I hit you with the baseball. If I hadn't been distracted by a vendor, it would have done more damage. And I wanted to watch you burn in that old house, but your boyfriend showed up."

My eyes grew large, possibly even bulging from both fear and lack of air. I wiggled my head enough to get a deep breath and squeaked out, "How did you know I suspected you?"

"I read your notes on your phone, amateur. Nobody leaves an open phone in plain sight on their seat. And you sure as heck shouldn't name the note—Baseball Suspects."

I refused to let a murderer criticize my investigative tactics and opened my mouth to debate him. But since I was being strangled and he had a knife, I decided I shouldn't worry about who was right or wrong. Instead, I asked, "Why did you poison Jason?"

"Because he poisoned his brother when he was little and killed him. I wasn't going to let him get away with that."

I would have put my hands to my mouth in shock if they weren't tied behind my back. How had that sweet redheaded Jason done something so horrid? My throat was screaming with pain, but I managed to croak out, "What about Marcia? What did she do?"

"She was having an affair–just like my wife did. I despise adultery. But you can stop with the twenty questions. Your life will be over soon, and you won't be able to tell anyone anyway."

He hauled me outside and towards the parking lot. I considered screaming, but we were on the opposite side of the tent from the people shooting off fireworks. With all the music, loud pops, squeals of fireworks, and laughing, nobody would ever hear me.

Grant said, "I heard a lot of these Okies don't lock their cars and leave the keys inside." He opened the door of a Cadillac and looked around but didn't see any keys. The next two cars were equally void of keys.

While leaning into a Cadillac Escalade he released his grip on my neck enough that I could breathe freely. I swallowed and said, "Grant, how do you think you'll get away with this? The authorities already know about you and have your information. They probably alerted TSA, so the airport isn't your ideal escape route."

He stopped in his tracks and looked up. "The Lord will provide a way."

I was glad he couldn't see my expression. The only God I knew wouldn't help this guy get away with what he had done.

The next vehicle was an early model Cadillac with giant Longhorn horns on the hood. It just screamed Texas, so I figured it had to be owned by Travis and Odette. I suddenly remembered what Shelly had said about the button you could push to play a song and came up with a plan. Glancing past Grant I saw two buttons on the dashboard: One to start the car and the other to play a song. Since Grant didn't drive, I thought I could trick him with my plan.

I said, "Oh, this car is keyless. I just need to push the button, and it should start the car. Can you loosen just one of my hands?" Of course, I knew you still needed a key nearby to start the car, but I hoped my plan might work with just the battery.

He growled, "Just tell me what to push."

I said, "OK, suit yourself. It's the one on the right."

He sat inside the car with one hand still holding my wrists. I held my breath, hoping I had guessed the correct button.

As soon as he pushed it, the song, *The Eyes of Texas Are Upon You* blared, played by what sounded like loud, tinny-sounding trumpets. It was so loud, I wanted to cover my ears but couldn't with my hands still tied behind my back.

His head whipped back at me. "That's obnoxious. Turn it off!"

"I can't! My hands are tied, literally."

"Why is it playing *I've Been Working on the Railroad?*"

I shouted over the song, "It's *The Eyes of Texas* - the theme song of the University of Texas–Austin."

He started punching buttons trying to stop the noise, but that caused even more havoc. The windshield wipers swished, the lights blinked on and off and the horn honked, but he still couldn't get the music to stop.

I brightened when I saw someone in a white shirt come around the tent. It was Mike, flanked by Travis, Odette, R.A., and Kim.

I looked over and realized Grant no longer had a hold of me. My feet weren't tied. What was I waiting for? I sprinted to my people.

Mike grabbed me. "What's going on?"

"Grant is in their car." I pointed my head at Travis. "He tied my wrists."

Kim and Odette rushed over and untied the string, then we three gals backed up as the men moved toward the car. Suddenly, Grant exited the car, holding a shotgun, and aimed it at the guys.

We all froze. Odette whispered, "I told Travis he needed to lock that thing up."

I whispered, "Is it loaded?"

She scrunched her nose. "I honestly don't know." When our guys backed up a step, I figured it must be.

A large group of wedding guests stood off to the side gawking at the man with the firearm.

Grant walked around the Caddy and headed to another vehicle, all the while holding the men at bay with the gun. He yanked on the door handle, but it didn't open. I wasn't sure what he planned to do if it did, since he didn't know how to drive.

Mike yelled, "Broken Arrow Police! Put down the weapon, Grant Green. You can't get away. More officers are on their way."

R.A. turned his back and started fiddling with something. What was he doing? We needed him to help stop Grant, not send a text. Then R.A. turned around. He did not have a phone in his hand, but a lit bottle rocket. He aimed right at Grant. Suddenly, it burst from R.A.'s hand and screamed towards the Hanson dude, hitting the ground next to his feet. It sizzled, then made a loud bang.

Grant jumped to the side and then pointed the gun directly at R.A. Kim yelled, "No!"

R.A. shot another rocket toward him, then another—none of which hit the man, but they were so expertly aimed that they hit close enough to freak him out.

Somehow, Grant gained his composure and steadied his aim at R.A. He pulled the trigger. I ducked down so I wouldn't see my brother-in-law get shot, but the loud bang made me scream.

Kim yelled again, "No!"

When I peeked up, R.A. was standing upright with nary a gunshot wound. Grant must have missed, but why was R.A. calmly lighting a fountain? He aimed it at the shooter and sprayed beautiful sparks. Grant dodged the colorful spray flying towards him and then clicked the trigger repeatedly before finally dropping the gun. He froze as if he was in some kind of a stupor.

Travis, who apparently was also a pyromaniac, lit a Roman Candle and shot different colored fireballs toward Grant.

Normally, the candles and fountains were my favorite fireworks on the 4th, but in this situation, I was worried someone would get badly injured.

In addition to the noise of fireworks, screams and the blaring *Eyes of Texas* song, I heard sirens.

As the police cars approached, everything got even louder. Within seconds, two police cars screeched to a halt in front of us. The officers, brandishing firearms that were probably loaded, carefully approached Grant. Within seconds they had him handcuffed. He looked traumatized by the whole ordeal. Good!

I almost collapsed in relief when he was taken away. Kim ran up and hugged R.A. Odette and I stood stunned while Mike and Travis talked to the officers.

Then I heard the most annoying noise of the night–Shelly. She screeched, "Of course, you found a way to ruin my wedding, Pity Kole! I knew you were behind all of this."

I looked up to find Shelly pointing to the police vehicle while glaring at me. The lights from the patrol cars didn't help her blue face look any better. It now had turned more of a purple hue.

I was about to go try to calm Shelly down, but my girls ran up to me and asked in unison, "Are you alright, Mom?"

"I am now." I hugged them both. "That was scary, but everything is OK now."

Ren cringed. "So, the Harry Potter dude really was a bad guy?"

I nodded, but Ree, who knew nothing about it said, "What? What did he do?"

I hugged both girls and said, "Let me tell you about it later. It's a long, crazy story, but everything is fine now. Just go back to shooting off your fireworks. Ree, you can even get the sparklers from my place on the table. I need to talk to Shelly."

They hesitated, then turned around to leave.

I walked over to Shelly, who was still in her full bridal regalia. The blue dye had smeared further across her cheeks somehow. Maybe she ate the rest of her slice of cake? Why hadn't anyone told her about her colorful face? They probably were scared of her.

I shook my head. "Shelly, I'm so sorry this happened. This will all be over shortly, and everything will go back to normal."

She screamed, "Who is that guy, and why is he at my wedding?"

"We met him on our bus tour, but he was invited by someone else – not me, I promise."

"Why was he arrested?"

I put my hand on hers. "I promise I'll fill you in later. Please just go enjoy your party. You don't need to worry about him."

Todd had been listening from the side and said, "Shelly. We just got married and you look incredible. Let's go celebrate."

"But…she…" The poor frazzled bride couldn't think of anything to say for a change.

Todd wrapped his arms around her and whispered something in her ear that made her relax. She sighed and said, "Okay, hot Toddy." Then she giggled, turned around, and hooked her arm in the arm of her groom. I was glad to see he knew how to calm her down.

I turned around to see what was happening with the policemen, and walked to R.A. "How did you know he wouldn't shoot you when you lit the bottle rocket?"

"Travis told us it wasn't loaded, so I took a chance that he was right."

"You are crazy. When I heard that bang, I was afraid you were a goner."

He said, "Sorry. It was just a firecracker that went off at the same time. Didn't mean to scare you." He nudged me. "But what I want to know is who uses flimsy matches to light fireworks? I always use a punk or at least a fireplace lighter."

I laughed. After a near-death occurrence, the firework lighting method was his biggest gripe? I hugged him. "Well, thanks for saving the day–again." I kissed him on his furry cheek.

I found Mike and started to hug him, but he grabbed my hand and put the fake priest's notebook in it. He said, "You need to check this out before they take it away as evidence. Be quick."

I couldn't read it in the dark and motioned for Kim to join me. Odette followed us and I asked, "Have either of you seen Kenny?"

Both gals shook their heads. When we reached the table, I frowned. This is where I had been kidnapped. I shook the memory off when I noticed my sparklers were gone. Maybe Ree and Caitlyn were having fun with them.

Still shaken, I opened the notebook. I exhaled a big breath and said, "Ok, let's see what's in here." It was written in neat, easy-to-read handwriting. The large title read, 'Confessions to a Priest.'

Before I could read the first entry, I was interrupted by Odette. "There is a note on this napkin. It's from Kenny."

I looked up as she read aloud, "My dearest Kitty, I'm very sorry to abandon you and your friends tonight, but I was bitten by a bug and am starting to itch. The noise is also bothering me, as is the smoke from the fireworks. To avoid any more annoyances, I am driving myself home. If Grant needs a ride, please use this money to pay the driver." Odette lifted the napkin to reveal a hundred-dollar bill.

Our eyes widened as she continued to read. 'Please forgive me if I caused a problem by leaving early. Yours forever, Kenny.'

What an odd guy.

Kim said, "I'd sure drive someone home for that–except I believe Grant is getting a free ride in a cruiser."

I snorted, then focused on the first entry in the notebook.

'Señor Herrera, a soft-spoken man of Mexican descent
sits beside me on the bus. The man in his seventies folds
his hands as he gives his confession in Spanish. Although

I am fluent in the language, I am unnerved by what comes out of his mouth and wonder if I have translated what he said correctly. Did he really say as a young man, he had murdered his boss while working in the lettuce fields? This is unnerving. What do I do? I'm bound to keep confessions confidential due to the Seal of Confession.'

My jaw dropped at this revelation. How could that sweet man have done such a thing? His family would be horrified. It was like I was reading someone's diary, but so much worse. I swallowed and read the next one.

'Marcia Baldwin – wife of Robert Baldwin approaches me while I'm having breakfast. She says she has something important to confess but cannot do it while her husband is around.

She admits that she's been having an affair with his best friend. It has gone on for three years and she can't seem to stop. She even talked her husband into moving near Yankee Stadium just to be near her boyfriend, who works as a manager of the team. Our conversation ends abruptly when Robert enters the breakfast area.'

This matched up with what Grant had said to me about Marcia being an adulterer. I started feeling sick having read about their sins. The next entry had Odette's name, so I handed the book to her and said, "Here are his notes about your confession. I don't want to invade your privacy, but perhaps you want to see what he wrote."

She took the book and as she read, her eyes grew wider and wider. She put her hand to her mouth and gasped. "This is slander. I never said that and certainly never did any such thing."

When she started to rip the page out, I stopped her. "No. That is evidence. Please don't damage it. I suggest you tell the police that it is not factual." But, after having read the other confessions, I wasn't sure our Texas lady was so perfect after all.

Odette's face turned red as she flipped to another page. "Here's yours, Pity. See if he lied about you." She handed the book to me.

I took a drink of my watered-down pina colada as I read.

'Pity Kole–Pity is an independent gal who doesn't know what she wants in life. I knew something was off as soon as she admitted she didn't like sports.

When Pity comes to me for atonement, I am shocked by her confession. While on a recent trip to Rome, she tried to seduce a priest and was so forceful with him, she actually ripped his frock. I don't want to imagine how she planned to desecrate my brother in Christ with her evil ways.

I absolved her but will stay away in case she tries to entice me into her web of sexual perversion.'

# Sports Joke #20

Why did the stadium get hot after the game?
*All of the fans left.*

At the word seduce, I spit out my warm, white drink onto the tablecloth. "Oh no he did not write that!"

Odette nodded. "See why I wanted to rip out the page?"

I nodded, dumbfounded, and handed the book to Kim. "Read this."

As she read Father John's note about me, her eyes widened, and she snorted. "That's hilarious, but not at all what happened. Why did you even tell him about Rome anyway?"

I made a face at her and shrugged. "I still felt bad about it and wanted to be absolved."

She finally stopped laughing long enough to say, "I think Jacob was embellishing the confessions to make his novel more interesting. He has quite an imagination."

Of course, Kim would pick up on that since she was a librarian. I said, "You may be right," and read what he wrote about other people. They all sounded far-fetched, except maybe the details about Gross Hair Guy assaulting women. I shivered, wondering if that was true.

I shook my head slowly as it all started to make sense. I looked at the two gals. "Maybe Grant read these notes, thought they were true, and went into full vigilante mode?"

Both gals considered the idea and nodded.

I needed to give the book back to the officer on duty and ran outside and handed it to him. "Here is more evidence for the Baltimore police, but please tell them most of it was fabricated. We believe Jacob, the guy who wrote it, exaggerated most of the crimes as part of his fictitious novel. Unfortunately, it seems that Grant…" I pointed to the culprit in the squad car, "read the book and believed it to be the truth, then took revenge on the people in the book."

Just then, a growl came from the cruiser. "And he shall get his day in Hell for deceiving me."

I looked at the creep sitting in the backseat and thought, 'Hey buddy, you may have your day there too.'

Mike approached me, took my hand, and pulled me towards him. "Are you alright?"

I snuggled in. "It's just all so crazy. He tried to force me to drive him to the airport."

"Why? Because he didn't know the way?"

"No. Because he never learned to drive."

"Well, I have something that will cheer you up." He handed me the blue shirt with the ripped section on top for me to see.

Wow, the hole was perfectly shaped like the Sooner State. I pulled out the missing piece and it fit perfectly. Then cringing, I yanked my hand back, not wanting to touch the creepy man's gasoline-smelling shirt. "Um. Please let the Baltimore police have it as evidence."

As Mike put the two pieces of shirt into an evidence bag, I took a few deep breaths. He came back to me and said, "Maybe you would rather have this." He handed me a Yankees hat.

"Oh, that's much better!!" I hugged it. "Yay. I shall return this baseball hat to its rightful owner. Thanks."

He raised his eyebrows waiting for something and I remembered what it was. "Dang. I'll never get that straight. It's a baseball *cap*."

"There you go."

I was glad everything was finally wrapped up nicely and said, "Hey, wanna walk around with me?"

Mike said, "Yes, but I can't. The police have a lot more questions. I'm sure they'll have you come in after the holiday to give your statement, too. Go take a relaxing walk."

I made my way past people who laughed as they shot off fireworks. There was so much space on Big Jack's ranch that people were spread out. The explosives weren't as dangerous as I had feared.

When I passed Ree, I stopped to watch her spelling her name in the air with a sparkler. She laughed as Caitlyn attempted to capture the dissipating name with her phone camera. I took my own photo of the scene before continuing on my walk.

A bit further, I witnessed Chris with his hand over Ren's hands as he "taught" her how to hold a Roman Candle. He probably had no idea she'd been shooting off fireworks since she was six years old. But she certainly seemed to be enjoying his lesson. Love will make you do funny things. I snapped a photo of them too.

I passed families enjoying the evening and then a few inebriated guys weaving through the cars. I hoped they weren't planning to drive anywhere soon.

Then I saw the sweetest scene. Far apart from the crowd, my ex-husband sat with his bride on the hood of their brand-new all-electric Cadillac. It was the present from her dad she had bragged about getting. The sleek, modern car was decked out with strings of cans tied to the bumper. Shelly's head was leaning on Todd's shoulder as he pointed up to the moon and she looked upward. I snuck around to the side of the car and took a photo of them with the moon in the shot. Awe.

Just as I was about to take my phone down, a shooting star passed over and she squealed in delight. I snapped a photo of that too, capturing what could be an award-winning shot of the newlyweds. They looked gloriously happy in their wedding garb.

The best thing about the shot was that it was not a posed photo, like most of the others taken today. It was a picture of true joy. I studied the photo, pleased to see I hadn't caught even a trace of blue on Shelly's face. I decided I would frame an 8x10 print of the shot and give it to them as a wedding gift.

As I walked back to the tent, the police car drove slowly past me. From the lights of the fireworks, I could see Grant sitting in the backseat behind a metal partition. I gave a sarcastic smile and waved to him. He scowled at me. Poor, poor man. At least he would have plenty of time to reminisce about meeting Hanson while sitting behind bars in the Tulsa County jail waiting to be extradited.

Back in the tent, our group rehashed the events of the night.

When Odette and Travis stood to leave, I said, "Travis, I hope you don't mind me using your Cadillac to distract Grant." I cringed.

He laughed. "It was ingenious. My old Texas Ranger buddies and the guys back at the dealership will love hearing about it."

Odette took my hand and said, "I hope you can relax now, dear. You had quite an evening."

"I'll be fine, now that the right guy is behind bars. Oh my gosh, I should tell Ava and Vince that I was wrong about Father John being the murderer. They won't believe how this all turned out."

Kim said, "I still can't believe you thought someone was out to get all the Yankees fans."

My face turned pink. "Well remember, I'm not a real detective."

Mike put his arm around me. "But you're my favorite non-detective."

I smiled and gave him a big old kiss. I sure did like this guy.

Mike and I walked Odette and Travis outside. I promised to visit them if I was ever in their part of Texas. As their enormous Cadillac drove away, I laughed as the horns blared *The Yellow Rose of Texas*. Who knew there was more than one song choice?

Mike took my hand. "Let's go get your girls, so you can get home. You had a big night."

We entered the tent to pry my daughters away from their friends. Then after gathering our red, white and blue swag bags, we walked back outside with R.A and Kim to say goodbye to the newlyweds.

To keep the peace, I smiled at Todd rather than hugging him. "I hope you two will be super happy."

Shelly didn't look at me, but Todd nodded. He shook Mike's hand and kissed the girls, goodbye. "Have fun at the cabin. I really do miss that place."

I was sure Todd missed going there with all the canoeing, fishing, and jumping off the rocks. But he would have new adventures with Shelly. Ooh, that would be a good book title if I were ever to write one–'Adventures with Shelly.'

The girls welcomed their new stepmom to the family by giving her hugs. I cringed when Shelly finally cracked a smile and displayed her still-blue teeth. She said, "Lauren and Marie, you were lovely attendants. Thank you for standing up for me."

Then she turned to me and pointed to my bouquet of silk flowers. She raised an eyebrow. "Let me know when your wedding is and maybe I'll crash it."

Everyone laughed as I turned pink. I couldn't even look at Mike, but cleared my throat and replied to Shelly, "Well, if it happens, you won't have to crash it. I'll invite you."

I made a quick exit from the couple before stepping over to thank Big Jack and Mrs. Jack for their hospitality.

Jack puffed out his chest and took Mike's hand. "It's always a pleasure to have you around. Sounds like things could have gotten a lot worse if you weren't here to capture the guy."

He turned to me, "And Pity, if I ever need a private eye, I'll call you. I hear you are quite the investigator.

Ren said, "Please don't call her."

Ree added, "Yeah, she gets in enough trouble on her own."

We walked Kim and R.A. to their car. "I'll see you at the cabin tomorrow."

R.A. shook Mike's hand. "You need to come along sometime. You would love it there."

Mike took my hand as we walked to his truck. "I hope you all have a relaxing weekend with family and playing in the water at this magical place I've heard so much about. You need a break after the last few crazy weeks."

I leaned in. "I really do. I'm just sorry you can't go with us. I'll take you to the cabin soon, but someone must stay behind to play with his new niece and more importantly, to protect the streets of Broken Arrow."

He said, "I'll do my darndest. And you stay safe. I've heard stories about people who live off the grid in the Ozarks."

I chuckled but then remembered some of the creepy hillbilly types who lived down the road from our cabin and cringed. Weird things could easily happen around there.

I shook it off and hugged his arm. "Thanks again for all your help with this mess, and for taking me on a baseball adventure. I still can't believe I enjoyed the games."

Mike smiled and started to reply but was interrupted by a scream coming from inside a tent.

"Todd! Why didn't you tell me my teeth were blue?!?!?!"

# AUTHOR'S NOTE

The idea for this Pity Mystery was initiated by my husband's quest to visit every Major League Baseball Park.

After I endured a seemingly endless bus tour of East Coast ballparks with Dan, it was a given that Pity would be forced to do the same - hence the idea for this book.

Luckily on our actual tour, nobody died. We did, however, see some amazing sights and meet wonderful new friends including, Sue and Frank from Long Island.

In addition to the crazy seven day/six game bus tour, we have continued our quest and have been lucky to meet up with family members at some other major league ball parks. Thanks to Emily, Tony, Ron, Linda, Kathy, Jeremy, Pati, Josh, Scott, Steve and Eve, for joining us for even more games.

As of now, we have made it to 22 of the 30 MLB parks, but who's counting?

The character, Grant, was inspired by an incident my sister, Kathy, experienced. While on a 2022 trip to Australia, she encountered a man who was overjoyed to learn she was from Tulsa. The stranger wanted to fly to Tulsa, visit her, and meet Hanson!

Even if I never become a sports fan, I have at least learned to appreciate the enthusiasm of real fans.

# About the Author

Martha Kemm Landes is a former Oklahoma public school music teacher. Besides writing musicals for her students, she is known for writing the Oklahoma State Children's Song, <u>Oklahoma, My Native Land</u>. After moving to New Mexico in 2011, she began her transition from composing music and musicals to writing light mysteries.

Martha lives with her author husband and their two adopted dogs in Rio Rancho, New Mexico. They enjoy spending time at their cabin in the nearby Jemez Mountains and traveling.

Besides writing mystery novels and renting out the cabin, Martha's other activities include quilting, playing pickleball, biking, gardening and hosting movie nights in their backyard theater.

*Scan the QR code for a quick link to Martha's website where you can find
fun news, giveaways, and even subscribe to her newsletter,
Mini Morsels from Martha.*